Two Lovers

by Beverly Adam

ACKNOWLEDGMENTS

Many thanks to Damon Leigh for encouraging me to write Russ and Carole's love story and to Leslie D. Stuart for her input.

ISBN: 13: 9781523402519
ISBN: 10: 1523402512
Library of Congress Control Number:2016919349
LCCN Imprint Name: Create Space Independent Publishing Platform. North Charleston, SC.

Dedication

To the fans of Carole Lombard and Russ Columbo.

Contents

Author's Notes

About the Author

Two Lovers

The love story of
Carole Lombard and Russ Columbo

by Beverly Adam

Chapter One

Heaven-Sent

On a star-studded August evening in 1933, the famed motion picture actress Carole Lombard arrived at a legendary nightclub on Wilshire Boulevard in Los Angeles. Located in the landmark Ambassador Hotel, the Cocoanut Grove was the hot spot for the Hollywood in-crowd. Its exotic décor resembled an alluring oasis, replete with Arabic archways, a waterfall, and desert palms. The ballroom's midnight blue ceiling was brightly adorned with constellations. Aladdin and his magic carpet would have felt instantly at home.

The Cocoanut Grove was a relaxing place for the rich and famous to rendezvous for cocktails, dance to the music of an exceptional orchestra, and enjoy the night. When the stars aligned and love smiled, the lucky ones might embark upon a path to an unforgettable romance.

Intent on enjoying herself that night, Carole had a date with screenwriter Bob (Robert) Riskin. She was a bright platinum blonde with wavy, shoulder-length hair, high cheekbones, winged eyebrows, and large, sapphire-blue eyes. She was breathtaking, her beautiful curves complemented by a tight-fitting black evening gown designed by Paramount's chief costume designer, Travis Banton. The silky fabric smoothly molded to her shapely body. No undergarment lines showed for one simple reason: she wasn't wearing any. The only embellishment was a strand of luminescent pearls dipping into the low *V* between her breasts.

A young photographer came up to her table, eagerly asking for permission to take her picture. "May I, Miss Lombard?"

She gave him a long look with an arched brow, those blue eyes surveying him. Carole knew every important photographer in Hollywood, but this one's face was unfamiliar to her. "You're new in town, aren't you?"

"Yeah," he shyly grinned, "and like you, ma'am, I'm from Indiana." He showed her his press badge with his name on it: Jake Froelich.

"It's Carole," she said, sweetly correcting the *ma'am*. "Sure, go ahead, Jake, take as many as you like." She sat back a little, artfully hiding in the shadows the barely noticeable scar on the side of her face. Flashing bulbs went off, momentarily blinding her. Other reporters had noticed she was posing for Jake. Good publicity was always welcome.

"That's swell, thanks."

"Anytime for a fellow Hoosier," she said, giving Jake a playful smile. "If ever you come by Paramount, drop by my trailer and say hello." She winked at him flirtatiously.

The photographer stumbled into the next table, where Cary Grant sat. The star held out his arms to keep Jake from falling into his lap. "Steady there," said Cary, holding him up.

"Thank you, Mr. Grant."

"No trouble at all." Cary patted him on the back and gave Jake a good-natured smile. Then he swung his charismatic gaze toward the cause of the commotion. "Hey, Carole, watch where you're aiming those blinkers of yours, will you? I think the poor kid was star struck."

"Sure thing, master." She touched the center of her forehead in a salaam, causing everyone nearby to laugh.

A heavy smoker, she lit a cigarette and looked expectantly to where the musicians were setting up. The headliner for the evening was Russ Columbo, a talented singer and composer. He was making a return engagement and was performing with the renowned Gus Arnheim Orchestra. It was well known that Russ had been elevated from first violinist to vocal soloist in the orchestra when he filled-in for the hard-drinking crooner Bing Crosby.

Russ was the reason she had come to the Cocoanut Grove tonight. He had performed in his first supporting movie-screen role in *Broadway Thru a Keyhole*, a gangster story in which he played the good-guy bandleader who gets the girl in the end. He starred opposite the beautiful actress Constance Cummings. One of the songs he sang in the picture, "You're My Past, Present and Future," was now a big hit on the radio.

For a rising star, Russ was already quite popular. Many fans were being turned away at the door. Carole could hear a buzz of expectation in the air, as if everyone in the audience knew that what they were about to see and hear was going to be truly memorable. No one wanted to miss out.

An unexpected bonanza of publicity had occurred at the film's release, bringing Russ even further into the spotlight. The newspapers told of the confrontation involving Al Jolson, the famous jazz singer, and his recent fight with the screenwriter, Walter Winchell, the fast-talking Hollywood commentator. The fight had taken place outside the boxing stadium of the Hollywood American Legion.

Walter had written the screenplay for *Broadway Thru a Keyhole*, and Al had punched him right in the kisser, believing that the storyline was based on his wife's life. Before marrying Al, the lovely Ruby Keeler had been involved with the bootlegger Larry Fay. Walter was now suing Al in court for assault, asserting that the movie was nothing but fiction. The controversy drew more attention to the picture, which in turn benefited from the additional publicity.

Russ had walked into the wings of the stage, but she could still see him from where she sat near the dance floor. There wasn't an inch of flab on his tall frame. He was naturally tall, a handsome swarthy Italian-American, with a strong jawline and dark eyes. He wore his signature look for the performance, an immaculate, custom-made white tuxedo with a black tie. He was twenty-five years old, the same age as her. But because he had a widow's peak hairline, he looked older.

Yes, Russ is definitely easy on the eyes, she decided, observing him. *He has good looks, personality, and talent. It isn't surprising that he became a sensation. But will he now make the leap from radio star to movie star?* That was the big unknown, but it was one Hollywood was already banking on. Tonight's performance was a result of the studio's campaign to promote him.

NBC, with whom he broadcast a weekly radio show, had named Russ "The Romeo of the Airwaves." And she had heard him introduced as "The Valentino of Radio." He was considered to be quite the heartthrob.

The orchestra finished its opening set of music and began to play a quiet melody. Russ stepped confidently up to the mike and into the spotlight. He began to sing in a soft, romantic manner known as crooning. He gave the audience the thrilling impression that he was singing directly to them. From the number of love-struck sighs she heard around her, his technique was effective on the female members of the audience.

She listened as he sang the love ballad he had written, "You Call It Madness, but I Call It Love." As he sang their eyes met, a flicker of recognition passed between them. Carole had met Russ before.

The first time had been at a Hollywood party hosted by director Wesley Ruggles. All the guests were sipping bootlegged liquor and drunkenly playing croquet. She had chosen to wear a light-blue tea gown with an uneven handkerchief hemline to match the color of her eyes. She had noticed Russ standing in the shade of a large California oak tree, talking to their host and a group of studio actors and directors.

Wanting to meet him, she had taken careful aim and hit her croquet ball intentionally in his direction. It had rolled to a stop by his left shoe. She'd casually strolled over to him.

All the men around Russ were wearing hats and button-up shirts with long ties, but not him. He was hatless and sported an unbuttoned polo shirt. Carole couldn't help but notice the firm bulge of his muscles beneath the short sleeves. She had heard he was a very good tennis player.

His brown eyes had held a friendly gleam as she approached. He bent down and picking up the ball, had handed it to her.

"Hello. I'm Russ."

They were then formally introduced by Wesley, but there were too many people present for them to converse beyond the usual shoptalk of the motion-picture business.

"I hope we meet again, Carole," he'd said when he bid her good-bye.

"Me too, Russ."

And she had *sensed* they would.

She had last spoken to Russ when she was living with William Powell in 1930, a few months before she became Mrs. Powell. Bill was sixteen years her senior. He had been married before to stage actress, Eileen Wilson, with whom he'd had a namesake son.

Bill had already made a name for himself in motion pictures playing the popular detective Philo Vance. For fun, she would call him by the name Philo, much like a stage performer does when rehearsing for a role.

Russ was invited to attend a Christmas party held at Bill's

white colonial mansion on Havenhurst Drive. He sang Christmas carols with Bill and the actor Edmund Lowe, bringing many holiday smiles.

Apparently, Russ was enjoying himself so much that he stayed up all night, taking turns playing the piano, entertaining the guests. Much to her delight, in the early morning, he ate breakfast with the rest of the gang.

They had briefly chatted when she poured him coffee, her heart making a funny little flip as she passed him the steaming cup. For once she had been completely tongue-tied, her usual witticisms forgotten.

"Thanks," Russ had said with a smile.

If any man could smile like an angel, he did.

"My pleasure," she had replied, retreating to the other side of the table, embarrassed by her girlish reaction.

Before he could say anything more, Bill, noticing the handsome singer, had come up from behind and put his arms possessively around her slim waist. He had silently let Russ know that although they were not yet married, she was taken.

She hadn't seen Russ again until tonight at the Cocoanut Grove. She had returned the previous month from Nevada, where she'd been residing while waiting for her divorce decree from Bill. It was granted by a judge in Carson City, carefully avoiding the circus that a high-profile divorce in Reno would have caused.

Her lawyer, George Thatcher, had advised her to divorce there. California had a long residency wait of one year. In Nevada, the requirement for divorce meant staying a mere six weeks. It had been like taking a long vacation, but in the end, she was single again.

The truth was that during the last year of their marriage, she had seen very little of Bill. She had been busy making eight films, while his contract had required him to make three.

Their schedules had conflicted to the point that they'd seldom spent any free time together. It had felt as if they were roommates, amicably sharing a house and beds, but not acting like husband and wife. Sex was nonexistent, well, at least not of the marital kind. Where once there had been a romantic friendship, a growing dissatisfaction had taken its place.

"I want to retire and travel like we did when we were first

married," Bill would complain between pictures, knowing full well she couldn't possibly leave because of her ironclad studio contract.

Thinking back on it, she realized that Bill saying he would quit the motion-picture business to travel was pure malarkey. At the time of their divorce, he had been offered the lead in Dashiell Hammett's murder mystery *The Thin Man.* He was set to play the detective Nick Charles, a suave character he closely resembled.

Ha! Bill will never quit, she decided, flicking the ashes from her cigarette into the palm-tree-shaped ashtray provided by the nightclub. *Not as long as he can speak standing on his own two feet!*

She wasn't naive. She knew Bill's true intentions. He had been trying to pressure her into giving up her acting career. She had dug her heels in, adamantly refusing to do it. She wouldn't quit. She had worked too hard and put up with way too much horse manure from the studio's producers and directors to stay home and simply knit herself back into anonymity. In the end, instead of quitting show business, she had said good-bye to her constraining marriage.

Carole and Marion Marx, (Zeppo Marx's wife), had spent one pleasant evening in the company of the famous gap-toothed aviator, Colonel Roscoe Turner, attending a show and gambling the night away in Reno. Roscoe told them he was preparing for the Macpherson Trophy Race and planned to fly a Boeing 247-D.

"How about I fly you back to Hollywood, Carole? I've begun a charter service, flying couples back and forth for weddings. It wouldn't be any trouble," he'd suggested.

"You would do that for me, Roscoe? Thanks a bunch!"

On August 18, she appeared at the courtroom in Carson City with her lawyer for her divorce to be signed by District Judge Clark Guild. The courtroom was jam packed with businessmen and had a strangely jovial atmosphere. She had commented on it to one of the clerks, "This is not at all what I expected. It feels like a stag party in here."

Lawyers, bankers, and accountants had stood around chatting amicably, shaking hands, exchanging business cards, and handing out cigars. The loss of confidence by the public after the fall of the stock exchange had led to a run on the banks, forcing the government to close them. Since then, with new federal regulations in place, Wall Street had stabilized and the men were there, asking that they be allowed to reopen. The divorce judgment was held between the bank hearings.

"Powell versus Powell," Judge Guild had intoned, peering over the rim of his glasses, looking at her and Bill as they sat in the front row with their lawyers. Behind them the bankers had continued to chat loudly. "Gentlemen, if you please, this is a court of law."

Silence reigned.

"No children. No alimony support requested. No division of property required, as both parties have settled the issue outside of court." The judge had flipped through the pages, his eyes lingering on Bill. "Mr. Powell will pay Mrs. Powell's attorney's fees. Dissolution of marriage granted."

The judge had hit his gavel against the podium with a loud *whack,* and it was done. The divorce had taken all of six minutes.

She had hastily exited after the judge's dismissal, not bothering to shake hands with Bill, knowing that a reporter and a photographer were waiting outside on the courthouse steps for a promised exclusive. Like a Hollywood pro, she had smiled for the camera and answered the reporter's questions, secretly relieved at how quickly the judgment had taken.

"Now that you're divorced, Carole, what do you think of Hollywood marriages?"

"I think they're swell. Why, I know several very happily married Hollywood couples. But mine, well, it just wasn't one of them." It would remain her take on the failed marriage whenever a reporter asked, but there had been more to it than that. Because there was no conflict, there would be no story—and therefore no prolonged press coverage.

Who knows, maybe a miracle would occur? One day she could fall in love and marry someone even more famous than Bill. Someone everyone liked better, eclipsing him forever in everyone's memory.

Word of the divorce quickly spread, a few local newspapers had raced over to the airport to take their picture moments before takeoff. She had worn a dove-gray tailored suit and a light-blue beret tilted rakishly on her wavy blonde head. Smartly dressed, she'd looked as if she were about to head off for a romantic rendezvous in Paris, rather than heading back to work in Hollywood.

She had been a little disappointed not to meet Roscoe's much-talked-about flying companion, his pet lion cub, Gilmore, with whom he had set several speed records and had flown over twenty-five thousand miles.

"Gilmore is a full-grown lion now, and too heavy to carry these days," Roscoe had explained. "He weighs almost five hundred pounds. I'm paying an exotic zoo to keep him for me. Besides, even when he was a cub, the clever fella would've snagged your stockings in no time."

Roscoe had glanced appreciatively down at her shapely legs. She hadn't worried about the aviator making a pass at her. He could look all he wanted. But she had made it very clear, touching was an entirely different matter.

Within a couple of hours of the divorce, she was back at the studio and in the wardrobe department at Paramount to be fitted for the gowns for the melodrama *White Woman.*

Tonight, she was with the modest and unassuming screenwriter Bob Riskin. He had been working on the comedy *It Happened One Night* for Frank Capra, who gave him regular work. Bob confided to her that he hoped it would soon be green-lighted for production by a small studio called Columbia Pictures.

The orchestra was playing and she was about to hint to Bob that she would like to dance when several of his intellectual acquaintances dropped by their table to drink and have a good look at her. She let loose under her breath several four-letter words.

"We call Carole the "profane angel," explained her friend Mitchell Leisen, the co-director of *Bolero,* to the newcomers.

"Why?"

"Because she looks like a beautiful angel. But watch out, she swears like a raunchy sailor. In fact, Carole is the only woman I know who can tell a dirty story without losing her femininity."

"Hey, if you're a young blonde around this man's town, you have to keep the salivating wolf pack off somehow," she defended.

She remembered how she had managed during the filming of the last picture she'd worked on, *The Eagle and the Hawk,* to avoid the casting couch with good humor. The persistent leading man, Fredric March, the star of the picture, had not been put off by her shocking potboiler language. She had realized, with some alarm, that her language had done quite the opposite. He had panted after her like a dog in heat, even after she had kindly told him to go play with himself.

The movie star was one of the studio's leading box-office

draws and was therefore treated like a king, while she was considered to be a lowly second-string actress who was easy to replace. All of the producers, directors, and leading men had a steady stable of women who were more than willing to spread their legs, thinking that by doing so they would be given a shot at making it big in motion pictures.

Fredric had simply to complain to the director that she was being "difficult," and the studio would have kicked her shapely backside to another less interesting picture. She had seen plenty of actresses descend the ladder that way.

What to do? Quit? Never! Although Paramount shuffled actors and actresses around like a deck of playing cards, frequently changing the casts at the last minute, she didn't request an assignment to another project. She had decided that she could teach the overbearing lug a lesson. But how could she do it without offending him?

"How about you and I share a drink?" she'd suggested, leading Fredric by his tie into her dressing room. The crew had watched, and a few shrill wolf whistles were blown. She'd closed the door and opened a bottle of bathtub gin, pouring it into paper cups.

"Here's mud in your eye!" she'd toasted, watching him drink. She then had lain down on the couch, giving Fredric a seductive come-hither look. The hungry wolf had almost drooled.

He began to tell her what a smart girl she was to give in to his attraction towards her, saying how he could help to further her movie career if she would behave like a good little girl and do as he asked. "Now, honey, tell me again what a bastard I am."

Fredric had begun stroking her, his hands sliding along her legs, reaching up under her skirt, then he had suddenly received an unexpected surprise. He had felt around where he thought her honeypot would be, but instead touched what appeared to be a long, hard, and very erect penis.

"You're a man!" he had shouted. He'd jumped away, pointing an accusing finger at her, as if she were an unclean abomination from the Old Testament about to sodomize him.

"You're fired!"

"No, I'm not," she'd countered with a grin. She had pulled out from beneath her skirt the fake penis she had strapped there. "And by the way, I'm not circumcised, either."

She then had boldly walked over and opened the door, holding up the plastic dildo in the air for all to see. The entire cast and crew had howled with laughter. Shamed, the actor never troubled her again.

It was true, she played by a rulebook of her own making. And like the tortoise, who by sheer determination won the race, she knew she would eventually reach the top rung of the entertainment ladder.

Carole was careful about her relationships with men. Fearful of scandals, she knew her studio had included a "moral turpitude" clause in her contract that could get her canned for any newsworthy indiscretion.

She might be sharing a house, pets, and everything else that was important with a man, but until a ring was firmly planted on her finger, the press would be informed that they were "just good friends." This personal code of conduct was kept in place with all of her relationships. She did not wish to be blacklisted. There were plenty of unemployed blonde actresses who would be more than happy to take her place.

What kind of roles did she aspire to? The thought stirred through her mind while she watched Russ sing. Here he was making his dreams come true, but what did she want? It was an important question that no one dared to ask her. The studios pretty much decided everything in her life, including the person they thought she should love and marry.

She wanted to stretch her acting abilities beyond looking like a beautiful clotheshorse and sighing like an idiot whenever the male lead made love to her. Her glamorous looks, she knew, undermined her ability to land more challenging roles. She yearned to receive the respect she needed from film critics and the studio in order to do so.

Yes, if only a plum role would come along and tap into my hidden abilities as an actress. She almost salivated at the thought. *Now that would be something!* But she lacked the star power needed to ask for better roles. For the moment, she was stuck accepting the typecasting as the pretty girlfriend.

She had no choice but to put on the skin-revealing negligees and let the camera look into her blouse and up her skirt. This on-film stripping for the voyeuristic viewing public paid the bills and kept her image firmly up on the screen. She couldn't afford to be a blue-nosed prude about it. And sometimes, she had to admit, being sexy was a kick.

Bob moved his chair in order to talk to a novelist. He no longer included her in the conversation.

The brainy bastard. She sighed. She was bored. Her romance with the screenwriter was fizzling out faster than the bootlegged champagne they were being served. To think she had gotten all dolled up tonight to become some man's gal pal. It was, well, laughable.

She turned and noticed that the fetching screen actress Sally Blane was gazing up at Russ with open adoration. Sally bore a strong resemblance to one of her more famous acting sisters, Loretta Young, having the same oval-shaped face and wide, soft brown eyes.

Sally blew Russ a kiss. It was obvious from the way in which the young woman's face lit up that she had a huge crush on the handsome singer. *Was Sally his girlfriend?* She couldn't explain why, but Carole's feminine intuition told her that if Sally and Russ were a couple, it was very much a one-sided affair.

Russ struck her as a man who would want a more mature and worldly woman, someone who would be his equal in every way, mentally, physically, and spiritually. He had charisma and deserved a woman who could walk beside him in life as an equal partner, not as a fan. She suddenly felt goose bumps rise up along her arms, a lightning-bolt premonition passing through her. *They would become lovers.*

Stunned, she looked back to the stage and at Russ. Was it possible he might be the man she was looking for, the one who would sweep her off her feet and make her want to put silk sheets back on the bed? He certainly had made her heart do flips at the Christmas breakfast all those years ago.

She intently watched as he began to sing "Prisoner of Love." He turned towards her, his eyes focusing on her face, as if he were reading her thoughts. He began to sing directly to her alone, ignoring everyone else in the audience. His voice was beautiful and stunning, enfolding her, his dark brown eyes connecting with hers.

She took in a sharp breath, her heart pounding. The deep intonation of his voice resonated in a place that had been empty for far too long. It struck her heart. His seductive eyes and sultry voice told her he wanted and desired her. She felt the same way, silently wanting him.

A slight smile curved his lips, he knew. Without ever touching, they were like one in both heart and mind. Their connection held until the last note faded away.

The audience applauded enthusiastically, thrilled with his performance; whistles of approval were heard from all over. For one last magical moment, it was Russ and Carole. The moment lasted until Russ turned his attention back to the orchestra for the next number.

The ballroom was buzzing, and it wasn't from the moonshine. She and Russ were a hot topic. No one had missed the smoldering looks that had passed between them, including her date.

Bob laughingly predicted to the others at their table, "I bet Carole hears from that crooner soon." He gave her a searching look, silently asking the question: *Do you want him to?*

She looked him squarely in the eye. "I wouldn't mind it if he did."

The next morning, a dozen yellow roses, matching the color of her hair, arrived from Russ at her home on Rexford Drive in Beverly Hills. She dipped her nose into the fragrant bouquet, enjoying the thought that the handsome singer was pursuing her. But would he catch her? She hadn't yet decided. For the moment it was exciting to think about last night and where the romance might lead.

Chapter Two

Jungle Fever

Carole stood on her mark chalked on the stage floor, wearing a black, form-fitting sheath gown. She began to sing. Russ, watching from the sidelines, smiled encouragingly. He had been giving her vocal coaching for the two songs she sang in *White Woman*: "He's a Cute Brute, a Gentleman and a Scholar" and "Yes, My Dear," which were by Harry Revel and Mack Gordon, Paramount's newest songwriting team.

The jungle film was a campy melodrama about a ruthless Malaysian rubber plantation owner, Horace H. Prin (Charles Laughton), who tricks a widowed singer, Judith Denning (Carole Lombard), into marrying him. She lives a miserable life of loneliness and abuse until she meets the handsome plantation worker David Von Elst (Kent Taylor), with whom she begins an affair. Her jealous husband sends the worker into headhunter country, hoping the natives will kill him, but David survives. The natives revolt, using genuine Indonesian poison-dart blowers for the scene, and a convict helps the couple escape. The evil husband is tidily speared to death at the end, providing the expected happy ending.

Russ had started coaching her shortly after they had begun dating, and his help wasn't costing the studio a penny. Unfortunately, the picture was already midway through production when he had begun, and she was going to tell him what Stuart Walker, the director, had decided.

She walked over to greet Russ after the director cried, "Cut! And that's a take."

Russ looked wonderful in his light-colored trousers, wearing a tweed sports coat and white patent-leather shoes. His hair was slicked back, and, as usual, he wore no tie.

"You were great, Carole."

"*Please*. I know better. Stuart has decided that my singing voice isn't good enough for the picture. He's going to have my voice dubbed. It's not the end of the world. There'll be plenty of other pictures where they might want me squawking like a parakeet, just not this one."

She drew him down closer to her.

"You were a real sweetheart for trying to help me. I won't forget it, Russ." She put both hands on the lapels of his jacket and kissed him. It was a good, slow, *I want you in my life* kind of kiss. Whistles and catcalls could be heard from the light and sound men sitting above and around the set.

Russ put his arms around her waist. "You got that right, fellas. Wow!"

Later, she almost regretted kissing him. Not that the kiss hadn't been enjoyably toe curling, but she was recently divorced, only a little over a month. What was she thinking? Did she want to become involved with someone who had thousands of female fans swooning at his feet? And she would also have to compete for his attention against other movie stars, like cute Sally Blane.

Determined to remain single, Carole denied the thrilling sensation she felt at the thought of being alone with Russ. It frightened her. He was getting too close too fast. She needed to slow things down. Maybe she should go out on a couple of dates with some other men? Have some fun, kick up her heels a bit?

Other than Bob Riskin, she had been out with the slow-talking hunk, Gary Cooper, whose trailer was located next to her own. Gary would come over and join the fun whenever she had a party on the studio lot, which usually occurred whenever there was a lot of illegal hooch around.

Over dinner Gary talked about the directors and actors they had both worked with at the studio. She jokingly told him, when they were discussing one particularly egotistical actor they both knew, "He's so vain that whenever he goes to the dentist he touches up his teeth!"

"You got that right!" Gary laughed.

When she mentioned Russ, she learned that Gary had encountered him several times on the set of the Westerns: *Wolf Song* and *The Texan*. In the picture, *The Texan*, Russ was one of the background singers sitting around a campfire.

"We got along fine, except in one area," commented Gary.

"Let me guess—a woman?"

"Yep."

"She must have been quite a woman. Who was she? Do I know her?"

"Lupe Vélez."

"Oh, no wonder. She's a known man-eater." The beautiful dancer's reputation for enjoying the company of fascinating men was legendary. The moniker, "The Mexican Spitfire," well suited the tempestuous dancer, who had been discovered by the famed Jewish vaudeville comedian Fanny Brice.

Gary went on to explain. On the set of *Wolf Song* both men had vied for the attentions of the actress. At first Lupe had been interested in Russ, but she then switched to Gary, who won the day and succeeded in carrying on a well-publicized affair with her.

"I was in love with Lupe," Gary eloquently confessed, "or as much as one could get with a creature who's as elusive as quicksilver."

Their passion had ended two years later, after Gary told Lupe that he had no intention of marrying her. She then had tracked him down at the train station. "She was angry," Gary related to Carole. "She drew out a gun and aimed it at me with shaking hands, and then pulled the trigger several times. I dove into a nearby train car, saving myself. The bullets narrowly missed my head."

Carole's heart gave a sudden lurch, thinking of how close Russ had come to being involved with the volatile actress. She decided to change the discussion to a safer topic, music. When the singer's name was mentioned again, Gary confessed that it was Russ's voice she had heard in his movies, *Wolf Song* and *The Texan*.

"I can't sing. Russ has dubbed my singing a couple of times," Gary explained.

"Me too, I can't carry a tune," Carole confessed. But something else at present was troubling her more than her inability to sing. It was the way her date tonight was wearing dark glasses and furtively looking around.

Is Gary ashamed to be seen with me in public? The thought went through her mind, but she quickly dismissed it as an improbability. She wasn't some fan-dancing showgirl from Minsky's Burlesque, wearing hot mama clothes that showed off her tits. She and Gary were both considered to be class acts in Hollywood. Her agent, Myron Selznick, brother of producer David Selznick, had nearly jumped for joy when he heard they were going out.

Observing Gary fiddle with his steak, she gave him a speculative glance. *What gives?* She knew that Gary, a tall Montana man, loved his beef, and usually ate a whole cow. Something was most definitely amiss.

When a reporter who was dining nearby began to take down notes, the handsome actor turned his body away from him. Carole saw red. She began waving and smiling at the seated reporter. All publicity was good publicity. It was the Eleventh Commandment that every Hollywood actor who wanted to remain up on the screen followed, and Gary knew it better than anyone.

She pointed to her dinner date. "He's Gary Cooper, you know—the famous film star. And I'm Carole Lombard. I'm pretty famous, too."

"Is that right," said the reporter. "What's with the shades?"

When Gary didn't give either of them an answer, she jumped in. "He didn't want his fans to recognize him. We're on a date."

The handsome actor looked sheepishly at her and gave the reporter a half smile. The reporter then left them alone.

"Gary, I've never known you to be shy around the press before," she said in a low voice, not wanting to be overheard. "You owe someone money or something?" She was both annoyed, as well as concerned. "Is someone after you for stealing his girl? Afraid you'll be shot?"

She wasn't used to having a man ignore her, unless he was secretly gay. But even Billy (William) Haines, her closest homosexual friend, knew better than to do that. *What was going on?*

She wouldn't acknowledge it, but tonight was a test. Could the most eligible bachelor in Hollywood, Gary Cooper, make her forget the equally charming and single, Russ Columbo?

Gary retreated farther back into the shadows of the dining booth.

Apparently not. If Gary kept up his strange behavior, she was going to use the restaurant's house phone and have someone come pick her up.

"No, no one is after me," he said at last. He took out a cigarette case and offered her one.

The truth hit her when he proceeded to mention ten times in a half hour the actress who had famously been dropped by the mammoth gorilla in the box-office hit *King Kong*, the energetic actress Sandra Shaw.

"Would you do me a favor, Gary?"

"Sure, what is it?"

"Ask Sandra to marry you and go have a whole bunch of kids, would you? And then would you do me an even bigger favor?"

"Anything."

"Don't ever ask me to babysit. Okay?"

He nodded his head and flashed his famous *gosh, ma'am, I didn't know I was behaving like an idiot* grin, the same one that beguiled movie fans the world over. "That obvious about her, am I?"

"Yeah, Gary, you're a man deep in love." She leaned over and kissed him on the cheek. "That's for good luck. You're gonna need it, I hear Sandra is quite a gal."

"She sure is. And I will, thanks."

Two months after the date, Carole read in Louella Parson's column that Gary and Sandra were married at the bride's apartment.

And then there was Bill. He was still very much in the picture. He had called a couple of times since the divorce, asking Carole how she was. He hadn't completely walked away from her. It was obvious he still felt something for her.

"Let's give the whole town something to talk about," Bill suggested. "Can you imagine everyone's faces, sweetheart, if you and I showed up together at the Barn Dance that Kay Francis is hosting at the Vendome Café, or at the opera gala? Think of what everybody would say. Wouldn't it be fun to surprise everyone?"

She agreed, but her heart had squeezed with pain when he used the word "sweetheart." Bill had broken all the dreams she had concerning marriage and what it stood for. Theirs had become an open marriage, whereby they both agreed to let the other date, acting single, while still being married. It was a big mistake.

Marriage must be a friendship, a calm companionship, she told herself. Her marriage to Bill had been far from calm. It had been horribly nerve wracking. She had been wrong about not wanting to possess the man she loved. The whole idea of an open marriage had been a complete sham.

She had spent many sleepless nights wondering who Bill was with and what they were doing. It had hurt like hell. Did she want to give him the opportunity to wound her again? No, but she wasn't ready to commit to anyone else, either.

"Sure, Bill, I'll go with you to the barn dance and anywhere else you'd care to go. Let's give everyone something to talk about."

She hung up and thought about Russ, and how sweet and wonderful he had been to try to coach her. He had been so patient. Then there was the way they had of connecting without talking, as if he really understood her. It was there in his eyes, at the corners of his smile, a silent acknowledgment that what they had was special.

What would happen if she let Russ into her life? She shuddered, remembering the hurt and betrayals she had endured during her marriage. No, she wasn't ready to let anyone in. No matter how attracted she was to Russ, she had to be realistic and be led by her head, not her heart.

They both had their respective careers to consider, as well. Russ had informed her that he was working on a couple of musical numbers for the picture *Moulin Rouge*, starring Franchot Tone and Constance Bennett, for Darryl Zanuck's new production company, Twentieth Century Pictures.

The studios kept him hopping. Russ was a hot commodity. The song "Coffee in the Morning and Kisses in the Night," along with the iconic "The Boulevard of Broken Dreams," both penned by the songwriting team of Harry Warren and Al Dubin, became tremendous hits. Russ performed them regularly on his NBC radio program and during live stage performances.

Carole attended *Moulin Rouge's* preview screening and was delighted to see Russ elegantly attired in white tails and top hat, dancing on a wide staircase while singing "Boulevard of Broken Dreams." She noticed that "Coffee in the Morning and Kisses in the Night" was also sung by the harmonizing jazz singing trio known as the Boswell Sisters (Martha, Connie, and Helvetia). They appeared in the musical number wearing glittery chef costumes, along with Russ and Constance Bennett, who played the roles of a daydreaming couple.

One of the sisters, Connee, posed seated on a grand piano. She was partially paralyzed from a childhood accident. Russ had told her during one of his visits to the set that he had worked with the talented sisters before in New York City, at the Brooklyn Paramount Theater. "The sisters were friendly and nice to me. One night I cooked a spaghetti dinner for them."

He became suddenly somber. "I experienced a dark period, both personally and professionally after that. I didn't record one song last year. To top it off, the woman I thought who loved me, Hannah Williams, up and married the prizefighter Jack Dempsey, instead. And then I had the inevitable parting of the ways with my manager, 'Conman' Conrad, who'd been mismanaging my career to the point that I was practically broke. It's taken me a couple of months to get my life back on track, but I'm feeling pretty optimistic now."

His career, she noticed, was in high gear. Russ was simultaneously promoting the movie *Broadway Thru a Keyhole,* with Texas Guinan, and the movie musical, *Moulin Rouge.*

When Russ called to let her know he couldn't visit her on the set, she was almost relieved. Their attraction for each other had been instantaneous and deep. However, she wasn't sure she was ready for a serious relationship.

"I'm sorry, Carole, they want me to sing a couple of the production numbers on the radio in the Midwest and make some personal appearances. I'll be out of town for a week or two. But when things calm down, can I take you out?"

"Sure, Russ, I'd like that. Call me."

She realized with an unexpected pang, that she would miss him. She had enjoyed giving Russ acting pointers and his presence on set always made her want to perform at her very best. And then there was the sizzling attraction she felt for him. Her body's heart-pounding sensations told her it was very real.

The following week she had one of the most frightening experiences of her life. She was calmly walking through the jungle set for *White Woman*, which contained a river dock, lush vegetation, and live animals from the studio zoo. Suddenly, the adult male chimpanzee named Duke, attacked. The primate jumped to the ground from a nearby tree, rising up on its hind legs to a full five feet. He loudly howled and in a rage, seized her arm, biting down on her tender flesh, piercing her skin with his sharp canines.

She screamed, alerting the animal attendants, who drove the animal away. The pain was excruciating. Blood seeped through her torn silk blouse. The thin garment hadn't provided any barrier against the primate's razor-sharp teeth.

Nobody knew what had triggered the one hundred and fifty-pound chimpanzee's fit of rage. It might have been anything, from being moved from his cage at the studio zoo, to a foreign environment, the set. She may also have looked the primate directly in the eye, which the animal would have deemed a threat. All that she knew for certain was that Duke had attacked without any warning.

The director and his assistant immediately took her to the hospital, where a doctor examined her and treated the arm with antiseptics. Nobody mentioned the word *rabies*, but it was in Carole's thoughts. The chimpanzee may have been infected by rats in his cage. There was no ready vaccination available if she developed it. She knew she could die from the bite.

She insisted on returning to the studio, although her arm was badly bruised and bore puncture wounds. She had to show everyone that the chimpanzee had not made a monkey's uncle out of her. She had a job to do. And she was darn well going to do it!

Unwavering, she was ready to be filmed within hours of the incident, wearing a long-sleeved silk blouse with revealing cleavage. She spent the night in her trailer at the studio, sleeping on the daybed, determined to finish the picture. Her head was throbbing and her bones ached.

Russ had read about the attack in the newspaper and called several times to ask how she was. He was in the Midwest doing promotions, making personal appearances and singing live at theaters and on radio programs.

He called her long distance from Cleveland with a suggestion. "I'll be back in town tomorrow, how about we go out to dinner?"

"I can't... I've got a fever. I think I've come down with the flu." It was a white lie, the same one she would later tell the studio.

"Oh, that's too bad."

"Russ, we have to leave for the theater now," she heard someone say over the wire.

"I have to go, but take care of yourself, Carole," he said.

"You, too." In the tradition of theater people who believe everything happens backward onstage, she added, "And break a leg, Russ."

"Thanks."

After Carole cradled the telephone, she almost regretted not telling him the truth, which was that bacteria from the chimpanzee's mouth had brought on a strong fever. She was now too sick to work, let alone go out to dinner.

Dr. Harry Martin, the physician husband of her entertainment-columnist friend, Louella Parsons, whom everyone affectionately called Docky, was sworn to secrecy when he examined her. He gave her some pills for the fever and promised not to tell his wife about her true condition.

Carole went back to work with steely determination, rehearsing for the over-the-top dance number in *Bolero* with the darkly handsome George Raft. The story focused on a dancer named Raoul Baere (George Raft) from New York City, whose dream is to make it big as an entertainer. He tries to entice Annette, played by Sally Rand (a real-life fan dancer), into becoming his dancing partner, but she turns him down. Raoul then offers the opportunity to Helen Hathaway (Carole Lombard). He creates a sexually charged acrobatic routine to be performed to the music by Maurice Ravel, which also gave the movie its title, *Bolero*.

Carole had to learn many complicated dance steps for the role of Helen, although the lifts would be body doubled. When she practiced with George during rehearsal a spinning turn, a sharp pain plowed into her head. She felt her legs begin to buckle. Upon seeing white starbursts, she inelegantly collapsed into his arms, her body falling limp against him like an unstrung puppet.

When she returned to consciousness, the crew was fussing over her, offering her water and a cold compress.

"Are you all right?" George asked.

She shook her head. She felt sick. No, this was no common flu that was going to pass in a few days.

"You're burning up," he said, touching her forehead. "You'd better go home and take it easy, Carole."

Nauseated, barely able to stand, she had to be driven home by a studio chauffeur. Louella's husband came and paid her another house call, but this time the good doctor wore a displeased expression on his face. She could tell he was concerned.

"Carole, you're very ill. I want you to promise me that you won't go back to the studio until I give you permission. Agreed?"

"Very well," she sighed, realizing the sanity of his request. She raised her hand as if taking an oath in the style of Groucho Marx. "I promise. So help me, Me."

The next day, Madalynne Fields, her secretary and live-in companion, entered the living room, where Carole was reclining on the sofa reading one of the trade papers. Her companion looked displeased. "Fieldsie," as she was nicknamed, was a large woman. She worked for Carole as her personal assistant and was one of her closest friends and advisers. "That Latin fellow is here. Do you want me to tell him you're sick and to go away?"

Carole knew very well who she meant. Her friend didn't hide the fact that if there was a tug-of-war for love to be won between the charming singer, Russ Columbo, and her debonair first husband, Bill, her trustworthy companion's money would be on the older actor as the winner.

"Send him in. And please, wipe that hangdog expression off your face. I don't want Russ to think I've contracted some kind of life-threatening illness."

"Very well, Miss Lombard," Fieldsie coolly replied.

Carole frowned. Fieldsie knew full well that she disliked it when people addressed her formally. Before becoming actress Carole Lombard, she had gone by her family name of Jane Peters. Her mother, Bessie Peters, had brought her up to treat everyone alike. Unless they wanted to anger her, everyone, including stagehands up to the director, knew to address her only by her first name, Carole.

She couldn't blame Fieldsie for favoring Bill. Many of her friends, as well as Bessie, considered Bill, with his impeccable manners and materialistic star trappings, to be the perfect husband for her. But then, none of them had been married to him.

Her mother didn't understand and was evidently baffled by her decision to divorce. "They just suddenly decided to disagree," she overheard Bessie tell her eldest brother, Stuart. "But they *do* intend on remaining good friends."

Bessie seemed to think there was a speck of hope that she and Bill might somehow reconcile and get back together. This hopeful attitude didn't surprise her. Her mother had lived a separate life from her own abusive husband, Frederic Peters, before quietly divorcing him. Carole's father had been in a work-related accident when she was seven years old, which lamed one of his legs and brought on severe headaches, resulting in outbursts of violent anger. Her mother had wisely taken evasive action by decamping from Indiana with

Carole and her two older brothers, Fred and Stuart, on a permanent vacation to California.

As for Carole's other friends, they only understood that Bill was white, charming, and an important movie star who had tons of money. What was there not to love?

Russ entered the room wearing two oven mitts on his hands. He was carrying in front of him a large cast-iron pot. There was something delicious percolating inside that smelled of tomatoes, onions, and chicken.

Carole sat up, astonished by the sight of this handsome man in domesticate attire. Russ was so tall that his dark head almost grazed the awning that separated the living room from the entry way.

It was the first time a man had ever cooked for her. All the men in her life had paid cooks. None of them would ever be caught dead in the kitchen cooking. It was considered women's work.

"Hello, Carole, I brought you some chicken soup. I made it myself." He grinned as he presented it to her.

"You did?"

"Yes."

"Where did you learn to cook, Russ? Did your mother teach you?"

"No, I used to help out at my brother Fiore's restaurant, Gigi's. Do you know it? It's a little south of Hollywood Boulevard on North Western Avenue, not far from Paramount Studios. The entire family helps run it. That's where I learned."

He looked over at a family portrait on the fireplace mantle that Carole had taken when she was a young girl with her two older brothers. "Like you, I'm the baby of the family, the youngest. I come from a big Italian family. When I was a kid I was pretty good at making the tomato-based sauces, but my mother, Julia, was strict. She wouldn't let me help out unless I practiced my music first. I hope this will make you feel better."

"This is sweet of you. Why don't we go into the kitchen and have some while it's hot?"

Once they were in the kitchen, he set the large pot on the stove. She opened one of the cupboards and began to reach up with her bandaged arm, wincing.

"May I?" He stood next to her, taking down two bowls. She

then set them on top of matching plates.

"Thanks."

"Here, allow me." He took down one of the hanging ladles from above the stove. Opening the pot's lid, he began ladling out the steaming soup. They sat down at the kitchen nook table and enjoyed the food.

"Oregano, chicken, tomato, and is that pasta? I've never had an Italian soup before," she said between mouthfuls.

"It's called 'minestrone.'"

"This is really delicious—thanks, Russ."

"The pleasure is all mine." He stopped what he seemed to be about to say next. He stared at her and reached out. He gently touched her face, his thumb lightly tracing the scar.

She flinched and moved his hand away. She never let anyone touch her there.

"Sorry," he said, apologetic.

"Don't be."

"The chimpanzee didn't do that, did it?"

"No, it happened a long time ago. I was in an automobile accident when I was seventeen. I was on a date, and the Bugatti roadster I was traveling in was at a stop light on a steep hill when the automobile in front of our sports car lost its brakes and rolled backward. All of a sudden—*wham!* It crashed smack-dab into our car, shattering the front windshield. I thought at the time it was like a beautiful fireworks explosion, and then I passed out."

She pointed to the jagged line running across the left side of her face, which she had disguised with layers of heavy stage makeup. She knew that Russ could see it in the full sunlight of the kitchen window.

"A sharp piece of glass left an open gash, which almost went to my eye." She gave him a look that said, *I'm a lot tougher than I appear.*

"The doctors performed a new procedure called 'plastic surgery' on me. I was immediately stitched up without any anesthetic for fear that the muscles might relax. The surgery quickly followed. I had twenty-five stitches and had to lay flat on my back for ten days, unmoving, with my eyes taped shut."

Carole grimaced in remembrance of the uncomfortable time. "My mouth was so stiff that for several months I could hardly move it. I had to, as the British say, 'keep a stiff upper lip.' In time, the scar diminished and I used the tricks of the trade, lighting and heavy makeup, to hide it from the camera. Fox ended my contract. They didn't want to risk using an actress with a facial scar. I ended up taking a year off from making pictures."

"Tough break."

"At the time, I thought my movie career might be over. Max Sennett's comedies saved me. His studio, Pathe, hired me because I looked good in a bathing suit. That's where I met Fieldsie. She was working there, too, as a comic. I wouldn't trade what I acquired there throwing pies for anything in the world."

She felt tears welling up in her eyes. She hadn't let herself cry about her most recent injury, not wanting to think about how suddenly the chimpanzee had attacked. Defenseless, she had been unable to prevent it from harming her.

She had hidden the truth. Nobody could know how badly she was hurt. It might damage her career. She had to be strong and get back to work as soon as possible. The studio wouldn't hesitate to replace her if they thought she had a prolonged illness.

What if she didn't get over this fever? What if she worsened and became permanently sick? She worried. It would be all over for her, the end of her career and the good life she had worked so hard to create for herself and her family. Tears began to slide down her face.

"Rats!" she exclaimed, wiping her eyes.

Russ stood up and put his arms comfortingly around her shoulders, holding her. "It's all right, Carole. You don't have to act tough around me. It's not only your beautiful exterior I'm attracted to, you're truly lovely inside, and that's what counts the most with me."

He gently turned her toward him and began softly kissing her, letting her know he thought she was the most beautiful, desirable woman in the world. She relaxed, kissing him back, feeling safe and accepted. It was a momentary reprieve from all the pretending. With Russ, she could be herself.

Chapter Three

Battling Baritones

Carole remained ill for a couple of weeks. The bacterial fever she had picked up from the chimpanzee had weakened her immune system. She was prone to picking up germs and became easily sick. Russ dropped by when he was free, which wasn't as often as she would have liked. The studio kept him occupied promoting a period movie called *The Bowery*, which was supposed to be based on the life of Steve Brodie, the first man to survive jumping off the Brooklyn Bridge. It costarred George Raft.

Carole had seen in a trade paper a picture taken of Russ at the studio party. He was dressed up like an 1890s Bowery toughie, wearing a striped turtleneck shirt with suspenders. He looked adorably handsome. He had received permission from NBC to appear in a four-station hookup on CBS for *The Bowery's* promotional radio show. The broadcast would be heard nationwide from California to New York.

She listened as a radio reporter interviewed him about it. "Russ, how do you feel about being heard across the nation, are you in any way intimidated?"

"No, there's a thrilling fascination in singing to thousands of fans over the radio. I very much look forward to doing the broadcast."

Carole read in the society column that Russ was still dating Sally Blane, as well as several other actresses, including June Knight and Mary Brian. But the actresses weren't the only ones interested in the good-looking singer. Hundreds of fan letters were arriving daily at the studio, some proposing marriage to the handsome singer.

Part of a fan letter was released to the press in which the young woman had made up a rhyming ditty using his name:

I sing of you, Russ Columbo…
You make my heart go jumbo, jumbo…
Russ Columbo.

"Talk about corny," Carole muttered upon reading it in the

morning paper.

Universal was pleased with their actor's immense popularity as a heartthrob, the studio had hired a secretary, Virginia Brissac, to answer his piles of fan letters. Carole had met the pretty young woman before on the lot. The secretary was a friend of Lansing Brown's, a photographer friend of Russ's, who had helped her attain the job.

Carole had turned down the opportunity to appear in the low-budget comedy *It Happened One Night*. The comedy starred Clark Gable, who was being paired in the movie with the French-born actress Claudette Colbert.

Carole had worked before with Clark in the romantic comedy *No Man of Her Own*, in which he received top billing. She had played an attractive librarian who unknowingly falls in love with a handsome con artist. In true Hollywood fashion, he reforms out of love for her and by the end of the picture goes straight.

A Pennsylvania-based reporter had asked her at the premier, "What did you think of *No Man of Her Own*, Carole?"

"I thought it was pretty good."

"Did you feel any sparks of attraction for the man you called a 'hunk of meat' while you were filming?"

"Do you mean Clark? Sorry, no—I didn't feel any sparks whatsoever for him."

"But you did some pretty hot love scenes, and he's one of the handsomest men on the lot. Didn't you feel anything?"

"Nothing."

She knew he was referring to Joan Crawford's interview, in which the actress had famously told a reporter that she "trembled all over with desire" whenever she was around the movie star.

Carole made it clear to the reporter. "It was strictly work and nothing more."

There was also the simple fact that they were both involved with other people. Clark was married to his second wife, the matronly oil heiress Rhea Langham. He was also having a not-so-secret affair with her friend Joan Crawford. The hot passion between Clark and Joan had started during the filming of *Possessed*, in 1931, and had continued into the following year, during the time Joan had become the wife of Hollywood royalty, Douglas Fairbanks Jr.

And as for Carole, her marriage to Bill at the time of the

filming was not running at its smoothest, but it wasn't yet down for the count. She had steered clear of the leading man and the messy love triangle Clark was involved in with Joan and Rhea. There had been no need for her to make it into a foursome.

Carole did give Clark a heavy gift at the wrap party, which was held upon completing the picture. When he opened the package, it turned out to be a ten-pound ham with his picture glued on the side. He found the joke amusing. She and Clark took their picture with it for the publicity department. Previously, Clark had given her a similar gag gift: a pair of elephant-size ballet slippers, which revealed his true thoughts about her at the time. The attached card had read: *To a true prima donna.*

Carole had not heard from Russ in a week. Was he still interested in her? Or was she simply a passing fancy? She wasn't going to stay home waiting for his phone call to find out. To prove her independence, Carole went out on dates with George Raft, her dancing partner in *Bolero.*

George was her current handsome distraction. She liked dancing with him at nightclubs. He was still legally married, although he lived as if he were single. He was separated from his wife, Grayce Mulrooney, who was Catholic and refused to divorce him. He had been a hoofer in vaudeville, as well as a professional ballroom dancer, partnering with him was a delight.

George had an interesting history. He told her he had grown up in the slums of New York, in Hell's Kitchen. He had underworld connections with the quick-tempered gangster Bugsy Siegel, as well as close ties with the mobster Owney Madden, whom he had openly admitted he wanted to be like. When George was with the mob, he had worked as a getaway driver. His gangster ties from New York had followed him when he moved to Hollywood.

George had recently appeared in Howard Hawk's famous gangster movie, *Scarface*, which was the fictionalized life of the Chicago mobster Al Capone, whom many believed had ordered the Saint Valentine's Day Massacres, in which seven rival gang members were gunned down. George's signature move in the film was flipping a coin and having it land back in the same hand.

"It looks difficult to do, George, is it?" Carole asked.

"It's not so easy, especially on command for the camera. I had to flip the coin and keep my hand nice and steady." He demonstrated, taking a nickel out of his pocket. He flipped it easily into the air and it landed back in his hand.

"I even managed to do it while staring at someone and saying my lines. During the filming, several highly questionable characters paid a visit to the set to watch. When it was screened, the picture received Al Capone's personal seal of approval, which he conveyed to me after he had kidnapped me to tell me so."

Sadly, mobsters in Hollywood were a dime a dozen. Prohibition had made the bootleggers as common as milkmen, and almost all the hot jazz clubs Carole frequented were run by them.

George had made dangerous enemies. He was followed around by brawny Mack Grey, a former boxing manager, who was his bodyguard and friend. The concealed heat both men carried didn't make her feel safe. When she accidentally brushed up against the heavy peashooter George had on him, she nervously stepped away, afraid it would go off.

Mack introduced her to a struggling actress he was dating, Lucille Ball. The studios were paying "Lucy" to be glamorous background decoration. She had appeared as an unnamed extra in *Broadway Thru a Keyhole*, *Moulin Rouge*, and *The Bowery*. Carole took an immediate shine to the vivacious actress and they quickly became friends.

Carole couldn't help asking about her favorite singer when she discovered what movies Lucy had been in. "Did you meet Russ Columbo? Isn't he wonderful?"

"Oh yeah, he's a great singer. He did a humdinger of a job promoting *The Bowery*, didn't he, George?" Lucy asked, her dark-blue eyes wide with concern as she nervously glanced over at him.

"Yeah, I guess so." He shrugged, putting an end to the conversation.

Carole, however, couldn't stop thinking about Russ. She listened to his NBC program every Sunday night and enjoyed hearing him sing on the radio. The presenter and producer for the show was Cecil Underwood.

Russ opened the show by greeting the radio audience with the words, "Good evening, my friends." His theme song, "You Call It Madness, but I Call It Love," followed.

A bright "Cheerio!" of recognition was heard from Jimmy

Fidler, the Hollywood commentator, when he was introduced after the music by Cecil.

The selection of music featured a blend of hit recordings and promotional songs from films that were currently showing on the screen, which Russ or his guests sang live over the wire with a full backup orchestra.

Russ had once modestly remarked to her, "You see, I've been studying music for quite a while now. I also studied voice and I've had a musical background playing the violin since childhood. So whatever I've done in my career has come naturally to me. Of course, I'm glad the public likes my singing, and I'm especially pleased that the radio has given me my big chance, otherwise I wouldn't have made it to Hollywood."

He called a half hour after the show ended. Carole sat near the telephone while reading over a script, *sensing* that he would. He asked how she was and he invited her to dinner. This time she gladly accepted. Her fever had weakened and she was already back at the studio working.

"We should go out and paint the town," he said. "Is there somewhere special you'd like to go?"

"How about the Colony Club? I hear it's reopened since the renovations. They're having a big party there tonight, and I've been invited. Why don't you come with me?" she suggested. The Colony Club was one of the few places in Hollywood, she knew, where they could meet and be untroubled by the curious public. It was a safe haven of privacy that provided an intimate setting to dine in.

Russ readily agreed. Carole told him she was rehearsing for her next role with the crooner Bing Crosby in the musical comedy *We're Not Dressing*. She would be leaving the following Monday for a couple of weeks of filming on Catalina Island, which would become the set for the shipwreck scenes in the picture. "The island is located a few miles off the coast. It has a resort town, Avalon, where Paramount plans to lodge us. The movie will be filmed in about three weeks, unless unforeseen difficulties occur."

"Say hello to Norman for me," Russ said, referring to Norman Taurog, the director, who had directed his adorable young nephew, Jackie Cooper, in the Academy Award–winning picture *Skippy*. "He's one of the first directors to befriend me in Hollywood. I've been to his house and Jackie's a couple of times. The kid's mother is Italian-

American."

"I will, although I'm afraid you won't be seeing very much of me in the upcoming weeks. I'll have only a few Sundays and Mondays available, but that's about it."

"That's fine. Anyway, I don't think Bing would appreciate seeing me on the set. It might make things uncomfortable."

"Because of the 'Battle of the Baritones'?"

She knew of the public rivalry created by his ex-manager, Conrad, who at one time was the trusted friend of both Bing and Russ. The cunning manager had pitted the baritones against each other in a battle for the listening public's hearts with competing radio and theater showings.

"I thought you said, Russ, that was all over when you came to Hollywood? Didn't you tell me the battle was just a publicity stunt that the theater promoters cashed in on? So why haven't you two made-up?"

"One word, opportunity. I haven't run into Bing yet, so I haven't had the chance to bury the hatchet. I never cared for the idea of the rivalry. It caused friction between Bing and I, where once we were the best of friends. I don't know what to do to end it."

"But I do. Pick me up at seven, Russ. I hate being late anywhere, so you better be on time."

"Don't worry, I'll be prompt."

He picked her up exactly on time in his brand-spanking-new silver Duesenberg, one of the first luxury items he had bought with his paycheck from Paramount.

Russ was clearly proud of his luxury car and told her that it had been built by hand in America by Frederick and August Duesenberg. Its supercharged engine could go over one hundred miles per hour. He boasted to her that the manufacturer claimed that the only car that could pass a Duesenberg on the road was another Duesenberg.

"How much did it cost?" she asked, wondering if she could afford to buy the luxury car.

"I paid nine thousand and five-hundred dollars for it."

She let loose a low whistle.

"That's almost three times what my friend Louella's husband makes as a doctor! I hope you're getting your money's worth."

"Don't worry, she's worth every penny." He confidently

smiled.

They talked over a romantic candlelight dinner at the Colony Club. As their after-dinner coffees arrived, Bing Crosby and his wife, Dixie Lee, walked into the restaurant with a group of friends, causing quite a stir. The couple had been married for a few years, and Dixie was wearing a new fur coat her husband had bought as a gift after she had given birth to their first child, Gary. She was visibly pregnant again.

Dixie waved to Carole and then, pointing to Bing, made an A-Okay hand signal. For a moment, Russ looked stunned. He clearly had not expected to meet his rival tonight.

Both of the singers were under contract to make musicals. The movie career plans for the two singers, however, were completely different. It was easy for the public to compare the two baritones, since their screen personas were nothing alike. Paramount depicted Bing, the deeper baritone, as a comical scallywag who wore fishermen sweaters, smoked a pipe, played golf, and was always chasing the pretty girls. Russ's character was Bing's complete opposite. He was portrayed at his studios as the sincere and manly lover, always sharply dressed in custom-made tuxedos.

In reality, to Carole's thinking, both men were equally gifted singers who had worked their way up the entertainment ladder. They had both started out in vaudeville, performing with singing groups and dancing. They then had taken it to the next level, as soloist performers, appearing with noteworthy orchestras in swanky nightclubs, where they were discovered by talent agents. Each went on to make hit recordings for phonograph labels and appeared on the radio on rival shows, winning the hearts of thousands of fans along the way.

Competing for the larger national listening audience on late-night radio shows, what was known as the Battle of the Baritones had begun. The media had a field day keeping score. Bing and Russ often sang and recorded the same songs, such as "Blue of the Night Meets the Gold of the Day." While Bing made it his signature song, as everyone soon learned, Russ had recorded it five days earlier than his rival.

In press releases to the entertainment newspapers and magazines, the publicity departments continued to play up their real and invented differences. The battle waged on as loyal fans argued over who was the better singer or actor, Bing or Russ? That question was certainly in everyone's thoughts as a sudden hush fell over the restaurant at the sight of the two famous men eyeing each other.

The moment had arrived for them to make amends and smoke the proverbial peace pipe. Would they call a truce? Or snub each other and have the Battle of the Baritones continue on indefinitely?

"Well," Carole breathed aloud, trying not to show concern.

"Excuse me," Russ said, "there's someone I have to talk to." He stood up and gave her a slight bow of acknowledgment, his eyes glowing with admiration. "Thanks, Carole, I couldn't have done this without your help."

"Go, already," she laughed, never comfortable with people thanking her for her good deeds. She took out her cigarette case and lit one, enjoying an after-dinner smoke while watching the two men.

Bing and Russ shook hands and talked. When their conversation had ended, they clapped each other on the back. Bing and his wife came by her table to say hello.

"Look forward to seeing you on Monday," said Bing with a friendly smile.

"Me, too."

She was relieved that the meeting seemed to have gone so well. Dixie waved a cheery good-bye, and Carole made a mental note to have Fieldsie send a box of orchids and an assortment of baby gifts to Dixie. She'd been a real peach to act as go-between and to arrange the meeting.

Russ sat down. He took her free hand into his own and kissed it. "Bing has invited me to attend their son Gary's christening party. I still can't believe this is happening. I don't know how you arranged it, but thank you, Carole. You're wonderful."

"My pleasure," she said, using the same tone she'd used all those years ago at the Christmas party.

They talked over coffee and cigarettes. She learned that his two closest friends were the actress Sally Blane, whom he had first met five years ago during a break when he was performing with the Gus Arnheim Orchestra at the Cocoanut Grove, and a professional photographer named Lansing Brown, whom he referred to as "Lansa." The photographer had been a close friend of Russ's older brother Fiore when Russ was a teenager.

Fiore had started the family restaurant, Gigi's, and had

unsuccessfully tried to break into the motion picture business, auditioning for small roles. Russ had worshipped Fiore, he told Carole, but his brother had died suddenly at the hospital, following a car accident. Fiore had developed pneumonia there, which the coroner declared to be the cause of death. Russ confided to Carole that his family did not believe that his brother's death had been natural. They suspected foul play.

"We believe my brother was killed by the mob in the hospital. He was smothered to death with his own pillow because he'd been dating a gangster's girlfriend. She'd been working as a nightclub dancer when they met. She was madly in love with my brother, but the mobster she was involved with wouldn't set her free, and they killed him. But there's no way we can prove it."

"I'm sorry to hear of your brother's death, what a terrible loss," said Carole. "And how do you know Lansing Brown?"

"I've known Lansa about eight years now," Russ told her, taking a sugar cube and putting it in his coffee. "I'd trust him with my life. He's never asked for any money from me. Everyone in Hollywood knows him. He's a great photographer. You should see some of the publicity shots he's taken of me. They're terrific. I don't know what I'd do without his help and advice—I can't wait to introduce you to him."

Carole had never heard of Lansing Brown before she'd met Russ and she'd been photographed by some of the best in the business. She realized Lansing was one of those photographers who took headshots for casting calls and agents. Her photographs were usually taken by studio-lot photographers and world-renowned photojournalists such as Cecil Beaton, George Hurrell, and Robert Eugene Richee, who were used on assignments by a variety of national publications.

She could tell that Lansing was important to Russ, though, and said nothing to disabuse his beliefs in the older man's abilities. She put two and two together and realized that Lansing had taken the place of Fiore in Russ's life and had become his closest friend.

"I'd like to meet your friend, Roogie," she said, using for the first time the nickname she had created for him by shortening his real first name, Ruggiero.

"I'll introduce you to him." He smiled, agreeing. "I'm certain you two will hit it off."

Carole was still dating Bill and had the following Saturday a date with him at The Pacific Southwest Tennis Tournament. She was expecting to watch an exciting final match between the Japanese tennis player, Jiro Sato, who was ranked third in the world, and the British player, Fred Perry, who was ranked number two. Jack Crawford, an Australian, was currently ranked number one, but he was not planning to participate.

The other two champions, Fred and Jiro, were to play against each other at the Los Angeles Tennis Club, where the amateur tournament was to take place. The club was one block south of Melrose, not far from the studios. She and Russ, along with many other Hollywood celebrities, took tennis lessons there.

Jiro and Fred had competed the previous year at the same tournament, and Fred had won. But Jiro was at the height of his form now, having won the recent quarterfinals at the French Open, where he had defeated Fred.

That Saturday at the club, Marlene Dietrich, the screen actress, waved to her in greeting before the tournament started. "Come by at the break and have a drink with me, Carole. I'll introduce you to some of the players." Marlene was currently dating Fred Perry, who was widely considered to be one of the most eligible bachelors around.

"Okay, but I'm here with Philo," Carole replied.

"Oh *vell*, in that case, darling." The German-born actress raised her eyebrows and shrugged. It was obvious she thought Carole could do better with a younger man than her ex-husband, and she knew plenty of younger men who'd fit the bill.

During the tournament Bill behaved as badly as he had during their marriage. He openly corrected Carole in front of their friends. "Now, you won't use bad words in front of Norma Shearer, will you?"

"No, of course not." Carole crossed her fingers behind her back. Norma was a high-ranking film star married to Irving Thalberg, one of the most important movie producers in Hollywood. Enjoying her powerful influence, Mrs. Thalberg often played queen bee over Carole, who resented it. It was no secret that there was no love lost between them.

While Carole watched the tournament her skirt hiked up, revealing her shapely calf. Bill eyed her silently in way which said, *lower your hem, woman, and behave like a lady!*

She sighed, adjusting the garment. She had forgotten during their separation how much Bill behaved like a middle-aged fuddy-duddy, chastising her for using foul language, reminding her to sit up and behave like a lady.

The final match at the tournament had indeed been well worth watching. Fred Perry won against Jiro Sato (6–4, 1–6, 6–3, 7–5). Fred went on to win Wimbledon. Sadly, it was the last time Los Angeles would see the gifted Japanese tennis star.

Jiro Sato, who was famous for his sense of humor and cheeriness, became severely depressed, doubting his abilities to perform at a world-class level. Carole later read in the newspaper that Jiro committed suicide after his request for a season long break was refused by the Japanese Tennis Association, jumping overboard into the Straits of Malacca during his voyage to play in the Davis Cup. He was twenty-six years old.

She had to reread the society column twice. Much to her surprise, after her appearance at the tennis tournament with her ex-husband, someone wrote in the newspaper about the possibility that she and Bill might remarry.

Was it the studio or one of their mutual friends who'd planted this gossip in the paper? She wondered if it was Mitchell Leisen, the movie director who was quoted in an interview as not understanding why she and Bill had split up.

She had no clue. She knew it wasn't Louella. Her friend would have asked permission first. Louella was oddly proud of her ability to be accurate about her gossip, enjoying chastising columnists, like Hedda Hopper, who weren't.

Carole concluded that it was probably one of the studio publicists who had planted the gossip. She knew that Paramount had tried, when she was married to Bill, to make them into Hollywood's next high profile couple, on the same level as Mary Pickford and Douglas Fairbanks. It wouldn't surprise her if the studio was now trying to push them back together, asking her friends and family to help. Normally a gossip item of this kind didn't trouble her, but she felt pressured and disliked the interference.

The press was impatient to pair her with someone. They had tried to marry her off to each man she'd been dating since the divorce was finalized. She denied reports that she was marrying Gary Cooper,

Gus Sonneberg, Gene Raymond, George Raft, her ex-husband, and, much to her amusement, Billy Haines, who was homosexual.

When a press agent called to ask once again for a confirmation, she coyly told the writer, "I can't marry all of Hollywood, you know."

Miffed by the incorrect gossip, Carole dialed one of the few phone numbers she knew by heart, Louella's. She gave her trusted friend a scoop by telling her about how Russ and Bing had made up at the restaurant and about the upcoming christening party. Louella thanked her and said it made her happy to have the news to share in her column.

"You're welcome, Lolly," Carole said cheerfully into the telephone, using her pet name for her friend. "I have a favor to ask, though..." and continued to talk.

Shortly after the suggestion in the papers that she would be remarrying Bill, an item appeared in print connecting her to a new love interest. He was someone no one had considered, but everyone knew. It read in eye-popping, bold type at the bottom of the column:

THERE'S MORE TO THAT CAROLE LOMBARD AND RUSS COLUMBO ROMANCE THAN YOU THINK!

Chapter Four

Burying Hatchets

Paramount posted guards on the set of *We're Not Dressing* out of fear that their original material might somehow be stolen by rival studios. The studio's press agent released a statement that said, in essence, that not only was the studio afraid of rival studio spies, they were also afraid of the many fans who tried to mob the sound stage, hoping to meet the film's famous stars. The last part was not entirely true, but it made for a good story, and Carole had to admit that it generated public interest.

One of the real problems in keeping to the schedule was the movie's leading man, Bing Crosby, who hadn't changed his wayward bachelor habits and in fact was often missing. On more than one occasion he had to be hunted down at a golf course or a restaurant and be dragged back to the studio to finish filming.

Although Russ was no longer at odds with Bing, his work kept him away from the set of *We're Not Dressing*. Much to the delight of the publicity department, his absence created rumors that he was afraid of an encounter with his supposed rival. That rumor would be set to rest when he attended the joint christening party on the eighth of October of Bing and Dixie's first child, Gary, and the son of two other actors, Richard Arlen and Jobyna Ralston, at the new Hollywood enclave of Toluca Lake.

The event was well covered by the entertainment press, as it was both a housewarming for the Crosby family and a christening party for the two Hollywood babies. Sally Blane and Lansing Brown accompanied Russ to the party, acting as his supportive entourage. Carole had wisely decided to stay away, not wanting the focus to be on her.

Russ's presence at the house party at Bing's new colonial mansion caused quite a stir. The glamourous white home was massive, with twenty rooms and over seven thousand square feet of space, as was gleefully reported in the papers. The minute Russ stepped in the door, all the guests turned to stare. The famous archrivals were together in the same room at last.

Upon seeing the tall singer, many of the guests nudged one another, exclaiming, "Russ Columbo is here! Russ Columbo is here!"

Bing quickly came up and welcomed his rival, firmly shaking his hands in front of the invited reporters. He then escorted Russ and his friends into the party. Dixie handed them drinks, and they began chatting like old friends, catching up on each other's lives. "Everything's going to be all right between those two fellows," said one of Bing's friends in an offhand way to a press reporter.

At their host's request, a well-known Broadway performer, Jack Durant, sang with Russ to the guests. The guests at the party were delighted to see the famous singers perform together at another vocalist's home. There appeared to be no sense of rivalry among the men— only comradeship and a desire to celebrate their renewed friendships.

The press had a field day and couldn't wait to send off wired reports. It was big news in the entertainment sections of three major newspapers. The Battle of the Baritones was officially over!

Russ called to tell Carole everything. "I couldn't have done any of this without your help, thank you."

"I was happy to be of help. When I've finished working on *We're Not Dressing*, let's meet up again...unless you have plans with someone else." She paused, thinking of the item in the newspaper she'd seen that declared that a wedding between Sally Blane and Russ appeared to be imminent.

"Plans with someone else? If I did, they're cancelled right as of this minute. I want to see you."

"Really?" She was pleased, while at the same time angry with herself for being so gullible. The gossip item about the possible marriage had obviously been left open at her kitchen table, either by her mother or by Fieldsie.

"Really, Angel," he said, shortening the moniker she's been given. "See you soon." He hung up, leaving her to wonder if her destiny might somehow be linked with his.

The fall weather on Catalina Island was mild, but the water was bitter cold. Carole wore light sweaters during the filming of *We're Not Dressing* to keep warm. They had already filmed all of the yacht and some of the island jungle scenes indoors at the studio set at Paramount. They were now working on the beach.

The movie was based upon the J. M. Barrie play *General Crichton*, which had previously been made into a silent movie. It was about a bratty heiress, Doris Worthington, played by Carole, who falls in love with a lowly but competent sailor named Stephen Jones (Bing Crosby). When her Uncle Hubert (Leon Errol) accidentally runs a yacht aground, they all become shipwrecked on what is believed to be a deserted island. Stephen, who proves to be a skilled outdoorsman, brings Doris and her snooty friends down off their high horses by forcing them to follow his lead.

The Broadway singer Ethel Merman, in her second movie role for Paramount, played the part of her character's sidekick girlfriend, Edith, who makes it to the island from the shipwrecked yacht by riding a bicycle between two floating planks with Doris's Uncle Hubert. In the movie, Doris's live pet bear, Droopy, also manages to survive and tows to the island a floating barrel that contains Stephen.

During filming, the director, Norman Taurog, and Bing had difficulty working with the two bears who portrayed Droopy. The stubborn animals had minds of their own and tended to walk away from the camera at the most inopportune moments during filming. The cantankerous animals had to be coaxed into obedience with bread covered in jam.

Norman was a large person who usually issued directions in a kindly manner. This time, however, frustrated by the bears' unpredictable behaviors, Carole watched him uncharacteristically swear and throw his hat on the ground, stomping on it.

"I never want to see a bear again as long as I live!" Norman shouted.

Gracie Allen and George Burns, the famous radio comedians, appeared as a couple of married naturalists. The pair did their part to add to the already zany mix by feeding each other comic one-liners. Their characters later helped to rescue all of the shipwrecked people off the island.

It was a musical comedy that was clearly meant to promote Bing. During the film, he sings no less than ten songs written for him by Mack Gordon and Harry Revel. The songwriting team had also written the music for Carole's previous picture, *White Woman*, which was their first collaboration for Paramount, as well as all four songs for

Broadway Thru a Keyhole, including "You're My Past, Present and Future," which Russ had made into a bestselling hit on the radio. It was obvious the studio hoped to do the same musical magic for Bing.

Carole noted that Bing wore eyeliner throughout the picture and a dark sailor sweater with a white crewman's hat, all of which were supposed to make him look matinee-idol attractive. Unfortunately, he had a tendency to pout during his close-ups.

To her thinking, the script was mildly entertaining but not remarkable. It was another lackluster glamour role for her, where once again she was receiving second billing. She knew it wouldn't add anything to her career. Still, she didn't complain and got on with the job.

During the filming on the island, the crew had set up a changing tent for her on the beach, where they would film the shipwreck scenes. She put a toe in the water and shivered. It was freezing cold.

"You know, Carole," said Bing, lazily taking a puff from his pipe, "if you put wintergreen oil on your skin, it'll keep you warm in the water. Isn't that right, fellas?"

The men who worked the booms and props looked at her and nodded their heads in agreement.

"It's a sure thing to keep you warm," added one of the older crewmen, Barney, who winked at the singer. He opened a tin pail and produced a bottle. "I use it for my arthritis, but I'll let you use it Miss…Carole."

"Okay, I'll give it a try." She gamely took the ointment and liberally applied it all over her body, getting ready to film the scene in which Stephen carries Doris to shore by walking on a sandbar, but then he accidentally stumbles into the water.

She had pulled on her full-length slip when she suddenly felt as if she were on fire. With a yelp, she raced out of her tent and ran toward the beach. She plunged into the icy cold water, not caring who saw her.

All of the cast and crew, as well as a good portion of the town of Avalon, who were standing behind a roped-off area observing the filming, watched her jump in with nothing on but her slip. A gasp of shocked surprise could be heard from the crowd of observers staring down at her state of half undress.

She sat in the cold water, waiting for the burning sensation to cease. She could see that the crew was nervously wondering if she would get mad and storm off the set. Despite her pretentions of asking them to call her by her first name, was she just another show-boating actress? Or was she a rare gal, one who could take a joke? She could sense them quietly waiting for her reaction.

Instead of being angry, Carole opened her mouth and began to laugh. Sitting neck deep in the frigid water, letting the surf wash over her, and uncaring of who saw or heard her, she laughed and laughed. She swore like a sailor, all the while laughing at herself, splashing and kicking the water around her. The crew joined her with admiration in their eyes.

Carole waded out of the water and went back into her tent, where she dried off, combed out her hair, reapplied her makeup, and put on another slip and the wrap dress she was supposed to wear for the scene. She reemerged from the tent and sunnily smiled at everyone.

"Now, where were we?"

The locals who had watched the drama unfold began to applaud.

"Wow, what a woman!" murmured Bing.

She made friends with him, despite the prank. Besides, they both knew sooner or later she would exact some sort of comic payback for the prank.

At Saint Catherine's in Avalon, the resort hotel where they were staying, some of the richer guests looked down their noses at the troupe of filmmaking bohemians who took up two of the large tables and a couple of the smaller side ones in the dining hall. They dropped snide comments about the thespians.

"You know how immoral these actors are," said one old lady to her prim companion, who eyed Carole as she walked by as if she had just arrived from Sodom and Gomorra and was about to strip for them.

"Scarlet women," agreed her friend. "They wear paint and dye their hair like common whores. They smoke and swear, and who knows what all takes place in their rooms at night?"

Not one to walk away without a fight, Carole decided to give the old biddies and everyone else at the hotel what they wanted: an unforgettable performance. At breakfast, when all the guests and the film crew were enjoying their meal, she made a dramatic entrance.

She slinked into the dining room, her hips swaying in a tight-fitting silk dress. She paused dramatically at the doorway, draping herself against the frame. "Bing!" she called out.

"What?" replied the actor, not bothering to look up from his morning newspaper.

"Did I leave my nightie in your room?"

The crooner's mouth dropped open, his pipe falling into his eggs. The crew burst out laughing. She had exacted her very public revenge.

The most difficult filming came near their last day on the island. They were filming the scene in which Stephen learns that Doris has known for some time about the presence of the naturalists and has kept the information from him, which causes him to become angry and to forcefully chain her to a pole. The dark undertones of the scene made it frightening. At one point in the script, Stephen slaps Doris.

During rehearsals, Carole had nervously asked Bing not to go through the slapping motions. He complied with her request. He ran through his lines, speaking the words, but not doing any of the required actions.

The day of the shooting arrived, and she was a bundle of nerves. She tried taking calming breaths before starting the scene, but all she could hear was the rapid beating of her heart. She was frightened. She would have run away if she could have, but she couldn't. She had to perform.

"Cameras roll," Norman said, cueing them to begin.

She said her lines without any difficulty. Stephen was going to slap her in the face. Protectively, she presented the side of her face that had not had plastic surgery. She tried not to flinch in anticipation of the fake slap.

Bing said his lines and raised his hand. *Smack!*

She felt a stinging sensation as his hand connected to the side of her face that had had the surgery. Something inside her snapped, and she began screaming at the top of her lungs. She kicked Bing in the shins, pulled off the toupee he wore to hide his receding hairline, and scratched his face.

Blood ran down his cheek. Several of the crew quickly restrained her from continuing the attack.

She cried uncontrollably as memories of the car accident began to flood her thoughts. She remembered the shards of glass slicing into her face and the trauma of being carried out of the wrecked car. The slap had reawakened everything she had tried so hard to forget. All of her fears about her body being hurt, including her most recent harrowing encounter with the frenzied chimpanzee, took control of her emotions. She lost control.

She tried to calm down, taking deep breaths as she gulped down her tears, explaining what had happened when Bing had slapped her. But Bing didn't seem to understand a single word she was saying. He took out a handkerchief and began to dab at the spot on his face where she had managed to scratch him.

"Thanks for telling me!" he said, and stalked off the set.

When asked what had caused her to become so angry, Bing told everyone, "Oh, it stemmed from some traumatic episode in her early childhood."

Carole watched him roll his eyes. He evidently thought she was a nutcase. She didn't bother to correct him. It was clear that Bing's pride had been bruised, he would misconstrue anything she said. She remained silent and finished the picture.

Opening the newspaper, the following day, Carole noticed, much to her chagrin, that word of the incident had leaked out. A reporter remarked in her column that both of them were carrying scrapes and bruises from the rough scene, although the writer didn't specify exactly what had taken place.

In the final cut of the movie, Norman decided that Stephen should rebuke Doris by saying that she's a spoiled brat who's not worth the trouble. Stephen then leaves her there, chained to a pole for the other castaways to release. Later, aboard the rescue ship, after Doris confesses her love to him, Stephen realizes that she is speaking the truth and sings her a love song. The picture finishes with them sailing away together to live happily ever after.

The picture became a mild success, ranking around eleventh at the box office. Two of the movie's songs: "May I?" and "Love Thy Neighbor," became immensely popular on the radio. Bing blissfully continued his career as a movie actor and singer. He, despite the slapping incident, remained close friends with both her and Russ, often playing tennis with them and she invited him to her home several times.

Not so, Carole, she felt awful about the incident and vowed to never again lose her temper on the set. She didn't want to be seen as one of those tempestuous, high-strung actresses whom directors and other actors dreaded. She didn't know it yet, but this attitude would cause trouble in her next picture, *Twentieth Century*.

She did, however, keep her sense of humor. At Norman's birthday party, she gave the director a very large gift. When it was ceremoniously rolled in front of him upon delivery, strange grunting sounds were heard coming from within.

When the director removed the cloth covering, his eyes widened. There sat the animal he least wanted to see. It was a real live bear!

Chapter Five

Open House

After acting in *Broadway Thru a Keyhole* and working on *Moulin Rouge*, the Hollywood producer Carl Laemmle Jr., the head of Universal Pictures, was ready to sign Russ to his production company. Everyone in Hollywood knew the handsome singer was a little camera shy, but many thought this could be overcome with experience and some good dramatic coaching.

Throughout November, Russ continued to promote *Broadway Thru a Keyhole* and *Only Yesterday* for Universal. By the beginning of December, he was back in Hollywood, enjoying the holiday parties. Carole caught glimpses of his tall figure at various celebrations that they both attended, but they had gone there with other people. She felt foolish for thinking that he was still interested in her when she watched him slow dance with a beautiful brunette at a Hawaiian-themed party.

Not one to hide her light under a bushel, at the encouragement from the host and hostess, Rena Borzage and her husband, Frank Borzage (the Academy Award–winning film director), Carole wrapped a long shawl around her body and performed the exotic Malaysian dance she had learned from the cast extras in *White Woman*. She stretched out her arms, gracefully lifted up the palms of her hands, and slightly bent her knees as she had been taught to do by the young women on the set.

Carole slowly moved around, her hips swaying seductively, a bright smile on her face. When she finished the dance, she bowed low, with one knee touching the ground.

Everyone applauded. Russ's piercing whistles were the loudest in the crowd when she finished. He kept applauding until his disgruntled date elbowed him in the ribs. "Cut it out, Russ! You're embarrassing me."

Carole winked at him, feeling she had scored a home run, and returned to her date for the night, George Raft. For the rest of the evening Mack, George's bodyguard, wouldn't let Russ near them. He always stepped in front of Russ whenever he tried to approach her, blocking his way.

In the morning, at her usual place at the breakfast table, someone had again left open the Hollywood gossip page from the newspaper. Rumors were running around town that Russ was connected with a lovely Broadway star from the Ziegfeld Follies named Dorothy Dell, who had recently arrived in Hollywood to work in motion pictures. Some said that the Southern, ex–pageant queen and Broadway showgirl had once been engaged to him in New York in 1931.

When Carole met Russ again, she asked him about this gossip. He didn't deny that he knew the Southern beauty: "Dorothy is a very sweet girl," he said, "and I saw her quite a number of times in New York at Ziegfeld's Follies—but we were never engaged." It was what she wanted to hear, but it was not entirely the truth.

Carole suddenly found herself spending more time at home during the holidays, she didn't enjoy it. The house on Roxbury Drive was a rental. It had been a place where she could live after the divorce from Bill.

She looked around at the dark wallpaper, the heavy furniture, the velvet curtains with their dangling pompoms, and the flock of dust-filled ostrich feathers stuck in tall art deco vases. She put a hand up to her mouth and stifled a yawn of boredom. She shook the dust out of one of the ostrich feathers and made a decision, it was time to move. She needed a place of her own. She was earning $1,000 a week and could well afford it.

"Fieldsie," she said decisively, turning to her friend, who had entered the room holding a pile of mail. "Call me a house agent, we're moving!"

In the foothills, on Hollywood Boulevard, Carole found her home, a Dutch colonial with four bedrooms, three baths, and a guesthouse in the back. At nearly three thousand square feet, it was a moderately sized home for a film star. It had good bones and was large enough to comfortably house Fieldsie, her mother, and herself, the live-in help, as well as her pet dogs.

This would be a home, she decided, where she could entertain and have fun, a place where she could showcase her success as a film star. It had to be both classy and Hollywood glamorous. But where to find a designer who could do all of that? And because she was not yet one of the best-paid actresses in Hollywood, where could she find one who wouldn't charge her a huge fortune to do it?

Maybe, although she hated the thought of asking, she could borrow some money from Bill to refurbish it? They were still on friendly terms, and he had made it clear that he would be more than happy to help her out financially if she needed it.

It was a delicate question, and she needed someone else's advice on the matter. Carole decided to ask the most stylish person she knew in town, the man she called her "closest girlfriend," the openly homosexual Billy Haines.

She found Billy's business and drove her car down to his little antique shop on Wilshire Boulevard. He ran the store with his dapper right-hand man Jimmie Shields, who would remain his life partner until his death.

The atmosphere at the store was not its normal cheery one. Instead of greeting her with his usual "Come take a look at what I found, darling. I never thought I'd find another of its kind outside of Khuzestan" (or some other exotic locale), Billy merely waved a dreary hello.

"Oh, hello, Carole. Good to see you."

"What's going on? Did I miss someone's funeral?" She pulled off her driving gloves and settled herself comfortably into a leather Edwardian club chair. Next to her stood a tall white statue of an Asian goddess that had been turned into a lamp. It was one of his unique creations.

He took out a silver cigarette case and offered her one. "They want me to get a beard. The studio thinks it would be for the best."

"Is that a problem? Or don't you think you'll look good wearing one?"

Billy had been listed in 1930 as the number-one box office leading man in film. He had recently performed in several movies with Joan Crawford.

"No, you misunderstand, Carole. They want me to marry a beard, or else." He pulled his tie away from his shirt and made it into a comical hangman's noose, crossing his eyes as he did so.

"I was caught by the police with a sailor friend I met at Pershing Square and arrested for lewd conduct. Most humiliating, really," he sniffed, wiping some invisible dust off the empire chair next to him.

"Jimmie had to come bail me out. And boy, did I get a tongue lashing when we got home, let me tell you. To make matters worse, the cat was let out of the bag. Apparently the studio found out about my arrest and made the usual ultimatum: either I iron out and make an honest, straight man of myself by marrying a beard, or I'll be blacklisted forever from appearing in another motion picture."

"Are you going to do it—get married?"

"No," he said. He firmly stubbed out his cigarette. "I'm not."

"Then what are you going to do?"

"I've decided to give up show business. Thank heavens I decided to invest in this place three years ago, or Jimmie and I might very well have found ourselves standing in the soup line over at the Salvation Army, waiting for handouts with the rest of Hollywood's unemployed."

"How are you settled?" She reached for her purse, ready to make a cash donation to help her friends land back on their feet.

"We're not a pair of desperate fairies in need of some pixie dust," he said, pushing her purse away. "We're able to get by, for now. What we really need is work." He gave her an assessing look. "Have you seen Joan's new living room? Isn't it the cat's meow?"

She was aware he was referring to Joan Crawford's startling white living-room showcase. She had heard that the plush white rugs covering the floors and the white grand piano had all been very pricey. The room was unconventional, Carole thought, and it definitely made a statement.

"It's very sophisticated and modern," she said, admiring the room's daring. She gave him an equally calculating stare. "And now I know why you wouldn't sell me that white lounge chair I was interested in. I saw it in Joan's living room. Nice. You and Jimmie did the decorating, didn't you?"

"Yes, we did. The chair wouldn't have suited you, Carole."

"No, I suppose not."

She shrugged, thinking about how much she loved to have her menagerie of pet dogs around, and how quickly they would have destroyed such a pristine piece. Feeling a little bit insulted, however, as if he had inferred that she lacked the necessary class to pull off such refined furniture, she couldn't help asking him: "And what exactly is my type, pray tell?"

The interior decorator sat back a little and examined her from head to toe, holding his hands up to make a square with his fingers as if he were about to direct her in a film. She was wearing a chic gray linen suit with a matching double-breasted jacket with broad shoulders done in the new Schiaparelli style, embellished with gray pearl buttons. A small oval-shaped Juliet cap with a fanned tail was perched on her curled blonde hair.

He gave her a friendly wink, having made his conclusion. "Carole, you are a seductive woman who, as a film star, requires some formality of living. Yet at the same time you're modern and sophisticated—like a piece of contemporary art set in an empire gold frame—and so needs some whimsy and fun in her life."

He tapped his chin with his pointing finger in thought. "I suggest an elegant blue drawing room done in six different shades to match the color of your eyes, and a den with a splash of bright color, possibly wallpapered in tartan. Other than blue, black, and white, what other colors do you like?"

"Green," she said without hesitation.

"And I suppose you want me to do up the rest of the house as well?"

"But I haven't asked you yet."

"Carole, darling, don't be coy. We're long past that. You need a decorator, which is why you came here today, correct?"

"Yes."

"And *I* need a famous client to showcase my talent and bring me more clients, and that, my dear, would be—"

"Me."

He went over to the table and drew out a work contract. He handed it to her.

"Jimmie and I, of course, will do the work pro bono, since you are a good friend. In return, you will promise to buy all the furniture and necessary bric-a-brac from us, and when it's all said and done, you will host an unforgettably fabulous party to which you will invite all of Hollywood. Agreed?" The last part he had asked with a hopeful lilt in his voice.

"Yes. I trust you, Billy. You can write your own ticket and do up the house any way you think will best suit me." She signed the contract and held out her hand to shake. He lifted it and bowed, bending over her hand in the Continental manner, as if she were a queen.

Carole enjoyed staging parties. She was hands down the most original hostess in Hollywood. It was a gift that caused pea-green envy among the better-paid, headlining actresses of film: the high-society studio queens like Norma Shearer and her ilk.

The house's redecoration would be finished around Christmas, a perfect time to have an open house, since all the studios were closed for the holidays. The entire house would be redecorated by Billy, which would launch his new career as an interior decorator.

She sent out invitations and made last-minute phone calls. Many of the invited declined, stating that they had relatives coming from out of town to entertain or a tickle in the back of the throat that might develop into a nasty cold—in other words, the usual excuses people made when they weren't certain they wanted to attend a party.

Carole didn't care. She went through her checklist with Fieldsie, not feeling the least bit concerned that half the people she invited had turned her down. She hummed under her breath the upbeat tune "Back in Your Own Backyard."

"Wesley Ruggles, David and his brother, Myron Selznick, and that cute director, Walter Lang, as well as comedic directors George Cukor and Ernest Lubitsch—you do realize, Carole, that you've asked almost every director you've ever worked with to this shindig? The men at this party will easily outnumber the women by three to one." Fieldsie said drily as she went over the guest list.

"This isn't a sit-down type of party, Fieldsie." Carole gaily waved an invitation in the air. "Besides, I'm planning on serving a buffet, and if I know those fellas, they'll bring their wives and sweethearts with them. Tell me, did I include Clark Gable? I hear they just screened *It Happened One Night*."

"Yes, you did," Fieldsie answered, picking up a note. "Joan Crawford and that new fella she's gaga over have said they might show. Do you think it's wise having Clark and that French fella in the same room?"

"His name is Franchot Tone, darling, and he's from Niagara Falls, New York. I hear he's an actor's actor, in love with live theater, Shakespeare, Ibsen, and all that. I had to invite Franchot. He was the big star in *Moulin Rouge*, and Joan won't come unless he comes. Besides, I promised Gloria Swanson when she visited me on the set to introduce her to the new Sadie Thompson—I mean, Sadie McKee."

"You felt sorry for her, you mean," her friend said, clearly knowing, as did everyone else in Hollywood, that the silent-film star's career was slowly declining.

Carole had invited Gloria in order to help put the lady's name back in the public eye and to introduce her tonight to Joan Crawford, who was reprising the role of Sadie Thompson in *Rain*, which the older actress had originally played.

"I see you invited that crooner Russ Columbo, George Raft, and your ex-husband." Fieldsie looked down at the guest list. "The only one of your beaux missing is Bob Riskin. Do you want me to call him? I don't see him on the list."

"No." Carole didn't look her in the eye.

"Not seeing each other, again?"

Carole shook her head. She had begun feeling as if Bob didn't consider her to be wife material, whereas she knew plenty of men who would gladly give their right arm to have the possibility to marry her, the screenwriter evidently wasn't one of them. Fed up with Bob's hot-and-cold attitude, she had gone sour on him, momentarily cutting him out of her life.

"Well, I hope you know what you're doing. Bob could've written you a peach of a part and gotten you in good with Frank Capra and a couple of the other directors."

"Maybe," Carole shrugged, "but for now, it's over between us." She remembered how she'd passed up the role in *It Happened One Night*, which Bob had wanted her to perform in with Clark Gable. Word of mouth about town was that the movie was a sleeper and on its way to becoming an unexpected popular hit.

"All right," said Fieldsie, "it's your party. But I hope, Carole, you won't regret this." She frowned, putting away the screenwriter's phone number.

The night of the party, Carole stood beneath a bough of mistletoe with a smile on her face, hiding her stage fright. *Remember, timing is everything*, she told herself. She had prepared for the party in the same way she would've before going onto a set, very thoroughly. She had to act as if what her guests were about to see was perfectly normal and, most importantly, fun.

This was the first house that Billy had entirely decorated himself. Both of their reputations were on the line. She glanced around. Drinks were at the ready, as were the canapés she'd had her cook, Edgar, prepare. It was show time.

The doorbell rang, and the hired maid opened it. A crowd walked in and gasped. They entered an empty foyer leading into an equally naked drawing room. The walls were bare of pictures, and all of the rooms, on further inspection, were entirely empty of furniture.

"What the hell?" said Louella, while surveying the empty rooms. "Carole, were you robbed?"

"No, Lolly," she cheerfully replied, handing her a glass of champagne from off a tray. She then placed herself in the center of the drawing room. "What do you think of my new place, everybody?"

"It's grand, Carole—that is, if you don't mind sitting on the floor," commented James Gleason.

To prove his point, the comedian sat down cross-legged on the new carpeting and began eating from his plate. Someone passed him down a glass of the recently legalized bubbly. The repeal of the Prohibition Act had been passed in Congress, just in time for the holidays. Everyone was drinking liberally.

James toasted those standing around him and drank. Her guests laughed.

Carole observed the loyal few who had managed to clear their busy schedules to attend, including the tall, handsome Latin who stood next to an elegant young woman in red who was wearing a big ugly hat, Russ Columbo. He smiled cheerfully at her in encouragement.

Carole herself was hatless and was wearing a hostess gown. She had decided to wear a long black-satin garment. It was a form-fitting, off-the-shoulder gown that belted in the middle, showing off her curves, with a trailing, see-though tulle train flowing in the back. She looked smooth and polished. The adjective *glamorous* described her well that evening.

"Isn't this fun?" she announced. "This is part one, everybody. Come back in two days, and I'll show you the rest." She realized she had been successful in her surprise, a real feat with this jaded crowd, and took a well-earned sip from her own champagne glass.

The entire assembly laughed and said how clever a hostess she was by whetting their appetites for more by showing them the bare, newly painted rooms and carpeted floors.

But not everyone wanted to come back for the real show, she found out. She overheard the brunette woman who'd accompanied Russ to the party remark at the door, after they'd said their good-byes, complain to him, "What a cheap trick. I thought you told me this was going to be a high-class party."

"It will be," he said. "This is the appetizer—the opening act, if you will." He turned, as if he wanted to say something to Carole, but the woman prevented him from doing so and impatiently pulled on his coat sleeve to go.

Carole tried not to let the incident bother her, but it did. After everyone had left, she turned to Fieldsie and asked, "Do you know the woman Russ was with? I saw her with him at the Mayfair Ball at the Wilshire Hotel and again at that Hawaiian luau party I attended at Rena and Frank's."

"Oh, her. Believe it or not, that was Mary Brian, the actress everyone has dubbed the 'sweetest girl in motion pictures.'"

"That's right! I should've recognized her. She was in a picture once with Bill a couple of years ago."

"*Forgotten Faces* was the name," Fieldsie said. "You didn't recognize her because she was wearing that ugly hat. She's been dating a whole string of men lately, from what I hear." She gave Carole a concerned look. "Hey, pal, you're not going to let that singing Romeo and his date sour your success, are you?"

"No, of course not."

Carole secretly wondered if Mary was now Russ's girl and she felt unhappy at the thought, yet she couldn't blame him for dating other women. They had gone out on a couple of unforgettable dates, intimate candlelight dinners at some grand restaurants and clubs, a drive to the ocean in his silver Duesenberg, dancing, romantic moments that any woman would have been thrilled by.

He must have thought he was getting somewhere with her, but then she had done an unexpected about-face. She had purposefully distanced herself from him, buckling under pressure from the studio to be seen as an unattached woman-about-town.

She had been publicly stepping out with George Raft, promoting their picture *Bolero*, which was to be released in February. The press turned a blind eye to the fact that the actor was still married, since he was now amicably separated from his Catholic wife.

The press focused on Carole and George as a movie couple. They were seen everywhere together, including Max Factor's makeup advertisements in the entertainment magazines, in which they were still framed in a romantic tango pose from the picture. A side feature of the ads had Carole giving step-by-step instructions on applying makeup, promoting the idea that rouge, lipstick, and foundation weren't forbidden products that were commonly used by prostitutes—ordinary women could use them, too. You, Miss Nobody Special, could go from being plain Jane Peters to becoming glamorous actress Carole Lombard, the woman whom men like the handsomely romantic George Raft desired to dance through life with.

Carole looked down at her guest list and frowned. *Well, you've got no one to blame but yourself if Russ walks off with someone else,* she told herself, thinking about Mary Brian. But she couldn't resist adding his name to the list of those to be invited to the second party.

What Fieldsie failed to notice when she went over the list was that Carole had invited not only every director she knew and wanted to work with, but also almost every leading man, including the one the studios weren't so certain about, the wild card, Russ Columbo. If she had noticed, Carole knew, Fieldsie would have asked what she was up to.

Chapter Six

Merry Gentlemen

The phone rang off the hook for the next two days. Curiosity, and the feeling you're missing out on all the fun, are great motivators for attending a party. Word spread faster than racecar champion Louis Meyer taking a hairpin curve at the Indianapolis 500 Speedway. Many of the leading actors, directors, and producers of Hollywood who had previously declined her invitation to come to the open house were suddenly free to attend the second party, to be held on Christmas Eve.

Billy Haines had been miffed with her at first, thinking her idea of an empty house party was completely nutty. "You're supposed to be showcasing my talent, not a bunch of empty rooms. What will people think—that I can't deliver on time or something?"

"Darling, stop fretting. You're as nervous as a stockbroker. Everything will be great, just you wait and see. You'll be the talk of the town. I promise." Carole drew a cross over her heart with a finger.

And she was right. Word spread around town about what had happened. Billy's little shop suddenly became the focal point of Hollywood's elite crowd, who dropped by to simultaneously discuss the unusual party and their decorating woes. The end result was a record-breaking week in sales for the store and numerous firm promises to attend her party to see his finished masterpiece.

Christmas Eve arrived, the night of the party. Bill Powell greeted her with a kiss on the cheek and told her he was certain she had a big hit on her hands—and, by the way, did she want to go away with him?

"I'm thinking of going down to Agua Caliente with a crowd and I thought maybe you'd care to join us in Mexico for the horseraces and gambling, like we did last year with the gang? We'll have a barrel of laughs."

She knew he was referring to their jaunt down to Tijuana last January. Sure, they'd had a grand time at the Hotel Agua Caliente Casino Resort, gambling at night and attending the horseraces during the day, even though she'd had to walk almost two miles from the luxurious tiled art deco hotel to reach the racetrack.

Of course, her millionaire husband had refused to let her ride in a hired car from the hotel—that would have been far too easy. "Let's walk and take in the scenery, darling," Bill had suggested. She'd reluctantly agreed.

They had walked. Bill wearing his flat loafers (the same ones he sported when playing badminton), she in six-inch high-heel shoes. The sun was high in the sky, and he wore a brimmed straw fedora to protect his face. She had followed behind her lord and master, swearing bitter epitaphs while balancing precariously on high heels.

"Bill, wait up!"

He slowed his walking until she'd caught up.

"What do you say we take the next cab that drives by, huh? My dogs are killing me. I've got blisters."

"But we're almost there, darling." He'd pointed to the racetrack, about a mile away.

As she limped by a lone cactus, she could have sworn that it saluted her. She sweated it out for a while longer until finally a covered donkey cart driven by a young boy began to pass her. Her husband had once again briskly walked on ahead without her.

She had waved to the boy to stop, gesturing her desire to hitch a ride. He had nodded his head, agreeing. Delighted, she had sat down on the covered cart's narrow wooden bench after handing the young driver a couple of pesos from her purse. The shade was heavenly, and her feet stopped throbbing. She soon was contentedly swinging her legs back and forth.

Cutting open a watermelon, the boy had handed her a slice to enjoy.

"Gracias," she'd said gratefully. She bit into the piece of watery sweetness.

When a minute later she passed Bill on the dusty road, wiping his sweaty brow with one of his perfectly folded silk handkerchiefs, she stuck her tongue out at him and waved.

"Enjoy the scenery, Philo!"

They spent the rest of the day in the starter's stand to watch the races, since they had been invited by the president of the racetrack to join him. When asked about it later, Carole told a reporter that the trip had been worth it, because they had not only seen the start of the race but were still there when the horses came out of the turn into the home stretch.

It had been thrilling to feel the horses running so close by them. She had felt the thunder of their moving bodies, the vibrations reverberating along the wood rails as the animals headed toward the finishing line in a quick flash of horseflesh and movement.

Carole had immediately started performing in the eerie film *Supernatural* upon her return to Hollywood from Mexico. She portrayed a woman who visits a medium and becomes possessed by the spirit of a vengeful dead murderer. To her thinking, the movie made her into a kind of female Boris Karloff. Her time in Mexico was now forgotten as her marriage began its slow descent to its inevitable end.

She looked tonight at Bill's hopeful face as he stood by the Christmas tree in the drawing room and realized that her heart wasn't in it. She didn't want to bend to his will.

"Sorry, Philo, I can't go to Mexico with you. I promised George I'd attend a boxing match with him on the fourth. The studio is counting on me to continue promoting *Bolero*."

"I see." He put his index finger up against the side of his nose in a knowing manner.

He walked over to the dining-room where a buffet had been laid out and began serving himself. The dapper actor Lloyd Pantages, who was talking to fellow actors Richard Barthelmess and Lois Wilson, warmly greeted him.

A simple, modern, three-tiered chandelier hung above the neo-classical dining table, which was surrounded by salmon-pink-covered chairs, the arms of which were shaped to look like Greek lyres. On the center of the dining table were some of her favorite flowers, sweet-smelling white gardenias in a cut-glass bowl from her garden, flanked by two double-armed silver candelabras lit with tall white candles.

The furniture of the dining room, living room, and bedroom had been carefully designed by Billy and had been built at his workshop. In the drawing room, done up in the promised six shades of blue, was a *directoire* chair, the curved tufted back resembling a seashell. It was perfect for lounging on and was situated near the white-painted brick fireplace. Above its mantle hung a large plain mirror that reached the ceiling. Christmas decorations added holiday cheer. Fake icicles and a white flocked Christmas tree hung with silver bells stood by the drawing room's wide front window.

Billy's signature looks, two small busts made into lamps, sat on pedestals on each side of the hearth. In one corner, overlooking the room, a large bronze emperor's bust sat on a taller pedestal. Across the room long empire-styled sofas and a custom-made, low, neo-classically styled coffee table. Billy had unknowingly started with her home what was to become known by decorators as the Hollywood Regency style.

"Did you see the piano in the den?" she heard one of her female guests asked another.

"Yes, I did, isn't it a hoot? Speaking of which, have you seen Carole's bedroom yet? It's to die for, completely over the top."

"No, I haven't seen it yet, but I'll make certain to before I leave tonight."

The bedroom walls were done in a dusty plum red with matching carpeting. The focus of the room was an oversize sleigh bed in rich velvet, with white buttons tufting the fabric. Most importantly to Carole, as she was frequently ill, it was comfortable enough to spend all day in. Two side tables holding lamps, covered with books and scripts, were at the end of the bed. Full-length mirrored panels, creating folding screens, surrounded the bed on each side, starting a new Hollywood trend.

Billy explained to the guests with a touch of humor, "You know how it is, motion picture people like to see how they look, even when they're sleeping."

Carole laughed. "And all this time I thought they were there to increase my chances of getting laid."

She noticed that Clark Gable had arrived at the party. He was his usual dapper self, wearing a black wool gabardine suit with a red tie. He was now sporting a thin mustache, which she had to admit looked good on him.

Clark was invited to the party tonight because he was one of Hollywood's biggest movie stars. Almost all of the stars from *Dancing Lady,* which had been released in theaters in late November, were there at the party, including Joan Crawford and Franchot Tone. Clark was talking to the hard-drinking actor John Gilbert; the latter having forewarned her that he would be leaving the party early to catch a train. The studio was debuting *Queen Christina,* in which he portrayed the lover, Don Antonio, to Greta Garbo's queen, in New York City.

Many of her guests were admiring the piano and the handsome performer playing it, Russ Columbo. The entire piano, except for the keys, was covered in green and pink tartan, which matched the den's walls. Russ was singing Christmas carols, much as he'd done all those years ago, with the actor Edmund Lowe, and, from the looks of it, having a marvelous time.

He looked in her direction as he played "God Rest You Merry Gentlemen," and as he did, she realized that she wanted things to end differently than they had a few years ago. He had shown up tonight minus a date and his usual entourage of Sally Blane and Lansing Brown.

Carole had read in the newspaper that he had other worries than his love life and career to occupy him. His ex-manager, Conrad, had filed a suit against him in court as an early Christmas present, stating that the singer owed him one-third of his net earnings for managing and promoting his Hollywood career.

"That's a complete lie," Russ bitterly told her. "I walked away from Conman Conrad ages ago, when he spitefully mismanaged my career in New York City. Conrad cancelled lucrative contracts without my knowledge, bringing my career to a near standstill in the process. He left me sick with the flu, skipping town with money in his own pocket, and leaving me almost empty-handed."

Everything Russ had negotiated in Hollywood since then had been without his ex-manager's help. The suit would be later "dismissed with prejudice". The legal term meant that Conrad had behaved badly in the eyes of the court. Because of his misconduct, Conrad was forbidden from ever filing a similar suit against Russ.

Joan Crawford was there with her new love interest, Franchot Tone. The newcomer, along with the talented Broadway dancer Fred Astaire and the Three Stooges, were making their film debuts in the film *Dancing Lady*. It was the first picture Joan and Clark had starred in together after their affair had been broken up by the studio.

Joan had been sent on a delayed honeymoon to Europe with her husband, Douglas Fairbanks Jr., in the hope of avoiding a public scandal. It hadn't worked, the couple had divorced upon returning to Hollywood.

"What's up with Pa?" Carole asked Joan, using the nickname she'd devised in response to Clark's new habit of calling her Ma, as his character had in the movie *No Man of Her Own*. "He looks glummer than usual tonight. Is it my imagination, or is he now wearing dentures? He keeps lifting his hands up to his face, as if to check that they're in the right place."

"That's right, you don't know what happened last summer!" Joan gave her a saucy *I've got something juicy to tell you* wink. "Come with me." She turned to Franchot. "I'll be back in a little while, darling. Powder room. Girls' talk, and I want to see the black lace curtains Carole put up. You can manage without me, can't you?"

"Sure. I'll go over and chat with Russ. I haven't seen him since we worked together on *Moulin Rouge*."

"You do that."

Once in the white-colored powder room with crystal doorknobs and swagged black-lace curtains, Carole sat down next to the vanity table filled with the collection of crystal perfume bottles she owned. Joan locked the door behind them.

"I don't want our conversation to be overheard. Although most of the gang out there already knows about Clark's health troubles, I'm supposed to keep this all hush-hush. The studio says we have to maintain his manly image. I hope Louella doesn't write anything." She gave her a meaningful look that said she would never talk to Carole again if Louella did.

"I'll ask her not to. So, what happened?"

"He passed out on the set of *Dancing Lady*. He and I were in the middle of a dance routine, when—*boom!* He passed out right there in front of me. I can tell you, Carole, I was scared. He didn't wake up. The studio called an ambulance, and they took him right away to some private hospital. He was really sick. I never felt so sorry for anyone in my entire life."

"What was wrong with him?"

"Pyorrhea, from infected teeth and gums. You know, he's always been a heavy smoker and had bad teeth. His first wife, Josephine Dillon, paid to have them straightened, but they were still pretty bad. The infection spread throughout his system and nearly killed him. The doctors removed most of his teeth, he's now wearing dentures. It's taken him a little time to get used to them. We had to shoot scenes around him for weeks. He could hardly talk when he was first wearing them."

"The poor man!" Carole exclaimed. "He must really be one of the saddest men in Hollywood. He always seems so depressed. His wife, Rhea, she must be a real harpy to live with, spending all his money the way she does. He needs a woman who can make him happy, someone who'll take an interest in what he enjoys doing and will try to help him with his career."

Joan gave Carole a look that stopped her in her tracks. The other film actress knew better than anyone how Clark operated with women, and it was a safe bet Joan thought Carole might very well be the next notch on his belt. The assumption made Carole uncomfortable. Yes, she had a tender heart, but she wasn't stupid.

"What about you and Franchot? I hear things have been sizzling between you two," Carole said, deftly changing the subject.

"Time will tell," her friend said with a laugh. "Meanwhile, we're having a lot of fun." Joan rolled her large brown eyes suggestively. She then unlocked the door and walked out of the powder room.

Clark walked by and smiled to them. "Hiya, Ma! Swell party you have going here. The food's good, and so is the company."

"Thanks, Pa."

He winked and headed to the den's bar, where he served himself a healthy tumbler of whiskey.

Joan frowned. "Look, Carole, be an angel and forget everything I told you about Mickey Mouse, will ya? I'm probably going to be working again with him soon on another picture and the last thing I want to do is get on his wrong side."

"Sure thing."

But Carole couldn't help wondering, despite her friend's obvious attraction to Franchot Tone, if Joan wasn't still in love with the big-eared lothario. Clark always acted as if he were the only cock in the hen house—could he ever settle on one woman? She briefly deliberated if it was possible, but quickly realized it wasn't her concern.

If she could pick any man in Hollywood to be by her side, whom would she choose? There were certainly plenty of good-looking, eligible male stars in her home that night. Besides Clark Gable, George Raft, John Gilbert, and her ex-husband, there was Richard Bethelmess, a very good-looking Hollywood star who was currently single. The trouble was that Richard was part of the trio of sophisticates known as the "Three Musketeers," consisting of Bill, Ron Colman, and himself, all of whom were close friends.

Carole wanted someone new, exciting, and romantic in her life. She wanted a man who wouldn't say to her, "Remember, darling, when you, Bill, and I did this?" Unthinkingly, she looked across the room.

A crowd was congregating around Russ at the piano. She could barely see him, although he was a head taller than most people there. She noticed that several women had tried to snare his attention during the evening, but he hadn't appeared to be interested in any of them.

Russ had barely spoken to her all evening. She had felt his eyes following her from time to time, and the attention made her happy. She had put on another gown by Travis, this time in one of her favorite colors, gray, because it brought out the color of her blue eyes and photographed well.

The long gown was made with tight long sleeves and a gathered fish-style train in the back. At the neckline, beading created the impression of a jeweled necklace dripping down the front of the garment's one-piece bodice. The beaded sleeves created the impression of multiple jeweled bracelets. When Carole went out at night, she wore a matching cape over it with loose sleeves and a long flowing train, trimmed with wide lace.

She played her part as hostess, occasionally bringing Russ coffee while he performed on the piano, lingering whenever she was able. It was nearing midnight and many of her guests were preparing to go home to rejoin their families. A crowd surrounded Russ, imploring him to sing at least one or two of his popular songs as a treat before they left. Franchot had earlier obliged by singing a couple of well-known show tunes.

"Russ, my wife Edna is a big fan of yours," said the one-legged veteran actor Herbert Marshall. He was a comrade of actor Ron Colman's, with whom he'd served in the London Scottish Regiment during World War I. Herbert wore an artificial leg, which was barely noticeable when he walked. He was sitting easily on one of the bar stools near the piano with his wife.

"Won't you sing a song for us before we leave, Russ?" Herbert asked. "It'd be something Edna could write her friends and family about, a Christmas present for her to remember tonight by."

"Sure thing," Russ replied, turning to the young woman.

"You're Edna?"

"Yes."

"Merry Christmas, Edna. What would you like me to sing?" Russ asked, running his fingers easily across the piano's keys before taking a final puff on the cigarette he'd been smoking.

"Could you sing 'Guilty'? It's a favorite of mine."

"It'd be my pleasure." Russ smiled at the young English woman and began playing without hesitation the introduction to the song on the piano. The room became silent as everyone waited with breathless expectation for him to open his mouth and begin to sing.

Carole stood still as well, putting a hand up to silence the person next to her who wanted to talk. She didn't look to see who it was; her entire focus was on Russ.

Russ began to sing, while his hands deftly played the piano keys. He looked across the room to her, their eyes meeting. His hands swept across the keys as his voice sang out the plea she knew he was directing at her.

Her heart thumped hard against her chest. She had been pushing him away these past couple of weeks because of her career. She was giving the public what it wanted by being with George, creating the impression that they were a couple of lovers, and that what was happening up on the screen was also happening off.

She had never felt more miserable in her life, running into Russ at almost every party she went to. Seeing him smiling and dancing with another woman made her jealous. It should have been her whom he held in his arms at the Mayfair Ball and the Hawaiian luau, not Mary Brian. In her heart of hearts, Carole knew she had invited him in order to see if he was still interested in her. And, if she was honest with herself, to see if she in turn could make him jealous.

He continued to sing, looking straight into Carole's eyes as he sang. He finished the song, and everyone in the room applauded. She knew the song was his open declaration of continued interest. He hadn't given up on her.

"Thanks, Russ," Herbert said, patting him on the shoulder. He turned to his wife. "I told you he was a nice guy, Edna."

"Yes, thanks, Russ." Edna smiled in gratitude.

The man Carole had previously silenced was now gently touching her on the elbow.

"Good night, Carole. Thanks for inviting me." She turned and

realized the person who'd been standing next to her d
was Clark Gable.

"Oh good night, glad you could come, Pa. I hope you an.
have a merry Christmas and a happy New Year."

"You too, Ma." He glanced in Russ's direction and quickly
kissed her on the cheek.

One by one, her guests hugged and kissed her good night,
wishing her a Merry Christmas. George, following the example of
Clark, kissed her on the cheek, his dark eyes narrowing when he
noticed Russ was waiting for his turn to take his leave.

"Don't forget, we have a date on the fourth," George said
pointedly, reminding her of the boxing match they were to attend
together in January.

"I won't." She knew that David Selznick and his brother,
Myron, were listening to their conversation. The two men beamed, she
was being a good studio player and putting her career first.

When it came to be Russ's turn to bid her farewell, he looked
up at the mistletoe that she had placed above the door. "There's one
more berry left, I see. You know what that means, don't you, Angel?"

He plucked it from the bough. In front of everyone, he took her
into his arms and kissed her.

She heard gasps of shock all around her, but she didn't care.
Carole closed her eyes, enjoying the pressure of his lips on hers. Her
heart sang, and she felt as if she had been granted wings and made into
a real angel. She could have sworn she heard bells ringing. When she
opened her eyes, she blinked, realizing they were real. It was midnight,
and the local churches were ringing in Christmas Day.

"Merry Christmas," he said.

He then walked out the door, down the garden path to where
his silver Duesenberg was parked. With athletic ease, he jumped into
the front seat of the car and drove off. She watched, placing her
fingertips up to her mouth. Her lips were still tingling.

"I think we'll definitely be seeing a lot more of that crooner,"
Fieldsie remarked to Bessie.

"Do you think so? But I thought Carole and Bill were supposed
to be getting back together."

"Look at her. That was some kiss he just gave her, nearly
knocked her off her feet."

"Oh," said Bessie, and then noticing that Bill had been witness .o the kiss between his ex-wife and the singer, "Oh!"

"Oh, *indeed*," reiterated Bill, kissing his ex-mother-in-law on the cheek. He then tipped his hat in Carole's direction, wishing her a Merry Christmas.

"And a Happy New Year to you," she murmured, never taking her eyes off Russ's car as it disappeared down the street.

"I'll try. Yes, I'll certainly try to make it a happy one." Without any further adieux, Bill walked down the path to his own car and drove away.

Chapter Seven

Boxing Day

Friday in Hollywood was boxing day, the main event leading up to the weekend. The boxing matches took place at the Hollywood American Legion Post 43 Stadium. Boxing notables such as Jack Dempsey (The Manassa Mauler), James J. Braddock (Cinderella Man), and Joe Louis (The Brown Bomber) fought there. George Raft, like many Hollywood celebrities, owned season tickets. Carole saw Boris Karloff, Charlie Chaplin, Clark Gable, the Marx Brothers, and Mae West, greeting one another as they took one of the valuable ringside seats close to the mat.

"Hey, Mae! How you doin'?" Carole's date, George, shouted out. The curvaceous actress was sashaying down the middle aisle alongside a muscular black man bearing a pile of gifts.

"Swell, George, just swell," replied the platinum blonde, throwing a white-fox stole over one shoulder. George and Mae had worked together on her first picture in Hollywood, *Night After Night*, in which he headlined.

"You know Gorilla, don't you?" asked Mae, introducing the man standing beside her, William Jones, by his boxing moniker. He was a National Boxing Association middleweight champion. When he wasn't in the ring boxing, William worked for Mae as a bodyguard and chauffeur. Carole had heard rumors that the biracial couple were also lovers, since the actress had bought the entire apartment building she was living in after the landowner tried to ban William from entering.

"Sure, I do," George replied. "Nice to meet ya, pal."

"Likewise," the boxer said with a nod. They didn't shake hands, since his arms were full of the gifts that Mae would later distribute to her favorite fighters.

"Have a great evening, Mae."

"You too, George. Good to see ya, Carole. Thanks for that fancy French telephone. It's a swell Christmas present. I use it every day."

"My pleasure, Mae. Glad you like it."

George was wearing plasters on his ears, and Carole could tell he was embarrassed by the curious looks everyone kept giving him. He was trying to hurry her to their seats, but that was not to be. Carole was immensely popular and many stars came over to tell her how much they had enjoyed her parties and the Christmas presents she had sent.

She was generous and didn't limit her gift giving to the stars and directors, she also had presents for anyone who worked on the set, from the cameraman down to the sweeper. To her, they were all friends.

"Were you two in a fight?" she asked George, voicing the question everyone must have been wondering, since both George and his bodyguard wore white medical tape on their ears, and Mack wore a wide strip across the bridge of his bulbous nose.

"No," George said, "we had some plastic surgery done." He pulled his fedora farther down on his head to hide the white tapings.

Carole knew George had boxed and played professional baseball but hadn't been very successful in either sport. He was known to have a quick temper and was frequently involved in brawls, including a couple that took place on the studio lot. She'd heard from Lucille Ball that George had had a fight during the filming of *The Bowery* with actor Wallace Beery (the lead) and a few extras. He'd also clashed in front of Carole with producer Ben Glazer on the set of *Bolero* over a scene where he was supposed to swear on his mother's grave, which he'd deemed blasphemous.

George had been so anxious to talk to the producer about the disputed scene that he dropped Carole in the middle of a dance rehearsal, when Ben walked onto the set. She landed smack-dab on her bottom with a loud *thump.*

"Thank you, George!" She had let loose a few scalding words, while rubbing her sore backside.

"I'm not going to do the scene—I refuse to do it!" George shouted.

"You're under contract, George. You'll do the scene exactly as I tell you to," retorted Ben.

That had set the hot-tempered actor off. He socked Ben squarely in the jaw, knocking him out cold. After several more arguments, involving agents and the studio's lawyers, a truce was eventually called, and they dropped the proposed scene from the movie.

Chunks of George's ear had gone missing du*/ creating what is known in boxing circles as *cabbage ea* had plastic surgery done on his ears and crooked nose, as well.

Carole watched the boxing matches with interest. When she was a young tomboy and saw her brother Stuart taking boxing lessons from their neighbor, the famed 1917 world lightweight champion Benny Leonard (The Ghetto Wizard), she insisted on learning, too. She did surprisingly well and, much to her pleasure, the boxer told her she was a better fighter than her older sibling, making up for her small size and weak strength with speed and gumption.

During one of their dinners, Russ had informed her that he, too, had boxed in his youth and had even fought once and lost. But his father had quickly snipped that youthful ambition in the bud.

"When Pops found out I'd been in a fight he was madder than hell with me. I can still hear him yelling at me for daring to risk breaking my fingers and crippling them, possibly jeopardizing forever my career as a violinist. Boy, did that get me! He was a professional, a vaudeville musician, and he wanted me to do better than him by becoming a violin virtuoso. He made me promise never to fight again and he swore he'd take a belt to me if ever I disobeyed him. As a result, I never did. I took up playing ball instead."

Carole knew not to look for Russ tonight at the fights. She knew that he was working almost every night now, performing live onstage with an orchestra or guest-singing on the radio. When he wasn't performing live he was recording for a phonograph company.

George was proud of his connections and had promised to introduce her tonight to the gigantic Italian boxer Primo Carnera (The Ambling Alp), the current NBA world heavyweight champion. At six feet seven inches tall, Primo was the tallest man ever to have boxed professionally at that time. He was managed by the gangster Owney Madden, George's former mob boss.

When the giant boxer came out to the center of the ring, loud boos came from all around the arena. Everyone knew the fights were fixed. The press had published reports that boxers and their families had been threatened by Owney's mob. The fighters claimed that if they had not pretended to be knocked out by a punch from Primo's glove, they risked losing not only the prize money but their lives and those of their loved ones.

Chunks of George's ear had gone missing during his fights, creating what is known in boxing circles as *cabbage ears*. Mack had had plastic surgery done on his ears and crooked nose, as well.

Carole watched the boxing matches with interest. When she was a young tomboy and saw her brother Stuart taking boxing lessons from their neighbor, the famed 1917 world lightweight champion Benny Leonard (The Ghetto Wizard), she insisted on learning, too. She did surprisingly well and, much to her pleasure, the boxer told her she was a better fighter than her older sibling, making up for her small size and weak strength with speed and gumption.

During one of their dinners, Russ had informed her that he, too, had boxed in his youth and had even fought once and lost. But his father had quickly snipped that youthful ambition in the bud.

"When Pops found out I'd been in a fight he was madder than hell with me. I can still hear him yelling at me for daring to risk breaking my fingers and crippling them, possibly jeopardizing forever my career as a violinist. Boy, did that get me! He was a professional, a vaudeville musician, and he wanted me to do better than him by becoming a violin virtuoso. He made me promise never to fight again and he swore he'd take a belt to me if ever I disobeyed him. As a result, I never did. I took up playing ball instead."

Carole knew not to look for Russ tonight at the fights. She knew that he was working almost every night now, performing live onstage with an orchestra or guest-singing on the radio. When he wasn't performing live he was recording for a phonograph company.

George was proud of his connections and had promised to introduce her tonight to the gigantic Italian boxer Primo Carnera (The Ambling Alp), the current NBA world heavyweight champion. At six feet seven inches tall, Primo was the tallest man ever to have boxed professionally at that time. He was managed by the gangster Owney Madden, George's former mob boss.

When the giant boxer came out to the center of the ring, loud boos came from all around the arena. Everyone knew the fights were fixed. The press had published reports that boxers and their families had been threatened by Owney's mob. The fighters claimed that if they had not pretended to be knocked out by a punch from Primo's glove, they risked losing not only the prize money but their lives and those of their loved ones.

"Whatcha doing in there, dago?" someone in the stadium shouted, using the derogatory word for an Italian. "Think you can take an American in a real fight?"

The Italian Goliath looked around him as if he were uncertain what to do. The David in the crowd was every person in the stadium who'd ever been harassed or frightened by the mob. The referee stood in the center of the ring, waiting to see if the crowd would simmer down. Someone threw an old shoe into the ring. A rain of peanut shells soon followed.

"What, your pal Owney Madden not gonna rescue you tonight?" Another angry spectator shouted out, "Afraid you might get hit and spill a little blood?"

"Come on, get out of there, you loser, and let some real fighters take over!" yelled out another.

George said nothing, but Carole could tell he was becoming uncomfortable as the crowd grew louder, and boisterous catcalls, boos, and hisses were heard all around them. No one was afraid of letting the boxer know what they thought of him and his mob connections.

"Let's get out of here," George said, rising up from his seat.

"But I want to stay and watch," she protested, curious to see if the boxer would abandon the ring.

"We're going." George none too gently grabbed her by the wrist.

"Hey," someone said, pointing at them: "Isn't that Carole Lombard with George Raft?"

"George, *dear*," Carole whispered sweetly into his ear, resisting her more natural urge to give him a good swift kick in the shins. "If you don't let go of me right now, I'm going to scream."

He immediately released his grip.

"I know you're eager to take me back to your apartment and show me your newly painted bedroom, darling, but can't a girl put her hat on first?" she said loudly enough for everyone around them to hear. Her remark caused several snickers.

The last thing she wanted was some innocent do-gooder to come to her rescue and end up being punched in the face by either Mack or George. She adjusted her hat and followed her date down the aisle.

"Slow down, George," she said, noticing gossip columnist Walter Winchell seated nearby. "Smile for Walter, will you, darling?"

other's eyes in the candlelight. It had been five days since he had kissed her at the Christmas party. An accordionist, a violinist, and an Italian singer serenaded them. When they finished, Russ asked if he could use the violin and the accordion. He then proceeded to play the Italian folk song "O Sole Mio," first on the violin and then, after a momentary pause, on the accordion.

The dinner guests around them applauded, enchanted. Carole noticed out of the corner of her eyes a reporter standing nearby jotting down notes. The writer pressed several green George Washingtons into the restaurant owner, Gino's hand. She overheard him make a request, "Call me if anything else interesting should happen."

"Sure thing," Gino replied.

"Russ," she said, nodding at the reporter, worried that the studio would find out they were now dating.

"Don't worry, Carole," Russ said soothingly. "I have everything in hand."

Nothing occurred that night. The following evening, however, who should walk in but Russ, this time on his arm was another lovely film star, the fetching Sally Blane!

The fact that Russ had taken Carole and Sally to the same restaurant was duly noted in the gossip column. Much to her amusement, Carole read about the two dates, knowing that they were successfully confusing the press. Sally was acting as their cover. She and Russ were secretly dating and were keeping their studios happy by pretending they weren't.

For the next couple of weeks, Russ would be seen publicly about town with both women. At a premiere at the Grauman's Chinese Theater, he escorted Sally, while Carole attended with a group of friends.

After *Bolero* was released into the theaters, Carole breathed a sigh of relief. The publicity build-up for *Bolero* had worked, making the picture an enormous success. To her delight, it was in the top five at the box-office, which meant a substantial pay increase for her.

Carole took a personal interest in Russ's career. She found out that he had operatic singing ability, which required a good ear, a wide voice range, and, very importantly, power, to sustain the notes. Early in his career, Russ had studied under Alexander Bevani, a world-class opera singer who coached him in Los Angeles.

Russ had been born in Camden, New Jersey, but his family had moved to California in his youth, and he had as a child been bounced back and forth between Northern and Southern California, finally settling in Hollywood. A false press release stated that he had been born in San Francisco. It also mentioned that he was the gifted twelfth child, born to a man, who was also a twelfth born child.

"All of which is false. I'm actually the thirteenth child born in my family, a younger sibling died as a baby," said Russ. "I guess the publicity department wanted to play up the fact that I'd been a child prodigy of the violin, connecting it to the Italian myth that twelfth born children are gifted."

Russ told her he hated the term *crooner*, along with all the negative misconceptions that went with it. He related to her one night, while they lay naked in bed, how when he was working in New York City, after reading a particularly scathing newspaper review that claimed crooners needed a microphone because their voices were too soft and weak to be heard in a theater without one, he decided to showcase his unknown operatic talent.

Russ had the houselights dimmed in the packed theater. Turning to the orchestra, he silenced them. A single spotlight was focused on him as he walked in a deliberate manner several feet away from the microphone to center stage. He opened his mouth and, without any further fanfare, sang an operatic piece by Puccini that could be heard all the way up in the rafters of the theater. Midway through the aria he lifted one hand up, and the orchestra joined him.

He topped the song off with one long, clear note that he held effortlessly for several minutes. He then quickly brought his hand down, silencing himself and the orchestra, and bowed.

"Silence reigned for a few seconds," he told her, "during which I wondered if I'd made a mistake by singing an aria. But then the house started jumping. The audience went crazy. Everyone was stomping up in the balcony, and I could hear shouts of 'bravo' coming from all over the place. Everyone, including the orchestra, stood up and applauded. I guess I'd made my point."

"I'd say so! I wish I'd have been there, Roogie—I bet it was something else." Carole loved their intimate pillow talk, where they could share thoughts they told no one else.

"You know, Russ, you should keep up your opera studies and find a teacher here. How about I introduce you to Maestro Pietro

Cimini? He's a darling man. Sometimes he coaches the singers on the lot. He's right now the musical director for *One Night of Love*, the operetta with Grace Moore over at Columbia Pictures I was telling you about. I bet you two would hit it off."

Her blue eyes lit up with a happy thought. "Hey, and if you do study under the maestro, maybe he'll recommend you for a light opera? And then you two could collaborate together and finish that operetta you told me you were writing."

"I'd like that. I've heard of the maestro. He was the conductor for the San Francisco Opera when I lived there. But I'm afraid I might be a bit too lazy these days to study."

"Why?"

"You see, a certain blonde has been distracting me lately. She's been keeping me up way past my bedtime. I don't know how I manage to make it to rehearsals sometimes." He lazily traced her exposed naked shoulder with a finger.

She looked down at her hands, suddenly feeling bashful. Russ made her aware that she was a beautiful, desirable woman. It was the reason she never played any pranks on him. He was her lover, *not* her pal. And she wanted all the romance he was offering: the candlelight dinners, slow dancing, beautiful music, and yes, oh yes, the wonderful lovemaking. She most definitely wanted that.

The joining of their bodies was as natural as breathing, effortless and fulfilling. They had taken their relationship to the most intimate level after his evening show on Valentine's Day. He was performing at the Cocoanut Grove with an orchestra and Jimmie Grier conducting. She'd arrived in time to watch the final set.

Russ was on stage singing for the audience, wishing them a good night and a safe journey home, when the orchestra began to play "Save the Last Dance for Me." It was one of the few songs he sang that showcased some of his operatic ability, and it was a delightful way to finish the evening.

During the last refrain, Russ descended the stage, where he found Carole seated at a ringside table in the audience. He held out his hand.

"May I?"

"Yes." She placed her hand into his. The warmth of him went directly to her heart. He gently led her out onto the dance floor.

He held her in his arms, and they glided and swayed to the

music as everyone watched. From then on, the song became theirs.

"How's Sally and Lansing been?" she asked while they were eating their dinner at the Ambassador Hotel.

"I suppose they're fine. Normally on holidays like this I'd go out with Sally, and we'd grab a bite to eat at a hamburger joint somewhere and then take in a movie. I've been so busy lately that I haven't spoken to her or Lansa in days."

"I could throw you a small barbecue party at my house and invite them over this weekend."

He leaned closer to her. "That's a great idea, but right now I want to spend the entire evening alone with you. I want a real Valentine's Day celebration. I know we discussed staying the night here, but I thought I'd make it extra special by reserving the honeymoon suite. That is, if it's all right with you?"

"Yes, I'd like that."

After a candlelight dinner of short ribs and a bottle of celebratory champagne, he leaned over and gave her a kiss. "Thank you for being my Valentine."

Carole felt herself warming at his words, thinking of what they were going to do after dinner. She was ready to take their relationship to the next level.

"I bought you a little something, too." She placed a small wrapped package on the table. He opened it. Inside was a Cartier watch, and the wrist band was inscribed: *To Roogie, with love, Angel.*

"Do you like it, darling?"

"Do I!" He kissed her again and immediately put it on.

"Russ, I'd like to go now." She wanted to be alone with him, away from the prying eyes of the onlookers observing their private moments.

The penthouse bridal suite he had booked had all the qualities of a romantic movie set. Carole enjoyed the luxury, from the large four-poster bed in a bedroom with an adjoining powder room to the tastefully arranged flowers in vases set about the suite on side tables. A baby grand piano stood in a corner of the sitting area surrounded by a sofa and chairs. Through the open French doors, a private balcony with Spanish iron railings overlooked the hotel's expansive Mediterranean garden.

She stepped outside. The moon shone high above, creating a

silver light, palm trees swayed in the mild California night breeze, and she could see water from a fountain splashing nearby. In the near distance, the lights of ranch houses shone in the dark hills. She breathed in deeply the scent of the night air, a mixture of desert sage and blooming roses. "This is lovely, Russ!"

"I'm glad you're pleased, Angel." He joined her, kissing her neck as he wrapped his arms around her. Carole turned and slowly kissed him, savoring the moment. When they stepped inside for more privacy, she took his hands and placed them on her.

Russ began to undress her, his hands shaking a little as he tried carefully to unbutton her beaded white gown. It touched her heart that this night was important to him, too. She tried to help him but, to her surprise, her hands shook, too. She had never felt more excited to be with someone in her entire life. Her heart was loudly beating in her chest.

"To hell with it." She shimmied out of the garment, while Russ quietly watched her remove the rest of her lingerie. She peeled them off until she was nude.

She touched him, loving the feel of his toned muscles. He reached for the condom packet on the side table and put it on. On the bed they made slow, gentle love, until she held him inside her and the tempo changed. Russ was sweet and gentle. It was a passionate night Carole would never forget.

Resting, he held her in his arms and spontaneously began humming a soothing melody in her ear. The vibrations touched the center of her being. His deep baritone reverberated beneath her soft, light soprano as she lay against his broad chest singing and humming, creating music together.

"Oh, nuts!" she swore vehemently. She quickly sat up, realizing that she'd forgotten to tap her cigarette ashes into a tray. It burned a black hole into the penthouse suite's carpet. Carole put a hand up to her mouth, a little ashamed of her eyebrow-raising language.

Russ let out a bellow of a laugh. He took the cigarette out of her hand and put it in the ashtray. "Don't ever change."

He kissed her until she felt a warm energy build up inside of her, causing her to reach up and bring his firm, muscular body down to hers, joining them together. It was wonderful and satisfying.

Much later, Carole woke up and found Russ playing on the piano, working out different variations on a melody she had heard him try out before, changing keys and rhythms and softly singing to himself the words he wanted to go with it. She put a robe on and sat down next to him on the bench, leaning her head against his shoulder, listening to him play. He kissed her forehead and played several parts of the love song he had been working on, "Too Beautiful for Words."

"This song is about you, Angel," he said. "I've been working on it since we first met at the Cocoanut Grove. Happy Valentine's Day."

He sang most of the song, and then paused. "Now, all I need is to find a word that rhymes with 'Berlin.' Any suggestions?"

She softly said with a laugh, "How about 'Gershwin'?" She knew he had probably chosen that very word in advance with his songwriting team, Bernie Grossman and Jack Stern.

"Great! I knew I could count on you. By the way, Angel, I love to hear you laugh." He leaned over and, kissing her quickly on the lips, pretended to write the word 'Gershwin' down for the first time.

He fiddled on the keys, changing the melody's chords several times. He played it fast and jazzy and then like a funeral dirge, which caused her to laugh even harder.

"Yeah, that works. You're laughing. Then, I thought maybe something like this..." he said. He then flawlessly played the rest of the song for her.

She was thrilled he'd written a song for her and clapped at his performance. "Oh, Russ, that was wonderful, darling! Thank you."

"I'm still fine-tuning it, but I thought you'd like it, Angel." He held her lovingly.

"Let's go back to bed, Roogie."

"Your wish is my command."

Carole told everyone who asked that the beaded white gown she wore that night was lucky. If someone were foolish enough to ask why, she would respond, "Because I got lucky in it."

There was no need to ask Russ if he cared about her, everything he said and did told her so. He showered her with gifts, jewelry, furs, and even a new pet, a sweet dachshund whom she named Brownie. In exchange, she gave him a malamute like the one she had owned when she'd first started out in pictures and a cigarette case embedded in diamonds that outlined his initials.

They shared tennis lessons together at the club and enjoyed

each other's company. But when he began to ask serious questions about their possible future together and where it might lead, she would shake her head and say, "Not now, Russ. It's too soon."

Even though everybody was saying that it was grand that she and Bill were now such terrific friends after their divorce, the past wasn't doing Carole's relationship with Russ any favors. She knew that Russ had the right to wonder if she were still in love with her ex-husband, otherwise why was she still going out with him?

Russ went to her house one morning to talk about it, and Carole *sensed* his coming. She had been avoiding him and had spent the previous evening laughing it up with her ex and some of their mutual friends.

She had been at her wittiest at the party the previous night. The director Howard Hawks was there, and she had a strange premonition—despite being somewhat less than lucid—that he was considering her for a role in one of his upcoming pictures. It had made her nervous. Carole had drunk more than usual, becoming even more uninhibited in her manner and speech than normal. It made the partyers laugh at everything she said. Today, lying in bed with a hangover and a queasy stomach, she was paying the penalty.

Carole let Fieldsie answer the door when Russ rang the bell. She wasn't up to facing him and pretended to still be asleep after a late night. But a gust of wind blew through the house, opening her bedroom door. She heard Brownie's joyous barking as he greeted him. The small dachshund adored Russ.

She dimly heard Russ's deep baritone addressing Fieldsie, answered by her friend's softer alto. Murmured words passed between them, followed by sudden silence. The front door closed. The small dog's paws pattered down the hallway, his nails clicking against the wood floor. A long, light-brown snout appeared, nudging the bedroom door wide open.

Brownie walked in, peeking his small head over the edge of the tufted bed she was lying on, stretching his long body. The dog, with a soft sigh, gazed at Carole. She placed a hand on his small head with a sigh of her own. *What to do?*

Russ telephoned that evening. She could hear in his voice that he was hurt by whatever Fieldsie had said to him at the door. Worse, he wanted her to know it.

"Carole, I have something to say to you."

"Yes, Russ," she answered in her most pleasant voice, while secretly knowing he ought to be yelling.

"Fieldsie told me that you were happy with our relationship, physically speaking. And I told her that that's fine by me, well, at least that part. And then she said that you and Bill were getting back together, and that I should butt out and step aside, to which I have no reply."

He paused for a moment. "I'm not some gigolo you can pick up and drop whenever you wish. And to be frank, I feel deeply wounded that the only part of our relationship that has made you happy is the sex. If that's so, then you're not the person I'm looking for. In which case, Carole, I'd prefer not to meet with you anymore, except on a professional level."

If she wanted to end the relationship, all she had to do was agree with him that this would be for the best. Then it'd be over, nice, neat, and tidy: no more Russ. That's what she wanted, right?

She felt a painful kick straight to her heart.

"Russ," she gasped. "I'm sorry for Fieldsie's behavior. I'll have words with her. I promise it'll never happen again. Forget what she said. I don't feel that way. I want to be with you, darling, not Bill. I confess that I wavered for a moment, thinking about what the studio expects from me, and about how Bill could help my career now that he's up on top, but not anymore. None of that matters compared to how I feel about you."

She added sincerely, "You have to believe me. I really do care about you, Roogie. Please forgive me. And please forgive Fieldsie—it won't happen again."

"All right, Angel, I do forgive you. I want to be with you, but only if you desire to be with me, too. It can't be one way. It has to be both. I thought you and I completed each other, but don't make me into some kind of romantic sap. I don't think I could bear it if you did."

"Honest, I do want to be with you. Just keep loving me."

"I will, and I do." His voice softened as he told her for the first time the words she wanted to hear. "I love you, Carole."

"Oh Russ, I love you, too!"

Carole felt genuine remorse for the pain she had caused him. She knew she had hurt him, wounding his manly pride, and she'd hurt herself. How foolish she'd been.

She knew she needed to be a better person. She had been studying the Baha'i faith with Bessie since she was a teenager, under the tutorage of a friend of her mother's. The religion believed that life partners, a husband and wife, had the responsibility of building each other up spiritually. She had known since the moment she'd met Russ that they were spiritually connected. It had been their destiny, she felt, for them to meet and fall in love.

Starting in April of 1934, they dated exclusively. Carole made it publicly known that she and Russ were now a couple. Their names began to appear regularly side by side in movie magazines and in the gossip columns. No more dates with Bill, George, or anyone else. It was as if Hollywood held a hoedown and somebody had shouted, "Everybody, change your partners!"

Bill had started enjoying the companionship of a much younger woman. He had begun dating the sexy bombshell Jean Harlow, who had been married three times by the time she was twenty-three years old and was almost twenty years younger than Bill. According to Louella, he drove the young starlet up to Santa Barbara for their first dinner date.

"Isn't it sweet that Bill calls her 'Baby'? Louella gossiped over the telephone.

"That's just darling." Carole wouldn't admit it, but she felt a small twinge of pain. She used to call Bill: Pops and Daddy. They had been her other pet names for him, and she had once been his Baby.

But not anymore, she told herself. She was a grown woman who was capable of handling her own life. But she was curious. When had Bill and Jean met? Everyone knew that they had both been in Mexico at the Agua Caliente Casino during the winter break. Maybe that was when they started dating?

She imagined Jean in her famous silk pajamas and platform sandals, pulling a handcart on a hot desert road with Bill sitting in it like a king, fanning himself, and grinned. She had absolutely no regrets about turning Bill's offer down.

The May-December couple came out during the hype for the musical picture *Reckless.* The picture had Bill cat-walking around the edge of an orchestra pit to show he was still young at heart at forty-two years of age. The schmaltzy storyline revolved around the suicide of an actress's husband, uncomfortably paralleling the real-life fact that Jean's second husband, MGM producer Paul Bern, had reportedly done the same.

Jean was to be featured on the same radio show as Russ with the personable host Jimmy Fidler, with whom they were both good friends. It made Carole a little nervous. What if Russ fell for the beautiful star? Jean was a funny, sexy comedian who often was up for the same movie roles as her.

Carole remembered with an uncomfortable pang that she had competed for the role of Helen in *Hell's Angels* against Jean during the time when she (Carole) was having a secret affair with producer Howard Hughes. Not surprisingly, Carole had lost the role when she broke up with him.

Carole suddenly felt uneasy at the thought of Russ spending any time with the platinum blonde, working and becoming acquainted with Jean in the close quarters of a radio studio booth. She wondered what she could do to be included in the radio gig without appearing to be insecure or jealous. She had heard that Walter Winchell would be there, as well. Oh boy, she would have to tread carefully. The gossip columnist could sometimes be a little too insightful.

Maybe she could attend the radio show with Russ and help him improve his dramatic presentation? Yeah, that might work. Actress Constance Bennett, had experienced a bad case of the jitters when visiting Russ's show the previous week, literally shaking in her shoes from nerves. Her nervousness must have been contagious, because Russ, a hardened veteran of the microphone, was soon jittery, too. Happily, as the interview was short, the listening audience at large had not noticed.

Carole's blue eyes widened with excitement. She had a great idea! She would start coaching Russ and then attend the show in order to give him vocal cues. Oh boy, it was perfect! She had already been coaching his acting. What could be more natural than doing the same for his radio presentation?

She did just that, instructing Russ not to end his sentences as if they were questions by lowering his voice, which helped him sound more assertive. She made certain he didn't nervously rush the words out of his mouth. He spoke in a steady, easygoing manner that the listening audience could understand over the radio. She taught him a few hand cues, so that he would know when to slow down or speak louder.

During the show Carole stood on the other side of the booth, signaling to him. Russ was wonderful, taking direction from her without hesitation. He sounded as manly as his fans would expect. The session went off without a hitch. Cecil Underwood, the producer, was pleased. To her relief, Jean was sweet and not at all a threat, the platinum blonde focused her attention on the other men present.

Russ hugged Carole afterward. "I'd have been completely lost without you, Angel. I don't know what I would have done if you hadn't been there. You were terrific!"

"I enjoyed it, Russ." She mentally patted herself on the back and decided to attend in the future as many of his radio shows as possible. She enjoyed coaching him. It wouldn't hurt her career, either, since she was often invited to be a guest on the radio when she was promoting a picture.

Carole saw George Raft with Virginia Pine and another couple dining at the Russian Eagle's gardens. Tables were spread out under the long branches of old oak trees. She and Russ were about to dine in the dim light of the Japanese lanterns strung from the branches as a strolling gypsy violinist played.

George had made an unexpected early reappearance in Hollywood. For lo and behold, he hadn't gone to Europe after all. Instead, he'd fallen head over heels for the socialite actress from Chicago, Mrs. Virginia Pine. The newspapers reported that George had faithfully followed Virginia back from Chicago to Hollywood on the train as soon as the ink had dried on her divorce decree. It was noticed by many that he gave up wearing high-waisted gangster trousers and polished his manners for the socialite.

He gave Carole a friendly nod of acknowledgment when she walked by his table, but that was it. Their romance had ended. She was thankful the studios weren't pressuring her anymore. Carole liked a different sort of man than when she was an impressionable twenty-year-old. Now she was more appreciative of a man's sweetness and thoughtfulness. Surface charm, she had discovered from her past relationship with Bill, wasn't everything.

Sally Blane, Russ told Carole, had started dating Dick Powell, who'd been in the very popular musical *42nd Street*. "Sally's relieved to no longer have to be part of the ruse to fool the press about our dating. She has her own romance with Dick to worry about."

"I like Sally," Carole said. "She's been wonderful to help us out as long as she has, Russ. Tell her thank you for me." She wasn't very close to either Lansing or Sally, but she wisely didn't try to keep Russ away from them.

As for Lansing, she saw him from time to time, but she still did not know him very well. He remained Russ's friend and was a bachelor who lived with his parents. A tall, heavyset man, with gaunt eyes and a thin mustache, he reminded Carole uncomfortably of a bouncer.

Russ told her over dinner of the present frustrations he was having with reporters and his studio, Universal Pictures. He was very unhappy. "It's the same close-minded thinking that I thought I'd left behind in New York, two years ago. Back then, I was informed by movie directors that I was 'too Latin' or 'too dark' to be cast in any important roles, which they usually reserved for Anglo whites. Nothing has changed."

"Yes it has, darling. You're now under contract with Universal Pictures and Laemmle promised you a musical," she said, referring to the head of the studio. "So, don't you think you're being treated better here?"

He frowned into his coffee cup, before taking a sip. "No, I'm fed-up. The musical that I was supposed to star in has been delayed by several more months. In the meanwhile, the studio has been offering me nothing but two-bit roles to fill in the time. I've decided to turn them all down."

"Russ, you should take the parts," Carole tried to reason with him, thinking of her own climb to stardom. "You're not doing your career any favors by refusing them. Consider my career, I started out in pictures by taking pies in the face and wearing bathing suits. I've worked my way up to having major leading roles. But that didn't happen overnight, darling. It takes time and experience to make it in this business."

"I know you're right. But I refuse to play some fast-talking mug who goes around beating up women. I won't do it. My fans will lose faith in me if I do. I'd rather not make any more pictures and go back to performing on the radio, if those are the kinds of roles they're going to keep offering me."

"Maybe you can convince Laemmle to offer you some other type of roles," she suggested.

"I doubt it. They promised me that I'd be singing and acting, and that I'd be allowed to use my own songs. But none of their promises have come true. My movie career is going nowhere fast. If only I could get released from my contract, then maybe I could work with a studio that would give me the musicals I want."

"Oh, Russ," she sighed. "You know they won't let you go. You're far too popular for them to let you off the hook. They'd rather have you sit around all day on the lot doing nothing than release you from your contract. I hope you can work something out with Laemmle."

"I'll try. Maybe something can be done."

The next morning, Carole received an unexpected phone call from her friend, the syndicated Hollywood reporter, Mollie Merrick. "You'll never guess who I ran into last night at the Colony Club, Carole."

"Who?" she asked, cutting to the chase.

"I met Lansing Brown, Russ's bachelor friend."

"Was anyone with him?"

"No, he was completely alone. We started talking and I asked him what he thought about you and Russ."

"And what did he say?"

"Lansa talked about your need to go to bed early at night for your health. And then what he said next I wrote down. He said, 'I wish Russ would fall in love with a big-breasted lass who doesn't have to face the camera in the morning. He drops by our house late at night and wants nothing better than to talk for the rest of the evening about Carole. And then he wants to go out to the clubs, and sometimes I'm too tired to start out with him at that hour. But he's my best friend, and I guess that's what friendship's for, to talk things over.'"

"What did you say to that?"

"I said, 'I suppose so,' and left it at that. There was something about the way Lansa said it, which made me uncomfortable. You don't think, you know, that he's *that way* about Russ, do you?"

"No, of course not. Billy would have told me if Lansing was homosexual."

Carole dismissed the idea out of hand, but the encounter nonetheless confirmed what she had known all along, that Lansing would like nothing better than to replace her with some dimwitted baby doll who knew nothing about motion pictures. Secure in her knowledge that Russ loved her, she saw no threat in the photographer and didn't give the incident another thought.

Russ finally came to terms with Universal. He had an uncredited walk-on role in the vapid drama *Glamour*, based on an Edna Ferber novel, starring Paul Lukas and Constance Cummings. He had fought against playing the role but, as a form of reconciliation with the studio, he complied.

Universal used his popularity to its advantage, naming him in the picture's buildup on the West Coast. It mentioned him in several newspapers in the hope of boosting the film's sagging box-office receipts by filling theaters with his numerous fans. When the film reached the East Coast, the studio tried to shorten the dull picture down to seventy-five minutes, and his scene was cut. It didn't work, though: the picture was a flop.

There was now talk of having Russ star in another musical, *Castles in the Air*, which was being written for him by John Meehan. It was later renamed *Wake Up and Dream*. He would star in the picture with June Knight and would sing several songs, including a couple that he had co-written. In the meantime, while waiting for rehearsals to begin, he appeared on the radio, sang with orchestras, and made records, as well as continuing to write songs and date Carole.

When he became busy off the studio lot, she suggested that he request a stand-in: someone who had the same height, color, and appearance as him whose job would be to stand around for hours on the set while the lighting people tried different filters and angles in preparation for the actual shooting of the picture. Universal agreed, realizing that they could use his considerable talents elsewhere during that time with personal appearances on the radio and on stage.

Carole went back to work acting. Howard Hawks offered her a leading role in his next picture, *Twentieth Century*, at Columbia Pictures. Her costar would be John Barrymore, the veteran actor.

The picture was part of a loan-out contract agreement between her studio, Paramount, and Columbia. It was an opportunity for her to work with the innovative movie director. She didn't know it, but the picture would change her acting style forever and was part of a new genre of comedy that was taking over the movie screen—the screwball.

Chapter Eight

Screwball

John Barrymore put his thumb and index finger up to his nose, pinched it, and began fanning his other hand up and down, his eyes raised heavenward. His face and actions revealed what he thought of Carole's acting. *She stunk! To high heavens, she stunk!*

Carole felt as if someone had punched her in the stomach. It was the second day of rehearsals at Columbia Pictures for the movie *Twentieth Century*, using a script adaptation of the play by Ben Hecht and Charles MacArthur. She was falling flat, sinking without a trace. She could tell by the cast's reactions how awful her performance was. Many of them couldn't even look her in the eye, it was that bad.

What am I doing wrong?

Carole played an inexperienced actress named Lily Garland (the former Mildred Plotka), a lingerie salesgirl who is discovered by Oscar Jaffe (John Barrymore), an egomaniacal Broadway impresario. In the film he successfully takes the bland Mildred and transforms her into the stage star Lily Garland, whose ego matches his own. He ends up losing her because of his overbearing jealousy, however, after tapping her telephone and setting a detective on her. Angry, she leaves him for Hollywood and becomes a famous movie star.

Several years later, Oscar has fallen on hard times and has had nothing but a series of flops. Running away from his debtors, he takes the train named the Twentieth Century, which runs between Chicago and New York City. In the story he learns that Lily is traveling in one of the cars and comes up with a scheme to use guilt to convince her to perform in his next production, *The Passion Play*, by pretending to be dying. Hilarious comedic mayhem ensues as the two verbally spar in the classic battle of the sexes with a screwball twist.

Carole was confused. She had her lines down to perfection and was doing everything possible to convey the right emotions. Hadn't she taken a backseat to John's acting, letting him take the lead and having him dominate the scene, as she had been expected to do for Bing in *We're Not Dressing*? Wasn't that what she was supposed to do now?

It was, after all, what was usually expected of her in a comedy: be pretty, say your lines, and then let them throw the proverbial pie in your face.

"Come on, Carole," said Howard Hawks. "Let's you and I go for a walk."

Her heart was pounding loudly now. *This was not good.* It was never good if a director wanted to talk to you alone.

"How much are you making for this picture?" he asked.

"About five thousand a week," she replied. She had received a big pay increase after making *Bolero.*

"What would you say if I told you you'd earned your whole salary this morning and didn't have to act anymore?"

She stopped walking and stared at him, stunned.

"Now forget about the scene. What would you do if a drunk said that you were a fat chick and he wanted to know why you had such small tits?" He then acted as if he were going to try to touch her breasts.

"I'd kick him in the balls."

"Well, Oscar has said something like that to you. Why don't you kick him?"

"Are you kidding?" She looked at him with disbelief, the *We're Not Dressing* debacle haunting her thoughts and emotions.

"No, I'm not."

He looked her right in the eye, and she knew he meant it.

They silently walked back together and when they reached the rehearsal room door, he turned to her with one last word of advice. "Now, we're going to go back in there and practice this scene and you kick, scream, and do anything else that comes into your mind that's natural. And quit acting! If you don't, I'm going to fire you!"

Carole mentally gave herself a shake. Determined, understanding now what was expected of her, she threw herself into the role of Lily Garland. She was going to go in and kick that self-satisfied egomaniac right where it counts.

"Carole, darling, so good to see you again," John said in greeting, standing up from the rehearsing circle. He pulled a chair solicitously out for her. "Do you need to go over your lines again, dear? Perhaps I can read them to you?"

"Oscar, you can go suck an egg," she growled at him with a glare.

"Lily!" he said with a delighted smile. He then kicked the chair out of the way. "Don't you respect me?"

"Who cares about your respect? I'm too big to be respected," Carole answered with one of the lines from the script, sticking her tongue out at him. She raised her leg and would have given him a good swift kick in the pants, too, but he saw it coming and dodged the attack.

He shook a finger at her. "Tsk, tsk. Are we getting slow in our old age? Hollywood's been too gentle with our Lily."

"I'm not yours, Oscar."

"Yeah," chimed in Walter Connolly, who played one of Oscar's partners and had been watching the whole interchange. "She's Russ Columbo's now!"

Every member of the cast laughed, including John.

"All right, Oscar," said Howard, stepping in. "Give Lily back her chair, and let's start from the top."

"One minute, Herr Director, before we begin, I have something to ask her. Carole…"

"Yes, John."

"Will you go out on a date with this old ham?"

"Sure, John, if you keep your hands to yourself."

"And that crooner fellow?"

"Oh, Russ? He'll be our chaperone." Everyone laughed.

Carole continued to perform the scenes as if she were living them. Her natural, liberated spirit shone through. Within five days, she and John Barrymore were hamming it up, seeing who could be the most outrageous. They would overlap each other's dialogue, interrupting each other in the screwball style, as if it were a real conversation, then slapstick their lines with a final zinger until they almost ran out of breath and energy. And she, living every single word, kicked, cried, threw tantrums, and sulked until she *was* Lily Garland.

From then on, Carole had no more troubles with her acting, and she earned John Barrymore's and everyone else's respect on the set as her performance went from bland, mousy Mildred to the outrageous, fiery Lily. She was a real queen of screwball!

The only time the picture had trouble was the day John Barrymore came onto the set drunk. He couldn't perform, slurring his words and forgetting his lines. It was embarrassing. She felt badly for him. He was having troubles with his family and his finances. Howard had to cancel shooting.

Remorseful for his behavior, the veteran actor offered to work for two days for free to make up for the lost time. Otherwise he didn't cause Carole or anyone else on the set any trouble and behaved in a professional manner. They became friends and he helped her with her acting.

He gave her suggestions that could make a scene funnier, spending extra time with her rehearsing until they could speak the rapid dialogue as if it were second nature, since the pacing was faster than normal. Carole was grateful to the veteran actor and told a magazine writer that John had taught her more in the six weeks she worked with him on that picture than she had absorbed in the whole six years she had been in pictures.

The filming took place on a specially made set that resembled an exact replica of a series of interconnecting Pullman train cars, sliced in half. The beauty of the set was that it could be moved around and fitted together like a puzzle, which made it possible to film any car at several different angles.

She and John would sometimes become so caught up in a scene when they were performing that Howard would have to step in during filming. He would appear on the set with his headphones on. "Slow down the pace here a bit. We can't catch the dialogue on the mike. You're both talking too fast."

Most of the time, Howard would stay out of the way and let the actors ham it up as much as they wanted. Carole watched John improvise during the "Kentucky colonel" scene, where he took putty out of his pocket and added it to his nose to extend it, then humorously picked at it—all unscripted. It was hilarious.

When the picture was "in the can" and ready to be edited, John and Carole went out on a double date with Russ and Fieldsie to an evening concert of the philharmonic. She kept her promise to John. He had behaved and had not touched her inappropriately during filming.

Russ chatted easily with Fieldsie, which made Carole happy. She loved Russ, and Fieldsie was one of her oldest and dearest friends. It would have broken her heart to have to choose between them. Thankfully, she didn't have to. After a heart to heart with her friend,

Fieldsie had promised she would give Russ a chance. That wasn't difficult, as he was kind and very personable.

She and Russ went with Fieldsie to the premiere for *Twentieth Century*. Carole felt nervous. What if the critics hated the new style of comedy? Would she be blamed if it failed? They walked over to a nearby steak house on Wilshire Boulevard, which wasn't much more than a hole in a wall, and ate steak sandwiches before the screening.

Elizabeth Wilson, an entertainment writer, recognized Carole and greeted them. "How are you doing, Carole? I'm about to preview your picture."

"I'm so frightened. Do you think it will be any good?"

"Really, you're scared?" asked the writer, her eyebrows raised in surprised.

"Yeah, I am."

"I'd have to see the picture first, you understand, before I can create an opinion."

"I understand. But could you do me a favor, would you call me up tomorrow morning and let me know what you think of it? I'm on pins and needles, wanting to know what the critics think of it."

"Sure, I'd be glad to."

Carole could see a light of admiration in Elizabeth's eyes. The writer was obviously impressed that she should ask her opinion.

The picture, much to Carole's relief, received rave reviews, but it didn't do well at the box office. It was too sophisticated for the general viewing public, who had trouble relating to the egotistical, less-than-sympathetic leading characters. Carole felt some disappointment upon hearing about the poor ticket sales, thinking that what she saw up on the screen was hilarious and clever. But her superb acting, however, wasn't overlooked by the film critics and studio directors who went to see the picture, some of whom had been watching her perform for her entire film career. They were impressed.

Carole played up her zany lifestyle. She let the newspaper reporters in on the fun, inviting them to the set and allowing them to pay visits to her home. She befriended writers, photographers, actors, directors, and gossip columnists—anyone she thought who could help further her career—keeping them in her corner by being accessible and down-to-earth. Her real life began to parallel the screwball one.

After making this picture, John Barrymore's star rapidly fell. She heard he was having trouble memorizing his lines because of his hard drinking and had found himself performing parodies of the Oscar Jaffe role in other pictures. She helped him when no one was interested in hiring him anymore, landing him a role in *True Confessions*, equally costarring with her and the genial Fred MacMurray.

It warmed her heart that John considered her to be "the finest actress he had ever worked with," which is what he'd written on the picture of the two of them he had given her as a souvenir of their time together on the set.

Howard Hawks, whom she learned from her mother was actually a distant second cousin of hers, was very proud of his Svengali moment. She heard that he told everyone he knew about how he had helped her stop acting and advised her to just be herself. As for Carole, thinking of how her acting style had changed, she fondly telegrammed the director when she performed in another comedy: *I'm gonna start kicking!*

Chapter Nine

Love Match

Russ was renting a large, Spanish-style home with five bedrooms at 1019 North Roxbury Drive. It had a tiled swimming pool with an adjoining cabana and guesthouse, as well as tennis courts in the expansive backyard. Carole liked the look of the home, which had been built in 1928 by actor Monte Blue. They planned to take a few publicity pictures there.

Russ had purchased another home on Outpost Circle in January, not far from Grauman's Chinese Theatre, and was currently living there with his parents, renting the Roxbury house for entertainment purposes and for privacy. Things were looking up. His contract with Universal Pictures had been renewed for another six months, during which time he was guaranteed starring roles in three movies, and his salary had been increased to $4,000 a week.

"Russ, how will your parents react to you bringing me home? Will they be upset?" she asked as they drove over to the Outpost Circle house.

"Are you crazy? They'll love you, Angel!"

"But I'm not Italian." She hesitated. "And I'm divorced."

"So? All of my brothers have married non-Italians, and so have a couple of my sisters. Not once did my parents object. As for you being divorced, a couple of my siblings have, too, and my parents didn't make a fuss over them doing so. Besides, you and Bill weren't married in a Catholic church."

"Why's that important?"

He gave her a fond look, and Carole knew the unspoken answer. If they did decide to marry in the church, they could. The pope prohibited divorce but made exceptions for those who converted to Catholicism.

Despite what Russ said, she worried that his family might not accept her. After all, she was a noted Hollywood personality, and her reputation was not what one would associate with a virgin bride. She had been married and had had lovers. Some people, she knew, saw only black and white. Either you were a good woman, like Rebecca of Sunnybrook Farm, or an evil seductress, like Carmen, leading men astray. How would they view her?

Russ must have noticed her frown, because he patted her hand. "Look, we're not back in the old country here, Angel. We may be Sicilians, but there are no arranged marriages in my family. Believe me, we marry whomever we choose. My parents are going to adore you. I'm glad you're finally going to meet them. Mama, in particular, has been wanting to meet you."

"Really?"

"Yeah. I told her how special you are to me. So you've got nothing to worry about, understand?"

"All right."

But still she worried, thinking about the upcoming meeting. She knew how important his family was to him. When they had first started dating, he had been reluctant to introduce them to her; they had quarreled once because of it. Now he seemed eager to have her meet them.

If his family didn't like her, what would she do? It hadn't helped her self-confidence when she'd run into Sally Blane at the Beverly Wilshire Hotel's ballroom powder room the night before.

"How's it going, Carole?" the light-brown-haired actress asked while applying some rouge on her lips in front of a gilded mirror. "How's Russ?"

"He's fine. He and I are going over to his parents' house in the morning and then over to Roxbury to take some publicity photos in the backyard."

"You're meeting his parents?"

"Yeah. Why?"

"Just asking." But the look that passed over the other actress's face forewarned Carole that Sally was none too pleased by the news. "In all the time I've known Russ, he's never once introduced me to his parents or invited me into his house."

"Really?" Carole was a little taken aback by this news, since Sally had been friends with Russ for several years now. Why hadn't Sally met his parents?

"Yes, I've driven over with him a couple of times to his parents' place," explained Sally, "but I've always stayed outside and waited in the car. He seems protective of them, especially of his mother, Julia. You know she's in poor health?"

"He told me."

"The girl who marries him will have to accept that his parents will probably be living with him under the same roof."

"I suppose so."

"And become Catholic."

Carole knew Sally meant "Catholic like her," inferring that she would be a better match for Russ.

And so what? she thought. *Lots of other women in Hollywood are Catholics, but that doesn't mean Russ is going to marry them. Anyway, she was thinking of converting to Catholicism. And as for his parents living with him, that wasn't so extraordinary. Her own mother, Bessie, lived with her. So why did everyone expect it to be such a big deal for her? It made no sense.*

"Well, good luck with Russ's family," said Sally before she left the powder room.

"Thanks."

Despite her kind words, Carole could tell Sally's feelings were clearly bent out of shape. She was about to enter into an exclusive part of Russ's life that he had never shared with Sally—and why would that be?

Because he's madly in love with you, a voice in her heart whispered. *He wants to marry you.* Her heart beat a little quicker at the second thought. Marriage, was she ready to make that commitment?

Carole met Russ's parents, Julia and Nicola, for the first time at the Outpost Circle home, as well as his older brother John and his sister Anna, in the sitting room overlooking the front yard. They said very little but were very welcoming. Nicola and John greeted her in English, but Julia, who wore dark glasses since she was slowly going blind, simply smiled, asking a few questions in Italian to Russ.

He answered them in his deep baritone. Whatever he said in Italian must have satisfied his mother, because Julia rose out of her chair and warmly kissed Carole on the cheeks.

"Bella Carole, I'm glad Russ brings you here to meet us. So glad you make him happy," said Julia.

"I'm pleased to be here. Thank you for having me." And that was it, she was accepted by his family.

At the breakfast table, Anna told a very funny story in Italian that made the others laugh. Carole felt excluded. It was hard for her, she who was used to being the life of the party, to sit there and say nothing. Maybe she didn't belong after all? Perhaps it would be better if Russ were involved with a nice Italian woman?

Russ, seeming to sense her insecurity, whispered into her ear. "You would have told it better. *Nessuna a come te...*There is no one like you, Angel. You are the one who lights up my life." He took her hand in his. "Stay by my side."

"I will, Roogie."

Comforted by his words, she made a decision to make an effort to fit in. But how? She looked at the food before her. She observed that most of it was Italian pastries and sausage.

That was it! She would learn to cook Italian. She might not have time to learn the language, but she certainly could make an effort and teach herself how to cook the food. Oh boy, she was a wiz at cooking!

She recognized a couple of film stars' homes during the drive over to the rental house on Roxbury Drive. Hollywood notables such as Jimmy Stewart, Jack Benny, and Ginger Rogers were Russ's neighbors. It was not too far from "the village," the local name for Rodeo Drive, where cattle had once been driven down the center of the road. Plus, it was less than a mile from her own home.

Today she was going to help oversee the publicity shoot of Russ for *Wake Up and Dream*. They decided to have the pictures taken at the Roxbury Drive house so that they would not be disturbed by curious onlookers at the tennis club. She would be the one supervising the photo shoot. Due to her years of experience in film, she knew almost as much as a professional photographer about lighting and film exposure.

The photographer whom Universal had hired for the shoot stood ready at the side of the pool as they prepared to take a few publicity stills of Russ. They wanted to show off some of the athletic side of his personality. Earlier that summer Russ had been forced to put his arm in a sling after developing tennis elbow from overplaying the condition's namesake sport.

"Russ, take your shirt off," Carole said, eying him critically as he prepared to stand on the pool's diving board.

"Who do you think I am, Buster Crabbe?" he said with a laugh.

He hesitated for half a second, knowing that by removing his shirt he would be bucking convention. Men usually wore knitted tank tops to hide their bare chests and nipples when they went to the pool or the ocean, along with matching swim trunks. The average Joe off the street did not swim without a tank top on. Only movie stars like the well-proportioned Olympic gold medalist swimmer in the freestyle, Buster Crabbe (*Tarzan*), did that.

She let loose a wolf whistle when Russ took off the tank top.

"Hot cha-cha!"

Russ had no reason to be ashamed. He had broad shoulders like a football player. Strong and muscular, his arms were well toned from swimming and tennis. His stomach was rock solid. He really was quite a hunk, she thought.

Carole had personally chosen the black swim trunks to show off his well-defined and muscular thighs. His trim waist was emphasized by the swim trunks' white belt, which was worn as part of the suit. His strong thighs and the bulge of his privates were shown off by the tight fit. She beamed with pleasure. It was perfect.

Her sapphire-blue eyes shone with womanly delight as she looked over his firm body. His fans were going to go gaga over the photos. And to think this gorgeous man was hers. Now, maybe she could talk him into plucking—

"I draw the line at plucking my chest," he said firmly, seeing her eyeing his chest and reading her thoughts.

"How about shaving your le—"

"No."

"Spoilsport." She turned to the cameraman who was standing by. "Okay, take the picture."

The photographer directed him not to look straight at the camera but at the pool as if he were about to dive in. Russ followed the instructions, and the photographer took a couple of still shots. When those were done, they moved onto the tennis courts, which were a little bit behind the pool.

She had invited their discreetly lesbian tennis instructor, Eleanor Tennant, to be a part of the storyline for the pictures. Russ had started playing tennis in his late teens in New York City and was an excellent player. When he began dating Carole, they decided to take private instruction together with Eleanor, who coached such tennis notables as Bobby Riggs, Pauline Betz, and Maureen Connolly.

Carole had been taking lessons since her marriage to Bill, who preferred badminton. She knew she was a pretty good player, and she and Russ had fun socializing together on the tennis courts with fellow film stars such as Ginger Rogers, Errol Flynn, and Gary Cooper.

"Should I go change?" Russ asked. At the club he usually wore tennis whites—the obligatory white shorts, sports t-shirt, and tennis shoes. He was wearing the white tennis shoes now.

"No, Russ, save time and simply take the white swimming belt off and don't put on a shirt. Eleanor can only stay for about half an hour and then she has to leave. Besides, the black looks good on you."

He quickly removed the belt. The photographer shot a couple of solo pictures of him, again shirtless, making him look as if he were about to serve the ball; he then took a few with Eleanor. The pictures were taken at the net, which made it appear as if the tennis instructor was showing him the proper way to hold a racket for a backhand. The afternoon photo shoot went off without a hitch.

Carole knew that Alice Marble, the young amateur tennis player who had been coached by Eleanor, had collapsed in Paris at the US Wightman Cup Tournament during warmups, and the instructor had assumed full care of her sick protégé.

"How's Alice doing?" Carole asked.

"She's not very well," the instructor replied. "She has been diagnosed with tuberculosis. Several doctors have informed me that she'll never be able to play tennis again."

The coach's face looked sad. "Quite frankly, I don't know what to do. She's at my home resting, since her mother's health is very poor and her family's financial situation is shaky. I hired a nurse to watch over her while I teach."

Carole's eyes lit up. Ever since the chimpanzee bite, she had spent a lot of time around doctors in an attempt to improve her own health with different therapies; she had in mind a doctor she could recommend.

"Don't give up. I know of a doctor right here in Los Angeles who might be able to help her. I'll call Fieldsie up to get you his number. You have to take Alice to see him. He's the best around. I'm certain he can help. The doc is a real wonder with ailments."

"Do you really think he can help?"

"Yeah, I'm telling you, he's the best." She turned toward Russ. "You don't mind if I use the house phone to call Fieldsie, do you?"

"No, of course not."

Carole went up to the house and asked for the doctor's telephone number. Hurrying back, she handed it to Eleanor. "Now promise me you'll take her to see him and then give me a call and let me know how it turns out. No, better yet, I'll call her. Poor kid, she probably feels like she's stuck in the doghouse."

From that day forward, Carole took a personal interest in the sick tennis player. She called Alice every day, encouraging her not to give up.

When she returned home Carole put her decision to master Italian cooking into action. She had Edgar, her cook, gather every Italian recipe he knew for her to learn and then she practiced cooking them.

There were some difficulties involved in learning how to make the Italian cuisine particular to Sicily, where Russ's family was from. She burned many pots and pans trying to correctly fry veal, chicken, and eggplant. And then there had been the dubious joys of learning to make pasta and sauces from scratch, and all the slicing, dicing, and peeling that went along with it. The stinging onions—oh, how they made her eyes water!

She felt squeamish when picking up her first live squid, having its wet, rubbery body slip out of her hands. The struggling octopod squirted water and black ink all over her. It fell to the kitchen floor and hid under the stove, leaving her angrily standing there swearing her head off. She had to kneel down and, using tongs, picked it up. Oh yes, learning to cook Italian food had been quite an adventure.

When she set the large platters of steaming food in front of Russ, she felt a real sense of accomplishment.

"Carole, this is delicious!" he exclaimed, after digging into the eggplant and tomato dish known as *pasta a la Norma* she placed before him. "*Deliziosissma!*"

"*Grazie.*" She held her wine glass in her hand and, lifting it, toasted him. She pretended that cooking the food had been a breeze to do.

"*Salute!*" she said.

"*Salute*, Angel."

They clinked glasses. She had done it. She had mastered Italian cooking!

In the back of her mind, she began to think that she would like to become Mrs. Russell Columbo. Yes, she would like to be his wife—but not yet. She wanted Russ to make it big as a movie star first.

It turned out that Carole was right about having Eleanor contact the LA doctor about Alice's ailment. He ordered a new set of X-rays. After viewing them, his diagnosis was different from the original diagnosis. Alice may have had TB in the past, but it was gone now, leaving her lungs scarred. It looked as if the tennis player was actually suffering from pleurisy and secondary anemia.

"As soon as my blood count increases, the doctor says I'll be able to play again," Alice excitedly told her over the telephone. "I'm taking iron pills now to help with the anemia."

"Gee, that's great news! Did you hear that, Russ? Alice is going to be A-Okay."

"Tell her I look forward to playing against her soon."

"Did you hear that? Russ says to keep a date open on your calendar so that we can play tennis once the doc says you're able. Well, I have to hang up now. He's taking me bowling with my brother Fred and his fiancée, Jane, to the Biltmore Bowl. Say 'hi' to Eleanor for me. Thanks for telling me the good news. Bye!"

When Alice's blood count reached a normal level, the doctor cautiously let her begin training again. Soon she was back on the tennis courts, and Carole had an opportunity to meet her. On a day when she and Russ had a private tennis lesson with Eleanor, the two met, talked, and played tennis together for the first time.

"Anybody up for a game?" asked Alice, her pale face looking eagerly at the court.

"What do ya say, Eleanor?" Russ asked.

"Sure."

Eleanor paired herself with Russ, and Carole partnered with Alice. The coach could not resist giving pointers while she played against the rest of them, despite the fact that Alice and Carole were winning. She interrupted the match to point out any small mistakes anyone made.

"Alice, you need to be in the far corner, ready to take that serve. You weren't in the right position on that shot. And Carole, keep your eye on the ball: watch it all the way as it reaches your racket."

"Yes, teacher dear," came her sweet reply.

Carole hit the next ball back but felt a twinge at her elbow.

"Keep your arm straight as an extension of the racket, Carole. Follow all the way through, like this." Eleanor demonstrated, using her own racket.

"Okay, teacher," again came Carole's answer, but she ran forward too soon to get a ball and missed. The instructor once more spoke out.

"Easy does it, Carole, you ran up too fast on that one."

"All right, Teach."

The moniker stuck. From then on, Eleanor Tennant was called "Teach" by everyone, including the press. Eleanor and Alice won the game, and Russ treated everyone to drinks up at the clubhouse afterward.

Alice slowly regained her strength. She climbed steadily back up the tennis ranks until she began to compete in major championship tournaments.

The young, ambitious player needed someone to help sponsor her amateur tennis career. Eleanor couldn't afford to pay all her travel and medical expenses, and many sponsors were leery about investing in a young woman who was still under a doctor's supervision.

Upon seeing how talented a tennis player Alice was, Carole decided to step in and pay her expenses herself, taking a personal interest in the young tennis player's career. Image conscious, she gave the young woman tips on how to look good on the court. She taught her how to style her hair, use makeup to hide acne, and pick out the right clothes to wear. She helped Alice improve the way the news media looked at her, from gawky teenager to poised tennis champ.

The talented tennis player, to Carole's delight, went on to win Wimbledon and eighteen other important and internationally recognized tennis championships.

Carole often recalled how great Russ had looked on the tennis court that day. He thought no one had noticed, but she knew he had purposefully flubbed his game. Alice hadn't regained her strength yet and was barely able to finish the match. Carole knew he'd thrown the match in order to encourage the sick tennis player. He could outplay almost anyone in the club, except the pros. It endeared him more to her, and she began telling the press, "I believe in giving the little guy, the person everyone considers to be an underdog, an even break."

Several weeks later, the journalist Warren Clark, upon learning that Eleanor was Russ's tennis coach, asked, "Say, Teach, what do you think of Russ Columbo's tennis playing? Is he any good?"

"Russ has the speed and agility of Bill Tilden."

The international tennis player Bill Tilden, to whom Eleanor compared Russ, was the current number-one hardcourt champion at Wimbledon. It was a high compliment, to say the least, coming from the professional tennis coach.

After reading Eleanor's statement, Carole began to kid Russ as they sat outside on her backyard patio enjoying the warm weather. "What, being a singer, a songwriter, and a radio and movie star isn't good enough for you, Russ? Now you want to become a professional tennis player, too?" She playfully threw a pillow at him.

"Hey!" He smiled, fending off the cushion. "I can't help it if I'm better than you, 'Tagalong'!"

"So, you overheard my stinky brother call me that last night, did you?" She grinned, delighted that he was getting along so well with her family and friends.

She pretended for a moment to be Mae West, putting a hand on her hip. "So, what are you going to do about it, big boy? Are you going to start crooning and mesmerize me with those big brown eyes of yours or take a peek in a mirror and preen?"

She pantomimed singing with a microphone and then, holding out her hand, she acted as if she were taking a long lingering look at herself in a mirror. She patted her hair and checked her teeth, picking out imaginary greens in a comical manner.

"So, you read about that, did you? That'll teach me. Some writer caught me checking my ugly mug in a mirror—yeah, exactly like Valentino used to. Well, I guess I got what I deserved. But now, young lady, you're going to get yours!"

He bent down and scooped her up, easily carrying her up to the pool. He pretended to be James Cagney. "Make fun of me, will ya. We'll see about that, Angel."

"No, Russ, *no!*" she squealed, kicking her feet as he dangled her over the water. "I've got an interview here in a couple of minutes and I'm all dolled up!"

"All right, Angel, I'm letting you off light this time, see." He gently put her down. He held her in his arms and gave her a long, sizzling kiss.

She put her arms around his neck, bringing him closer, and kissed him back. But as fate would have it, at that exact moment her high-heeled sandals slid out beneath her on the smooth, wet cement. She frantically grabbed hold of him for support, tightening her grip. They both fell backward into the water with one loud *ka-splash!*

Their clumsy fall was witnessed by the prudish writer of a woman's magazine.

Carole emerged out of the water several seconds later, sputtering. Russ popped up beside her. Soaking wet, they both crawled out of the pool and walked to the cabana to dry off and get out of their wet clothes. Once toweled off and dried, they reappeared in matching striped lounging robes. The lady writer had already done a vanishing act. Two weeks later, Carole discovered why.

"Balderdash!" Carole angrily murmured after reading the magazine, which stated that she had spontaneously jumped into the pool with all her clothes on after "going Hollywood" crazy.

"As if I could afford to destroy a one-of-a-kind dress by jumping into the pool!" Disgusted, she threw the magazine into the garbage bin.

Chapter Ten

The Game of Kings

The flat triangular field of the Uplifters Club was set in the Rustic Canyon area of the Santa Monica Mountains; the field was manicured by the groundskeeper for the game of kings—polo. It was one of several polo fields in Southern California at the time, including three at the nearby Riviera Club. A famous Hollywood star once described the fast-paced game, which was played on horseback with a mallet and ball, as being like trying to engage in golf during an earthquake.

The Hollywood crowd enjoyed the great outdoors of Mediterranean California and were fanatical about the sport. It was an exciting way to get exercise and blow off steam for those who could afford it, and it was an opportunity to be seen having fun by the general public.

The popular cowboy comic Will Rogers, who had pioneered the sport in California, invited Carole to throw in the first ball and to hand out trophies to the winners of the match. She had accepted and was now seated up in the viewing stands with Russ on a mild, cool day in May. They watched the game being played below between the Actors Team, captained by the gum-chewing Will Rogers, and the Producers Team, captained by the gung-ho producer Darryl Zanuck.

The sport was played by two teams consisting of four players on horseback who competed on a three-hundred-yard-long rectangular field. The way to score points was to hit the ball between two goalposts, which were evenly spaced eight feet apart, one on either end of the field. The sides were changed after each goal. The players used long mallets to hit the ball; they could hook their opponents' mallets in order to prevent them from scoring.

Polo was played on even-tempered and well-trained horses that could perform at quick gallops for up to seven minutes, which was the amount of time the sets, known as chukkers, lasted. Each game had six chukkers, so the entire game lasted around an hour. A fresh string of horses was needed to play the game, and players changed mounts up to six to eight times per game. Carole knew that teaching the animals to be responsive to the riders' commands took hours of practice, and special horse trainers were required. It was a game that only the very rich could afford.

Carole liked being around horses and had learned to ride when she had starred in "horse operas" in the late 1920s. She would have enjoyed owning a riding mount, but because a stable was expensive, she didn't. Instead, she enjoyed the vicarious pleasure of watching those who could, the Hollywood stars and producers who played on the polo fields. She often went with Zeppo Marx and his wife Marion to watch the celebrity matches.

"Come with me," she'd said to Russ, inviting him. "You told me you used to ride in Central Park on a roan when you were living in New York City. I think you'll find this interesting. The ladies get dressed up like they're all duchesses, and the fellas play a fast-paced, dangerous game. Besides, it'll be great press for both of us. There are always a couple of newspaper reporters and photographers at hand."

"Have it your way, Angel. I'm sold—let's go."

In the stands, Russ sat next to her, wearing a lightweight brown sports jacket, a white-buttoned shirt, and a matching long tie with a folded white handkerchief stuck in his pocket. In Carole's eyes, he looked like a modern-day prince: handsome, well groomed, relaxed, and very personable. He was the perfect companion. Nobody ever criticized his social manners, since they were always impeccable.

Russ told Carole that it troubled him that so many people in Hollywood still assumed that he was simply acting as her escort, squiring her around town, and that nothing romantic was occurring between the two of them. "When are we going to start setting everyone straight about us? Don't you think it's time, Angel?"

"It's best for now that the public see you as an available bachelor, someone women can fantasize about. For the present, darling, we have to continue telling the press that we're simply friends. It'll only be for a short while, until you release your first big picture. Pretty soon we'll get married."

A pained expression passed over his face.

"Russ, are you sick? What is it, darling? You gave me the oddest look."

"It's nothing."

But she could tell something was amiss. His feelings were obviously hurt. Maybe he thought she was behaving like his ex-fiancée, Hannah Williams.

Couldn't he see she wanted to build him up into a bigger movie star before they married? If he became a top box-office draw, she could then retire from her own career and focus solely on his. She wanted to stop performing when they started having children. She would then take a backseat, managing his career behind the scenes, but without the extra burden of maintaining her own career.

Carole fondly remembered the way he encouraged his nieces and nephews to study music and would listen to them perform at family gatherings. After meals he would go outside and play ball with them. She'd observed him gently persuading a little five-year-old nephew to throw a baseball to him. Russ caught it, and the little boy's face lit up with joy. A maternal warmth entered her heart. Carole had never thought about having children when she was with Bill, since he seemed happy with the one son he'd had by his first wife, but with Russ it was different.

She was proud of being his girlfriend and wanted so much to become his wife and have his children that sometimes it hurt. Now was not the time to start a family, however, they had to focus on building up his career.

There was the added reality that taking care of his family as well as hers was going to cost lots of money. He had recently hired a caregiver named Carrie to watch over his ailing mother and fragile father. And her own mother, Bessie, wasn't getting any younger. They each had an entourage of servants and family to support. In order for them to survive financially once they'd married and had a family of their own, she thought that Russ had to make it to the top as a movie actor.

After this month, Carole knew that Russ would be spending most of June at the studio with the music-writing team and scriptwriters who were preparing for the filming of *Wake Up and Dream*. She wanted him to come with her today to the polo match to receive more exposure from the press before he disappeared behind the studio's iron gates for work.

The polo match was the perfect opportunity to be seen by the general public and to have their names printed in the papers.

Sometimes as many as forty thousand people would attend, and the local radio would broadcast the matches live. Out of the corner of her eye she spotted the comic actor Ken Murray filming them. Accustomed to being photographed by all kinds of photographers, she ignored him, her attention remaining on the polo match before her.

Russ put his arm casually behind her. She looked at him and gave him a warm smile. It was wonderful having him beside her.

"You look like a queen today, Angel."

"Thank you, Russ, I feel like one."

She had carefully chosen her attire for the polo match, styling herself after the English ladies she'd seen in newsreels. Carole dressed as if the match were taking place at Ascot Park, England's premier polo fields, and had worn the most impressive hat she owned.

She had pulled her shoulder-length blonde locks back and had put on a black, wide-brimmed cartwheel hat with a small bunch of removable flowers decorating the shallow crown. She wore a plain long-sleeved linen coatdress that buttoned on the side. Her hands were covered by black kid gloves, and a red fox stole, a gift from Russ, lay draped around her narrow shoulders.

She watched Will Rogers on his favorite polo horse, Bootlegger. He missed a couple of the easy shots but returned a difficult one, scoring a goal. Cheers and applause could be heard across the viewing stands. His playing kept the audience on the edge of their seats.

The cowboy humorist played only one way, and that was full out. He swung his mallet around his head like a rodeo star about to rope a steer and he really was that accurate in hitting the small white polo ball. He was immensely popular with both celebrities and the public. A real chatterbox, Will talked and joked nonstop during the entire time he was on the playing field. Carole knew he was the key reason the sport had gained such wide acceptance in the movie colony.

Will owned a polo field in Pacific Palisades, the first in the area, and had built a large house there after selling his Beverly Hills home. On Sundays when she and Russ dropped by, they would find Will with his family and friends playing polo before brunch. She envied them. Away from Hollywood they had created their own private little slice of paradise. Maybe, she thought, when she and Russ got married they could do the same and buy a ranch.

Playing on the Actors Team that day was another familiar face, her friend James Gleason, whom Russ had met at the Christmas open house. James was known to be a true devotee of the sport. He had been playing since the 1920s, when he'd started writing Broadway shows and screenplays, such as the first talkie she'd starred in, *High Voltage* in 1929.

Out on the field, she spotted producers Hal Roach (*Little Rascals* and Laurel and Hardy movies), Walt and Roy Disney (Animation), and Darryl Zanuck (Twentieth Century) on horseback. Carole knew from experience that the left-handed Darryl took the sport quite seriously: he carried around with him on the studio lot a riding crop that was weighted in the same way as the polo mallet, which he was now swinging around out on the field.

Her friend Gary Cooper also played, but she did not see him that day. Instead, English actor Leslie Howard was on the Actors Team, sporting protective glasses. Leslie owned a stable of polo horses and was generally considered to be a decent player. Carole could see that out on the field he was maintaining excellent control over his mount and had made a few well-aimed whacks at the small ball for his team.

"Good shot," she exclaimed under her breath, when the Englishman put one of the balls between the goal posts. Russ nodded his head and politely applauded in agreement.

At halftime they stood and stretched their legs, joining the other spectators on the polo field. Everyone stomped down the torn divot grass on the field, which helped save money in grounds keeping. A couple of fans took the opportunity to approach Carole and Russ, asking for autographs. They kindly obliged. After some refreshments of hot coffee, cold lemonade, and sandwiches, they returned to the viewing stands.

The game restarted, and a collective gasp came from the crowd as Walt almost took a spill from his mount while using his mallet to reach for the ball. Carole knew, he could have fallen off his horse and broken a limb, or worse.

"Be careful there, Mickey!" said Will, who as usual was chewing gum. "You want some of my gum so you can stick your pants to the saddle?"

Walt made a wry face, ignoring the jibe.

"Oh, applesauce!" said Hal Roach as he tangled mallets with Spencer in an effort to score.

"Yeah, that's what I thought—mighty tasty, too," commented Will, grinning wickedly as he stole the ball away from the producer when it rolled in his direction. He then went on to pass it to James Gleason, who quickly ran it down the field and put it between the goalposts, scoring another point for their team. Everyone in the stands stood up and applauded.

"That was something to see!" said Russ as they clapped.

After changing horses, Darryl Zanuck showed up out of the blue. For a while he and Will ran the ball neck and neck, nearly colliding their mounts, until finally the producer scored by putting the ball in on the other end.

"Can't let you have all the fun, Wild Will!" said the producer with smug satisfaction.

"Dang! And all this time I thought you were asleep there in the saddle, Darryl. Like maybe you forgot we were playing—whatcha think?"

"That you're full of it, Will."

The polo match went on like this for another twenty minutes until the timekeeper rang the thirty-second bell during the last chukker, signaling with his head to have the horn blown, which ended the game. The Actors Team won with nine points to the Producers' three. The team captains and players shook hands.

Carole was then invited to come out onto the field to pass out trophies to the winning team by the master of ceremonies. When she handed James Gleason his, he kissed her fondly on the cheek. A couple of photographers, as well as Ken's movie camera, took pictures of the moment.

Russ beamed proudly at her from the sideline, where he patiently waited.

She overheard someone comment in admiration to Will about his ability and stamina in the saddle as they walked off the field: "Boy, Will, you sure have a great pair of legs on you!"

The gray-haired, fifty-four-year-old wit smiled, his blue eyes twinkling: "Well, why do you think Florenz Ziegfeld kept me in the Follies all those years?" He gave Carole a saucy wink.

Carole laughed, knowing that the Ziegfeld Follies was where Will had performed as a cowboy comic long before he was snagged by

Hollywood. The Follies at the time was famous for its beautiful, long-legged showgirls. She repeated the joke to Russ in the car on the way back, and they both got a kick out of it.

Chapter Eleven

Now and Forever

"Dorothy Dell is dead, Shirley," the camera operator on the set of *Now and Forever* informed the young five-year-old performer, whom everyone knew had been befriended by the beautiful and recently deceased nineteen-year-old actress. Dorothy and Shirley had both previously appeared in the child's first major picture, the smash hit *Little Miss Marker*, at Fox Studios.

Tears welled in the blonde, ringlet-haired child's china-blue eyes, and Shirley Temple began to earnestly cry into the pillow of the set's bed. The director, Henry Hathaway, cued the cameraman, Harry Fischbeck, who filmed close-ups of the child's tearstained face and heartfelt sobs. Miraculously, the child was able to say her lines to Gary without faltering.

There's nothing like stepping into someone else's more-than-perfect shoes to make you feel uncomfortable, and this was what was happening to Carole.

The director had purposefully withheld the information from the child star about Dorothy Dell's death in order to use the tragedy to invoke a heartbroken emotional reaction from Shirley for their picture. It made Carole wish to high heavens she hadn't agreed to step in and take the role that had been vacated by the southern beauty.

Dorothy Dell had been much beloved. The young actress had been discovered in the Ziegfeld Follies in New York City and had been brought to Hollywood by Paramount to become a film star. The lovely actress had recently been featured in her first leading roles in the films *Wharf Angel*, *Little Miss Marker*, and *Shoot the Works*, the movie where she made the song "With My Eyes Wide Open" a success. Dorothy, with her natural talent for acting, had seemed headed for stardom.

Then, she was tragically killed in a car accident in Altadena, California, in the San Gabriel Mountains. The doctor she had been on a dinner date with, after drinking liquor from a flask, had failed to take a curve correctly as he raced along the serpentine mountainous road.

Instead of turning, he drove straight ahead. The car jumped the curb, catapulting into a canyon. The vehicle crashed first into a telephone pole and then a palm tree, then rolled downward to a deadly standstill. Both passengers were killed.

Carole had just walked onto the set from her dressing room when she saw them filming Shirley and was appalled at the use of the tragedy to make the little girl cry. *How could they do that to the kid?*

The camera backed up, and Henry said quietly, "Cut—and that's a take."

Carole strode onto the set and stopped herself short from saying aloud a bad word in front of the kid. She sat down on the stage bed and held Shirley. "Darling, I'm terribly sorry you found out this way. Dorothy is with the angels, dear."

The little girl sat up and looked at her through tear-filled eyes. "Is she really in heaven, Carole? No kidding, is Dorothy really dead?"

"Yes, darling. There was a car accident, and she died. She's gone to be with God and the angels, and they're all having a marvelous time together in heaven."

Her own blue eyes began to brim with tears. She had never met Dorothy Dell, but thoughts of a young woman's life taken too soon pained her and brought back painful memories of her own car accident, which had marred her face. She easily could have been the southern belle. It was also terrible to see how genuinely grief-stricken Shirley felt over the loss of her beautiful friend.

"I bet she's the prettiest angel there, don't you?" asked Shirley.

"I bet you're right, darling."

"Dorothy was my friend. We used to play together, and I loved her. I'm going to miss her terribly. Do you think, as an angel, she can come down and see me perform? She always said she liked my singing."

"Yes, dear, I'm sure she can. We just can't see her."

Carole continued to hold the youngster until Shirley's mother appeared on the set. The little girl began crying again as she went running into her mother's arms.

"Dorothy's dead, Mama! She's gone!"

"If you want," Carole volunteered, "I'll hold down Henry's arms while you sock him."

"That won't be necessary," replied the austere stage mother,

Gertrude Temple, picking up her daughter.

"Suit yourself."

If it'd been my kid, I'd have thrown a hissy fit. Carole decided that she never wanted any of her children, when she and Russ had some, to become child actors.

"You mustn't cry like this," said Gertrude. "It isn't fair, Shirley. You see, everybody here today feels sad, but they have work to do and they're trying to control their feelings. And you're not helping. And Dorothy, she's all right now."

The child began crying harder. "But, Mama, she's dead."

"All right, Shirley, that's enough. Do you hear me? She'd be the last person in the world who would want you to cry."

At last the child's sobs ended. Under the direction of her mother, Shirley walked over to Henry Hathaway. "I'm ready to work, Mr. Director." And they resumed filming.

The news of Dorothy's death had been announced on the radio. Russ, who had been seated next to Carole the night before while going over the script for *Wake Up and Dream*, suddenly stood up, abruptly dropping the script to the floor. He openly cried.

"Russ, darling," Carole walked over to him, concerned. "What's happened? Why are you crying?"

He turned to her, tears running down his face.

"Dorothy Dell's dead."

"Yes, I know, dear. But why are you so upset?"

"I loved her."

Her heart squeezed. She *knew* he was speaking the truth.

"We were once engaged."

"When was this?" Carole held her breath, waiting for his answer. Had she been a fool? Had Russ been seeing Dorothy behind her back all this time?

"When I was working in New York City at the Paramount Theater, I met her. She was in the Follies then, and we fell crazily in love. We nearly eloped, but Conrad broke us up—made us believe it wasn't the right time to get married, started rumors in the papers about her and about me," he said bitterly.

"Conrad had me dating and marrying Greta Garbo without having once met her. It was a sideshow fiasco, involving telegrams sent to her hotel room and expensive bouquets of roses, and all of this—all of this he did behind my back!" He angrily reached for his cigarette case.

She could tell Russ was shaken up and helped him light a cigarette. He took in a deep puff and released the smoke into the air. She lit one for herself and waited for him to calm down before he continued.

"Funny thing, Greta didn't deny it. I guess she liked the press. But Dorothy was upset. Conrad had tarred and feathered her good name in the papers, making her look bad. She decided we should separate for a time. I, like a fool, agreed. We never got back together. I saw her twice after that, but never alone. One time she showed up at one of my gigs with Jack Dempsey, the same heavyweight who later married Hannah! Dorothy went her way, and I selfishly went mine. Man, I should have busted Conrad in the chops when I had the chance!"

Carole then understood the pained face he had made at the polo field. He thought she was going to be another Dorothy Dell, the woman he'd loved and lost, and he was fearful that the right time for them to marry was going to be never. She secretly felt some relief as well, since the romance with the beautiful young actress had ended long before he met her. He had never betrayed her with another.

"Russ—oh, I'm terribly sorry, darling. She must have been your first real love."

He confessed that he had tried to contact Dorothy's mother to tell her how sorry he was for her loss, but he was sternly informed that she didn't want to speak to him.

"Are you going to attend the funeral?"

"No, I don't want to upset her mother any further."

"You should write her a condolence. I think that a note would be acceptable. Maybe she'll change her mind and ask you to attend?"

"Yeah, good idea. I think I'll do that."

"Russ, I'm here for you if you need me."

"Thanks, Carole. I don't know what I would do if you weren't here. I'd probably go crazy."

He sent the card but never received a word back. He did not attend the funeral. Paramount paid for Dorothy's casket to be sent by train to the South to be buried in her family's cemetery there.

After the young actress's death, Carole would sometimes catch Russ staring off into the distance and knew that he was thinking of the deceased beauty.

The next day the studio called to inform Carole that she was to report to the set, where she was to take Dorothy Dell's place in *Now and Forever*. The sentimental melodrama revolved around a vagabond confidence man living in France named Jerry Day (Gary Cooper) who in the end goes straight to please his daughter Pennie (Shirley Temple) and his girlfriend Toni (Carole Lombard), both of whom wanted a normal family life. When Pennie and Toni discover that Jerry has stolen a jeweled necklace from the child's adult friend and has hidden it in her teddy bear, trouble soon follows.

On the set, Carole was surprised to find that Shirley, who was on loan from Fox Films, knew all Carole's lines as well as her own. Many of the scenes she performed with the dimpled child star could be done in one take. It was unnerving.

"Nuts!" Carole exclaimed. She had blown one of her lines in front of the kid.

"Oh, you've got a Dorothy, too, don't you, Miss Carole?" asked the child, looking up at her and patting her arm.

"Yes, dear, I do."

She could see that the child was clearly traumatized. Everyone on the set was making excuses for Shirley's odd behavior, doting on her, giving her gifts, and pretending that Dorothy was her make-believe friend and not a beautiful young woman who had suddenly been killed. Gary Cooper, whom Shirley had dubbed "Mr. Wigglebritches," drew pictures for the child while she sat on his lap, trying to distract the little girl whenever her innocent blue eyes filled with tears.

The press, of course, was told that the child star was having a grand time playing games with Gary and Carole. It was no big deal that her adult friend Dorothy had been killed in a car crash. One Dorothy had died, and an invisible playmate named Dorothy had simply taken her place. Everything was honky dory on the set. The kid was a living doll, lots of fun.

Give me a break. Shirley should have been given some time off to come to terms with her grief, decided Carole, stepping outside to have a much needed smoke. The abnormality of it all was making her ill at ease. She wished she could light another, but both she and Russ were trying to cut back. Other stars drank, took drugs, had serial affairs, gambled, or played polo to relieve the pressure; they both chain smoked.

After the break, she was going to have to go back and argue with the director. There was an upcoming scene where she was supposed to spank Pennie (Shirley) because she refused to go to bed as told, and Carole wanted to have it deleted or rewritten.

"Look, Henry, the kid's been through enough. I want it taken out." She talked to him privately in the control room, really hating what she was supposed to do in the scene. She didn't believe in corporal punishment and would never in her life hit or slap a kid.

"Shirley doesn't mind if you do."

"Let me put it to you this way, *I mind.* I don't want to do it, Henry. I won't spank Shirley and see her cry again. Take it out, or let me play it a different way, please!"

"Okay, okay, settle down. Give me a chance to take a look at it." He perused the scene she had underlined. "All right, you can play the scene the way you want. It won't make that much of a difference to the picture."

"Grand! I'll go tell Shirley's mother."

But when it came time to do the scene, the little girl faithfully remembered the way it was originally written. The bright child informed her, "You have to spank me now, Carole."

"But darling, I don't want to. I don't want to spank you, Shirley. I like you too much. And, thank heavens, it's been taken out."

"But you have to do it. That's the way I memorized it."

"Very well," Carole agreed, gently tapping the child's bottom with all the hardness of a butterfly, and the little girl giggled.

When they finished the long good-night scene, Shirley commented, "My, that was a short scene." She then turned toward Henry. "Was that a take, Mr. Director?"

"Yes, it was, Shirley."

Everyone laughed at the precocious child's comments. She was adored on the set by both the cast and the crew. It was obvious the little star thought that this was a normal way of life.

Carole was never again in another Shirley Temple movie, although from time to time she met Shirley at different Hollywood events. The picture had given her a sour stomach. She went back, without any regrets, to acting in adult romances and helping Russ prepare for *Wake Up and Dream.*

Chapter Twelve

Wake Up and Dream

Carole was taking copious notes during the rehearsals for *Wake Up and Dream*. She had noticed the pretty blonde singer June Knight's face fall upon her arrival at the script reading. June and Russ had once been a hot item in New York City when the actress was in the Broadway musical *Hot-Cha!*, starring Lupe Vélez. The studio's weekly rag said that June was the last showgirl Florenz Ziegfeld had made into a star before he died in 32'.

Russ admitted to Carole, "For a short time, June and I renewed our romance here in Hollywood, but we were never suited as a couple." He stopped, as if remembering an unpleasant incident. "She's nothing like you, Angel."

"What do you mean?"

"We never had the kind of connection you and I have."

She knew Russ meant their ability to understand each other without having to speak.

He continued. "It never existed between us. And then when she told me she didn't want to have kids, I lost all interest and broke it off. You know, Angel, I'd like to have a couple—at least three or four. Don't you?"

"Yes, I know, Russ. God willing, we will, darling."

Carole pictured what their child would look like. She would love to have a little boy first, with straight brown hair and sweet, round chubby cheeks and a little bow of a mouth. Maybe the shape of his eyes would be like hers. And when he grew up he would have his father's wonderful musical talent and be athletic like both of them. But most of all, Carole hoped that their child would be kind to others and feel safe and loved, something she had never experienced in her own childhood because of her abusive father.

Yes, she secretly hoped she would be able to have children. She tried not to think about the possibility that she might not be able to. Not only did her weakened immune system trouble her, but she suffered from unusually long menstrual periods, which made her very tired. She commented on it once to Fieldsie: "I'm afraid God must have gotten the formula all wrong when he made me."

Her ability to have children was not important. She was young and still had plenty of time to find out what (if anything) was wrong. Sex was usually uncomfortable for her, but she was fortunate, Russ was an extremely gentle lover. He was like no man she'd ever been with before.

She had woken up, after having fallen asleep after their lovemaking, to find him sitting on the edge of the bed, gazing down at her as she slept. He didn't touch her; he simply sat there. She could see in his gentle brown eyes a bright, tender glimmer... love.

"Roogie, how long have you been sitting there?" She looked out the window. It was starting to become dark.

"For a little while now, I thought I'd let you rest."

She picked up the clock by the bed and looked at the time. Due to the summer heat wave, his picture was being filmed at night. "But you're supposed to be over at the studio in a half hour. Hadn't you better get going?"

"I don't want to go. I'd rather stay here with you."

"Oh, darling, don't be childish. You better hop in your car and hurry over there. They'll be expecting you at makeup."

"All right, but I'm going under protest."

"Sometimes, Roogie, I don't think you want to be rich and famous."

His brown eyes warmly studied her naked body. "If it means leaving you like this, I'd gladly give them both up. In case you didn't know, Angel, you're the most important person in my life."

She, in turn, reached up and pulled him down to her for a loving kiss.

"I think you're pretty marvelous, too. Now, young man, you better get going. I don't want you to be late for your first big day of filming."

"Very well, Mother dear," he said sarcastically. "You're joining me later, right?"

"Yes. I swear, one would think you would be lost without me." She pretended annoyance, while her heart sang with happiness. She loved having a hand in his career. She enjoyed the fact that Russ respected her opinions and took her advice as seriously as the director's.

"That may very well be, but let's not find out just yet, Angel. Be there, please, I'd like your input."

"I'll be there. You know I wouldn't miss it for anything in the world."

Before filming they had gone over the script together with the film's writer, John Meehan Jr., who had written the pleasant romance *Let's Talk It Over*. The new musical was showcasing Russ's singing and songwriting abilities. *Wake Up and Dream* played up the real-life fact that Russ had once been a vaudeville performer who had sung and danced with a family group when he was still in his teens.

The story revolved around a dancing and singing trio composed of Paul Scotti (Russ Columbo), his lifelong friend Charley Sullivan (Roger Pryor), and Charley's pretty fiancée, Toby Brown (June Knight). The storyline follows them through their bumpy ups and downs to Hollywood once they find themselves in trouble after Paul is mistakenly hired to replace a Broadway star at an audition. The trio is forced to flee town after Charley kidnaps the expected star, leaving him gagged and bound in an abandoned house.

The trio then make their way across the United States by bus, fearing the police are after them for kidnapping, taking along with them Paul's newly arrived Italian friend, the eternally hungry Cellini (Henry Armetta). In need of money, Cellini romances Madame Rose (Catherine Doucet), an eccentric wealthy fortuneteller guarded by comic Joe Egbert (Andy Devine), who carries an unloaded gun in his pocket for protection.

During one of their stops, Paul performs the song "Too Beautiful for Words" with Toby as a duet and is discovered by a film star named Mae La Rue (Wini Shaw) and her important Hollywood protector, Mr. Roger Babcock (Richard Carle), who helps launch Paul's film career. Paul has been secretly in love with Toby all along and pretends to become an egomaniac who has "gone Hollywood" by dating Mae in order to help save his friend Charley's relationship with her. But when Charley realizes that Paul and Toby love each other, he nobly steps aside and announces the engagement of the couple at a Hollywood party, giving the film its upbeat happily-ever-after.

John Meehan, the writer, let Carole and Russ make changes to the screenplay. Apparently, the studio heads had told him that they wanted to showcase Russ's talent and to stay in the singer's good books. Carole knew that they didn't want their popular star to break his contract and sign with another studio.

She suggested, looking down at the script, "Wouldn't it be funny if Russ's character said 'I wrote it' right before singing the song?"

"That would make a great inside joke," agreed Russ, who had co-written most of the songs he was singing in the picture. The song he had written for Carole, "Too Beautiful for Words," was to be featured several times throughout the picture.

"I bet we'd get some laughs from the audience with that one," Carole said.

"Good idea, let's add it in," John said, concurring.

All the other cast members' performances in the picture would be secondary to Russ's. This was supposed to be the long-overdue buildup for his movie career. It didn't sit well with June Knight, who had wrongly assumed that she was to have a bigger singing role and announced that she didn't like the fact that she was to be listed third on the screen credits after the charming Roger Pryor.

Roger, the second billed lead, was a newcomer to Hollywood, but he had already been in several motion pictures. Like Carole, at one point Roger was working on three movies at the same time: he was finishing one film, rehearsing for *Lady by Choice* (which he was about to perform in with Carole), and working on this one. He had a very easygoing personality and was not difficult to work with.

Carole heard June loudly complaining to the director, Kurt Neumann: "I only get one song in this picture? That's it?"

"Yes. In case you didn't know, this is supposed to be a Russ Columbo picture—not a June Knight production."

"As if I could forget!" June shouted. The taffy blonde flounced out of the room and would have her pert little nose out of joint for the rest of the filming.

Not shy about her desire to sing solo in the picture, June let everyone know what she wanted. The cast and crew were filming outside when suddenly a horrible, piercing sound disrupted work.

"What the hell was that?" muttered Kurt, removing his headphones. "Can someone find the source of that racket and get it to stop!"

An assistant director went on the errand, but failed to return. The noise now became someone loudly singing one of the picture's songs, "Wake Up and Dream."

"Oh, for heaven's sake, it's June!" swore Kurt, as the familiar voice of the picture's leading pain-in-the-neck could be heard singing at the top of her lungs through a nearby open window.

"Come on, Phil," Carole said, turning to the soundman. "Let's get to the bottom of this."

They walked over to June's dressing room, where a stagehand supervisor stood pounding on the door. June had not only disrupted their picture but two others as well. Several minutes passed as they stood there listening as the singer went through an entire repertoire of songs, wasting everyone's time.

At long last June opened the door, wearing a dressing gown and a staged look of bewilderment, as if she couldn't understand why they would possibly be standing there frowning.

"What can I do for you?" June asked brightly, as if she expected them to hand her a bouquet of roses for her performance. "I was just warming up my vocal chords."

"We can't hear our signal bells," complained the stagehand, referring to the bells that the stagehand supervisor telephoned in as a cue for moving props. A whole entire wall or staircase could be placed at the wrong time, crushing an actor or another stagehand. Everyone on the lot was forewarned of the potential danger if a stagehand missed his bell, deaths had been known to occur.

A soundman from another picture chimed in, "Nobody can hear anything through all that caterwauling. Are you skinning a cat in there?"

"What do you mean by that?" June cast a frosty glare in Carole's direction, as if she were the one at fault.

Carole had heard enough. "June, *dear*, these gentlemen and myself are here on behalf of the entire lot to kindly tell you to *shut up*." She said this in a calm, firm voice that left everyone with their mouths open. She then turned on her six-inch heels and left.

"Well, I never!" exclaimed the singer, but Carole's intervention had worked. June ceased her self-centered attempts to impress after that.

Carole returned to the set and related what had happened.

"So it's lucky for June that 'peril serials' aren't popular these days, or she would probably kill herself in one," Russ dryly commented, referring to the short films that used to be made involving beautiful damsels in distress, placed in potentially deadly situations.

"Isn't that the truth!" laughed Carole.

The other cast members, like singer Wini Shaw, were perfectly happy to be appearing in Russ's picture. The actors enjoyed one another's company both on and off the set. Many of them had performed with Russ before in New York City, so there was a sense of comradery on the set as old theater friendships were renewed.

The most frequently discussed subject wasn't about people, the past, or filmmaking, but the weather. California had joined the rest of the country in its long heat wave that had created the Dust Bowl and was currently inflicting drought across fifty million acres from New York to California. The temperature in the studio lot buildings was an intolerable 120 degrees Fahrenheit—and that was before the big set lights were turned on.

Not willing to put the production on hiatus until the weather cooled down, the studio decided to have the picture filmed at night. This resulted in a good portion of the storyline taking place in the evening. The cast and crew were now sleeping during the day and working all through the night.

It was evident during the making of *Wake Up and Dream* that June still hoped to get back together with Russ. She didn't hide her feelings very well. It was disconcerting to Carole to show up on the set and find the singer, whose real name was Margaret Rose Valliequietto, cozying up to him between takes.

Observing the performer when filming began in July, Carole decided that for a woman who had supposedly been released from the hospital only a short time ago for appendicitis, June certainly had a lot of energy.

They were in the process of filming the vaudeville dance routine with Roger Pryor, the secondary male lead with whom Carole had begun rehearsing her next picture, *Lady by Choice*. The scene was being filmed at the Hollywood Theater, although in the movie it was supposed to be Atlantic City.

She tried hard not to be jealous of June by comforting herself with the knowledge that the starlet was engaged to Paul Ames, a New York stockbroker whom June had met in Miami. They had begun building a home in the hills in preparation for their marriage. Then again, as a movie weekly noted, "June is always engaged to someone." Before she'd met Paul, the gossips had her engaged to the boxing champion Max Baer. Who would be next?

Russ and Roger both wore white captain hats with dark-blue sport jackets and long neckties for the vaudeville scene. June had on a white sleeveless knit sailor dress with a matching beret.

Carole had to admit that the taffy blonde looked pretty cute, and starting with two happy songs: "Wake Up and Dream" and "Let's Pretend There's a Moon," both of which Russ had co-written, was a good way to begin the picture on an upbeat note.

Carole heard June coyly ask, "Russ, don't you think you and I should go over 'Let's Pretend There's a Moon' one more time?"

Carole had just arrived on the set, and Russ stared down at her as she took a seat in the front row behind the live orchestra to watch. They were about to begin filming the "Wake Up and Dream" dance number and song. Her shiny blonde hair, hatless, stood out from the rest of the audience of extras. She was wearing the black dress with the white bib front she had worn in *Now and Forever*, since she'd come directly from the studio.

Russ looked marvelously at ease onstage. She was pleased. When they had first started filming, he had confided to her that he thought his eyes were too close together. After many reassurances that this wasn't so, he had begun to act less self-consciously. It showed now in his performance, which was a vast improvement from his last picture.

"Ahem," said June.

"Oh—what was it that you asked me, June?"

"I said, don't you think we should rehearse the song once more?"

"Naw, I'm sure it'll be fine. We've gone over it plenty. What do you think, Kurt? Are we ready?"

Kurt Neumann was standing to one side of the stage, preparing to film. "Sure, we've done enough takes of the 'Wake Up and Dream' number. We can move on, Russ. I think you two have the next number down solid, so let's start filming."

"Shall we?" Russ turned to June.

"All right." She walked to her mark, which had been chalked on the stage floor.

Kurt cued them to begin.

"'Let's give the old goat what he wants,'" said Russ, speaking his line. He then escorted June out onto the stage where a bench had been set up. After an orchestral introduction, he began to sing "Let's Pretend There's a Moon."

It was a charming number in which his friend Charley provides an artificial moon for the song. All of the extras in the audience applauded. Carole sighed, looking into Russ's eyes as he looked down at her from the stage. He had such a wonderfully smooth voice. It was always a delight to hear him sing.

"That was great, Russ," Kurt said. "Now, if you and Carole don't mind, could you, as Paul, sing it to Toby?" Everyone in the audience laughed. No one had missed the amorous looks between the couple.

In the next take, Paul cozied up to Toby and sang the song with his arms wrapped around her waist and his cheek pressed up against hers. They sang the song a couple of times, which enabled the camera to film them from several different angles, including a backstage one.

The rest of the picture went off pretty much without a hitch. It was only toward the end of production that Carole realized that Russ's emotions should be shown more in the film. Kurt agreed, and they did a couple of reshoots in August.

The studio previewers for Universal noted that in the scene in which Paul "goes Hollywood," Russ demonstrated a wide range of emotions, from playful to dark to seriously romantic. One poor reviewer at the time, who must have gone to the men's room at the end, actually thought his character, Paul, was a bad guy! Carole gave the reviewer a good ribbing the next time she met him in the pressroom.

It was true that Russ's acting was still a little self-conscious, but noticeably less than before. The love scene at the end of the picture in which he tells Toby he loves her was considered to be a real "toe curler," and many studio reviewers thought the combination of sublime music (which one could whistle), lots of laughable comedy, and the sweet romance would have general appeal at the box office. All of which was good news.

She read in a trade magazine: "Columbo's acting is less self-conscious. The picture should go over well with the feminine contingent for if his profile doesn't get 'em, his crooning will."

On a personal note, an item was printed about her and Russ as a couple. Her presence on the set had not gone unnoticed. It stated that friends were predicting a wedding but that they kept telling everyone, "We're just friends."

Carole had to admit that it was becoming ridiculous to deny that they didn't plan to marry, since she had input on his picture and was a constant presence on the set of *Wake Up And Dream*. She no longer confirmed or denied that they might marry.

Photographers took romantic photos of them together as a couple at Hollywood events, gazing fondly into each other's eyes. They attended an award banquet together where she wore her hair shoulder length and loosely curled, making her look years younger, as if she were one of Russ's teenage fans.

Russ proudly looked down in the photo at the eighty-carat cabochon-sapphire ring encircled with diamonds she wore on her ring finger, silently indicating the direction their romance seemed to be heading. She had given him a gold ring with a solitaire diamond set in the center, which he faithfully wore. She was gradually introducing the idea that they would be marrying. When the time was right, they would be.

In early August, she was finishing up *Now and Forever* and was in the middle of preparations for *Lady by Choice*, another Columbia picture, as well as trying to help Russ with *Wake Up and Dream*. She had renewed her contract with Paramount for two years; as an added incentive to stay with the studio, they'd written into her contract that she had the right to have opinions about her role choices and could use her favorite cameraman, Ted Tetzlaff.

Ever since the making of *Twentieth Century*, the studio heads had sensed that she was going places. Although the picture itself hadn't been a box-office success, they had raised her salary again and had praised her performance in the entertainment magazines.

Paramount loaned her out to Columbia Studio. She often ran from one end of the lot to the other in one day, from the sound stage to wardrobe for fittings, and then in a hurry, to rehearsals. It was becoming both tiresome and awkward for her.

She absolutely hated the idea of being late anywhere. The way in which the assistant director looked at her, as if she had stayed up all night partying, when the unglamorous reality was that she'd been up memorizing a script, made her want to say language that would have given a censor apoplexy.

Today, as sure as God had made dictatorial autocrats, this one was striding toward her. She knew in advance what the director wanted to say. She could see it in his narrow eyes, his twitching mustache, and the tightening of his face. He wanted to give her a dressing down. *He must have taken instructions from Charlie Chaplin with that twitching lip hair!*

"You're late!" he shouted, reprimanding her.

"You don't have to tell me—I know I'm late. It couldn't be helped. I was stuck at wardrobe for fittings. Do you know how many ostrich feathers it takes to cover this body? Well I can tell you, quite a few." She referred to the fact that she was about to be playing the part of a fan-dancing stripper in her next picture, *Lady by Choice*. "I'm terribly sorry, but I can't possibly be in two places at once."

"Very well, but don't let it happen again, Miss Lombard."

When his back was turned, she stuck her tongue out at him and shouted, "It's Carole!"

She thought about bringing her bike to the studio. She'd had her picture taken once for the magazine *Modern Screen* with her dog Brownie seated on a cushion on the back of her bike. But she knew riding a bike would be impractical, since trousers and shorts on the lot were strictly forbidden. The modest skirted garments she owned fell well below her knees, and they would become caught on the greasy bike chain, ripping holes in the hems. What to do?

Between takes, Carole smoked and watched a group of kids who were in the movie playing outside. One of the little girls still wore a party dress for the singing scene in which Shirley sings "The World Owes Me a Living" and was rolling around on a pair of roller skates. She was having a marvelous time zooming back and forth. It looked like a lot of fun.

That was it, the answer to her problem. Carole summoned the little girl. "Hey, kid, how much for your skates? I'll pay you double."

Several minutes later, Carole had laced the roller skates to her small feet and she was off. She zoomed first to the publicity office and dropped off some notices, causing papers to fly through the air as she sailed through. She skated right to wardrobe, where she stopped and was fitted, and feathers took flight as she careened her way to the other end of the studio lot, barely missing hitting Columbia producer Harry Cohn, who was carrying a mug of hot coffee in his hand as he walked toward his office.

"Watch out! Watch out!" she shouted, waving her hands and brushing past him.

He spilled some of the scalding brew and swore vehemently, "Carole Lom-bard!"

"Sorry, Harry!" She flew past him and down the studio lot's hill. "Whee…whee…watch out, coming through!"

She zipped by several startled actors and crew, unsteadily rolling down the center of the studio street to her next appointment, the rehearsal room for *Lady by Choice*. There she burst through the door, where she finally collapsed, legs spread eagle out in front of her, roller skates still strapped to her feet, into a chair with script in hand, and a pencil behind her ear.

The assistant director entered the rehearsal room and stared. He seemed to want to say something to her, but wisely decided not to. Carole looked him right in the eye, with one-winged eyebrow arched upward, and dared him to speak.

Cowed, he silently walked away.

The entire cast broke out laughing and applauded her. May Robson, the elderly seventy-five-years old actress, leaned toward her and said, "That's showing him, Carole!"

On the last day of filming for *Wake Up and Dream*, icy cold beer was ordered and picnic tables were set up outside under the shade of a grove of large California oak trees. Italian food was served on red-checkered tablecloths, and everybody drank, enjoying the sunshine. Carole and Roger sat next to each other and chatted as a photographer took their picture. A funny one was taken of Russ, who, mugging for the shot, held up a big mug of the cold brew before taking a sip.

Everyone toasted the end of the picture and to the director's newest addition, a bouncing baby boy who'd been born before filming began. It was a fun way to end the production.

Not surprisingly, the minute the picture was finished, June Knight, who felt she'd been treated badly by the studio and considered *Wake Up and Dream* to be the last straw, announced that she was breaking her contract with Universal. Carole heard June didn't give up her career, though, but continued to make pictures and eventually married Paul Ames, the New York stockbroker. Louella informed her that the long-anticipated marriage lasted exactly thirteen days, for, much to the stunned bride's surprise, the groom brought along his best man with them on their honeymoon!

The day of the wrap party, Carole and Russ celebrated some more by going out to dinner at the Cocoanut Grove with Marlene Dietrich. Carole invited the film star along, since Marlene's current boyfriend, Fred Perry, was out of town playing in a tennis tournament and Marlene was alone. Walter Lang, the director, and Fieldsie completed the group at their table.

A photographer visited and took pictures. Russ danced with everyone, and the rumba he danced with Carole resembled a professional routine. There was no question that they put the rest of the dancers on the floor to shame. What surprised many was how effortlessly they danced together without ever having practiced.

Carole overheard a woman comment to her partner as they danced past them, "Darling, don't you think Russ and Carole look as if they'd been made for each other?" but she didn't hear the man's answer, since Russ twirled her around at that moment. It was true, he was an excellent dancer.

The nicest surprise for her was to see Fieldsie having such a wonderful time with Walter Lang. She had never seen her companion so caught up in a man before. She was positively glowing.

On the way back from the powder room, Carole asked, "Hey, what's up with you and Walter?"

"Carole, I think…oh, do I dare say it?"

"Go on, tell me."

"I think I'm falling in love!"

"Oh, honey, that's the best news I've heard yet!" She hugged her longtime friend. "I'll keep my fingers crossed. Walter seems equally taken with you, too. I can tell he's smitten. Look, he's staring at you right now—he can't keep his eyes off you."

Fieldsie looked over at their table. Walter was indeed sitting there, staring at her. Fieldsie's face turned a bright shade of red. Carole thought it was too sweet for words to see her usually self-assured friend falling head over heels in love.

She whispered into her ear, "I hope your love for Walter becomes as deep as Russ's and mine. Now, I gotta get back to the table. I don't want Marlene to get into a snit, thinking I've abandoned her."

She needn't have worried. Russ played host for their little party, chatting easily with the famous film actress and making certain she didn't feel like a wallflower by taking Marlene out on the dance floor several times. He was the perfect gentleman. She and Russ had already gone out on a couple of fun group dates with Marlene, which always included a male film star, such as, Ronald Colman, to escort her. They had double-dated the week before, while attending actor Clifton Webb's housewarming party together.

At the request of Paramount Studios, where both actresses were under contract, Carole was helping the German actress to be seen in public and to receive ink in the press.

"Darling," said Marlene, looking in Russ's direction as he was dancing with Fieldsie, "That one, are you thinking of keeping him? Otherwise, if you don't want him, I could take him off your hands."

"Oh no you don't, you she-wolf!" Carole exclaimed, knowing Marlene's reputation with men. "Pretty soon Russ and I are going to announce our engagement, so hands off."

"Okay, darling. I was just asking."

Carole was willing to share space in her car for the sake of the studio and to let Marlene have a couple of dances with Russ, but that was as far as it went. *That Valkyrie siren had just better keep her hands to herself!*

Chapter Thirteen

Dark Shadows

Carole looked up from the script she had been reading. It was late, nearing midnight. It was Saturday night and she'd decided to quietly relax at the Roxbury house. The picture *Now and Forever* was in the editing room, and she and Russ were waiting on the "rushes" for *Wake Up and Dream* to see if any reshooting needed to be done. The front door slammed shut, and Russ strode into the living room, visibly upset.

"Darling, what's wrong?" she asked, seeing his stormy expression.

"I just had a fight with Lansa."

"What about?"

"I don't want to talk about it."

She *sensed* that it had something to do with her. Lansing Brown was having a difficult time accepting her relationship with Russ. He used to be the one who helped Russ run his career, or at least that's what the photographer had led himself to believe.

"Maybe you two need some time apart? Then, after a cooling-off period, you can talk and be friends again. Look at Fieldsie and I, why, sometimes she drives me right to the edge with all her demands, and she tells people she'd like nothing better than to cut my throat because I drive her crazy. Darling, it's only natural that something like this should eventually occur between you and Lansing."

"I suppose so. Maybe I should tell everyone about all the help he's given me and what a great guy he's been as my best friend in my next interview. That might make everything all right between us. He seems to think I don't appreciate everything he did for me in the past."

"You could do that, Russ." She shrugged, secretly doubting that it would make any real difference. For the past year of Russ's career, she, his brother, John, and a paid talent agent, had been doing the actual work of negotiating contracts with Universal Pictures and Brunswick Records, as well as helping Russ with his acting, recording, and radio performances—all abilities that Lansing Brown had never possessed.

She wanted to say to him, "What has Lansing done to help further your career? Not much, unless you consider hanging out with you and Sally Blane, meeting celebrities and partying, to be counted as so called 'work'." She held her tongue, though. It didn't matter if Lansing remained Russ's friend, as long as he didn't interfere, he wasn't important.

She had her own career to think about. The magazine writer, Dorothy Manners had written that the reason *Now and Forever* had been delayed was because of Carole's health, and not because of Dorothy Dell's death. The interview was set-up by the studio and was supposed to distract everyone from the young actress's sad demise by focusing on Carole's madcap lifestyle and frail health.

The writer had noted that Carole wasn't a typical temperamental actress: she'd had an amicable divorce from Bill (with whom she'd remained friends) and was known for her well-thought-out practical jokes. As for her current love life, Carole didn't confirm or deny rumors about wedding plans with Russ, purposefully remaining ambiguous.

They were in Carole's trailer on the studio lot at Columbia, which she had decorated in Southwestern decor. An Indian blanket was thrown over the back of the sofa. The reporter asked, "Carole, I hear you've been unwell. Want to put to rest a rumor? What's causing you to be sick, if you don't mind my asking?"

"I've had a bad cold—the flu," she said, reaching for a cigarette. She took a puff from her cigarette and released the smoke. "It's just that simple, nothing more, nothing less."

She hid the real truth, that she was suffering from another one of her unusually long menstrual periods, which left her exhausted. She also couldn't mention that she was working night and day on several pictures at once, or that Dorothy Dell's death was the real reason for the filming delay.

She had to maintain a glamorous image for her fans and maintain the Hollywood fairytale that everything was picture-perfect. It had been drilled into her years ago that feminine problems were forbidden subjects that were not to be openly shared with the general public. It would detract from her sexy persona.

The character she and the studio had created for her was that of a sexy, young, carefree star. She admired and copied President Franklin D. Roosevelt, who suffered from debilitating polio but always wore a bright, optimistic smile on his face, hiding the real truth, which was that he could barely stand, let alone walk.

Russ knew her health wasn't good and treated her as if she were a glass figurine. He confided that his worst fear was that something should happen to her. He was always afraid that she might be taken away from him through illness, just like his brother Fiore, who'd died in a hospital. His beloved older sister Fannie, who'd raised him, had also passed away from influenza during the 1919 flu epidemic. He placed Carole high up on a pedestal and adored her, but not many knew that he did this out of a mixture of love and genuine fear.

He was always gentle with her and was unquestioningly kind, doing anything she asked of him. If it would make her happy and would help her feel better, he would bend over backward to make sure it happened.

She glanced over at a photograph of his handsome profile that she kept on a nearby side table. *Oh, how much he loves me! Surely no woman has ever been so loved and adored by one man as I have.*

Dorothy Manners interrupted her reverie. "Can I ask you one more question, Carole, for a future column we're doing on fear?"

"Sure, go ahead."

"What are you the most afraid of in the world?"

It used to be spiders, but she decided to answer the question truthfully, remembering what had happened on the set of *White Woman.* "Chimpanzee bites."

The reporter closed her notebook, stood up, and held out a hand. "Well, that should do it. Thank you for your time, Carole."

She shook it. "My pleasure. If you have any more questions, call Fieldsie. She'll write them down for me to answer."

"Sure thing. Nice to have met you."

"You, too."

After the door closed, Carole lay back down on the couch and took out a small bottle her LA specialist had ordered for her. Opening it, she swallowed one of the tablets.

The picture she was currently working on, *Lady by Choice*, was a follow-up to the box-office success, *Lady for a Day,* from the year before, which had also starred May Robson, the elderly actress whom the media had named the "American dowager queen of the film and stage." *Lady for a Day* had been nominated for two Oscars, which was a first for Columbia Pictures. Carole knew everyone was wondering if this sequel would measure up to the first? While the title was similar, it had a completely different plot.

The plot revolved around Georgia "Alabam" Lee (played by Carole), a fan-dancing nightclub stripper, who as a publicity stunt, adopts Patsy Patterson (May Robson), a homeless drunk who is under a court judgment and has been sentenced to living in an old people's home. The role of Judge Daly was performed by character actor Walter Connolly, with whom she'd worked in *Twentieth Century.* His character sentences both women: one for indecent exposure and the other for public drunkenness.

Patsy is touched by Alabam's kind nature and starts to take her mothering role seriously. She reforms her life and starts drinking less in order to help her benefactress, Alabam. Roger Pryor, the good-looking leading man with a trim mustache, who'd been the second lead in Russ's picture, played a lawyer named Johnny Mills in the picture. His character falls in love with Alabam and, in the end, over the vehement objections of his wealthy family, who threaten to disinherit him, they get married. This happy-ending is mainly due to Patsy's nudging and from the kindly judge's interference.

Carole had no difficulties working with Roger. Although he was not yet divorced from his estranged wife, Priscilla Mitchell, with whom he'd had a daughter, Roger had fallen in love with the lovely blonde actress, Ann Sothern. He had arrived in Hollywood after appearing in the dramatic medical hit *Men in White* on Broadway and had since then appeared in a series of movie musicals. Carole and Russ had become friends with the couple, as Roger and Russ shared similar backgrounds, and Ann had a charming personality.

The movie critics were very kind to *Lady by Choice* when it debuted. Carole was happy, since her performance and May Robson's had received favorable reviews. Noting how well she had performed, one critic wondered, when Carole would again be given a juicy role like the one she'd played in *Twentieth Century?*

I would like the answer to that one, too, she thought when she read the comment. *Maybe I should retire and content myself with being Russ's wife instead. There's no such thing as a perfect acting career in Hollywood for a married woman, for the great god Studio is the most jealous lover of all.*

The picture, *Twentieth Century,* was supposed to have been her big break, but it had bombed at the box office. But she wasn't a quitter. She would have to work harder. Something would pan out for her sooner or later, she knew. The right picture was just around the corner; she could feel it.

"What did you think of the picture, Carole?" Louella asked after *Lady by Choice* was screened.

"It was good box office, wasn't it?" came her tactful reply. What else could she say? The role was another clotheshorse role, but she did it anyway.

Meanwhile, Russ's career was humming along smoothly. His radio show with Jimmy Fidler on NBC had been moved from Sundays to Friday nights, which helped the show gain more fans. Music enthusiasts were simply crazy to hear Russ sing. He was immensely popular.

She and Russ were nearly mobbed by his fans whenever they went to the radio station. It was calculated that he had made approximately half a million dollars from his vocal recordings that year at Brunswick Record. The recording company eagerly had him sign a long-term contract.

The smell of money also brought the vultures out. Russ found himself besieged by lawsuits from companies that wanted to milk him for money that was supposedly owed them from questionable contracts Conrad had arranged for him in the early 1930s. Russ countersued in a couple of cases, stating that they in fact owed *him.*

No one was fooled. Russ knew that Conrad was behind some of the lawsuits and that he'd been trying (fruitlessly, it turned out) to repeat the success he'd experienced with Russ by signing other singers.

Meanwhile, they had to finish work on *Wake Up and Dream,* hear what the critics and studio heads thought about it, and then take Russ's movie career to the next level. There was talk of possibly starring him in a few operettas, since word about his extraordinary talent had spread. He was taking voice lessons, and the quality of his voice had improved.

Pietro Cimini, the opera conductor at the Los Angeles Philharmonic, had been greatly impressed. He commented to Carole on Russ's singing ability after he visited the set to listen to him sing. "Columbo has the voice and aptitude to be an opera singer of the first magnitude."

MGM now wanted Russ for the operetta *Naughty Marietta*, where he would costar with the lovely opera singer Jeannette MacDonald. In the movie they planned to reprise the Harry Warren song "You're My Everything," which Russ had previously recorded. The studio approached Universal Pictures to ask to borrow him, but to Carole and Russ's dismay, Carl Laemmle turned their request down.

The producer had recently acquired the rights to the Oscar Hammerstein and Jerome Kern musical *Show Boat*, which had been a success on Broadway. He told them that he wanted Russ to play the lead, Gaylord Ravenal. Word spread fast. The entertainment magazines began to receive concerned letters from Russ's fans, who wanted him to remain a crooning ballad singer.

Russ confided to Carole that he wanted to sing opera and introduce it on the radio. "I'd like the general public to enjoy the music," he said. "They think only intellectuals and the very rich can understand and appreciate it. I think everyone can enjoy opera. Maybe if I sang it on the radio I could make it popular, like the Great Caruso did?"

"It's worth a try," she agreed.

Despite how well his career was moving, a dark shadow would soon hang over them. She sensed something had happened. A dark feeling of dread cloaked her entire being on Wednesday morning. She felt a dead weight hang heavily on her heart. Something was wrong with Russ!

Worried, she glanced up at the clock on the wall and began to count down the minutes until he returned from a friend's funeral service he was attending at the Church of the Blessed Sacrament on Sunset Boulevard. It was the home parish of many of their Hollywood friends and was where she was being instructed in the faith in preparation for converting to Catholicism. Her good friend Louella

Parsons, who was born Jewish, had converted, as had Dixie Crosby and Gary Cooper.

An hour later Russ drove up into the driveway, and Carole calmed down. Maybe she had merely imagined something was wrong. Could it be that her overly active imagination was playing on her fear of losing him when they were at their happiest and most in love?

She had only to look at his frightened brown eyes and pale face when he walked into the living room to know that her premonition had been correct. Something had happened.

"What is it, Russ? Did you have another run-in with Lansing? Was he at the funeral?"

"No, nothing like that. I was sitting in the pew, during the service, when I had… oh, Angel!" He gathered her into his arms and tightly held her. She could feel his body trembling.

"What is it, darling? What happened?"

"It's too incredible to be believed. I had an overwhelming premonition that God was planning to call me home. I felt a coldness cloak my entire body. It was as if Death himself was sitting right next to me, whispering the news."

"Are you sure? After all, if anybody should be shaking hands with the grim reaper, it ought to be me. I'm the one who's always sick."

"No, I pray to God it's me. I don't think I could go on if anything should happen to you."

She felt a similar coldness. They had previously dismissed the significance of a series of dangerous events that had occurred during the previous months as mere coincidences, but not anymore.

One evening they had been ice skating when a fire broke out at the Ice Palace. She had remembered smelling smoke and a man blowing a whistle at the moment the back wall burst into flames.

"Ladies and gentlemen, please quickly evacuate the building in an orderly manner. Walk, don't run," an employee of the Ice Palace had announced.

She and Russ had done as they were asked and made it outside the building just as the fire brigade pulled up. A crowd of rubbernecking onlookers had soon noticed them, as did the fire chief. The uniformed officer had approached them as a large crowd began to gather.

"Can I be of any service, Officer?" Russ had asked.

"No, thank you, Mr. Columbo. But you could do us a favor by taking yourself and Miss Lombard somewhere else. Your presence is attracting people to the vicinity, and we don't want anyone getting too close to the fire, a safety precaution, you understand. The building might collapse."

"Of course, we'll leave right away."

Russ had taken her by the hand and guided her through the crowd. There were so many people present she hadn't been able to see the pavement beneath her. One of the local newspaper reporters had also noticed them and had tried to speak to them. Eager to leave, they'd pretended not to notice her.

When they had at last arrived home, she had noticed something they both had forgotten. She'd burst out laughing, pointing down at their feet. "Look what we forgot, Russ!"

He had started laughing as well. In their anxiety to leave the burning building and to avoid the large crowd out front, they had forgotten to retrieve their shoes!

Another dangerous event was not so easy to dismiss, especially in retrospect, considering Dorothy Dell's tragic death. Late one afternoon, they were taking a leisurely drive in the countryside in Russ's Duesenberg, after viewing a morning polo match. Russ pulled over after he'd been driving for some time and asked her, "You want to drive for a while?" He'd dangled the car keys temptingly in front of her.

"Really, you'd let me?" she'd asked.

"Sure. You've always wanted to drive her, why not today?"

They had been headed back to town to a radio station where she and John Barrymore were supposed to be interviewed. She was supposed to be featured that afternoon in a fifteen-minute promo with John for *True Confessions.*

The feel of the powerful engine beneath her was intimidating, which had at first caused her to drive cautiously. Unfortunately, her fear hadn't lasted. She had glanced down at her wristwatch.

If she didn't hurry up she was going to be late!

Overconfidence took control during a long stretch of the road, and she had pressed her foot down hard on the gas pedal. She'd felt a rush of excitement course through her as the car easily had accelerated. The Duesenberg had quickly sped up to sixty-five miles per hour. The car had raced at ten…twenty…thirty miles per hour above the posted speed limit.

"Oh boy, this is fun!"

"Carole," Russ had cautioned, a slight edge in his voice, but it was too late. Before you could say *police patrols park pretty principals*, they'd heard a siren from a nearby constable's vehicle. A policeman on his motorcycle had signaled to her to pull over. It was only then that she had become frightened. Instead of slowing to a gradual stop, she'd abruptly slammed on the brake, which had caused the car to skid dangerously off the road. The car had fishtailed out of control, swerving back and forth until it had whipped around and had come to a standstill in a cloud of dust beside a grove of orange trees.

"Drat!" she'd exclaimed, turning off the engine. The officer had followed them, cautiously approaching the car with his gun drawn.

He had stopped and lowered it, when he reached the car's left side door, staring at them. "Carole Lombard and Russ Columbo. Well I'll be…" He put his gun back in its holster.

"Hello, Officer," she'd greeted him with a sunny smile, trying to act as if nothing out of the ordinary had occurred.

"Who do you two think you are, Bonnie and Clyde? Miss Lombard, you had to have been driving at least thirty miles over the speed limit, possibly more. Now, which of you two is the owner of this fancy hotrod?"

"He is, but it was my fault, Officer. I was the one driving. I should get the ticket."

"No!" Russ had interrupted. "This is my car, give the ticket to me. I should never have let her drive."

"But darling, I was the one who was speeding."

"Angel, I insist. This is my car and I'm the one responsible for it. I should pay."

"I see, two lovebirds, huh?" had commented the officer. "How about I make this easy for the both of you?"

"Yes, please do," she'd said with a bright smile, hoping against hope that they could charm their way out of a fine. "Would you like our autographs, Officer?"

"Yeah, sign right here." He had indicated the sheet he held. "I'm giving you both tickets. And this isn't Hollywood, Miss. Lombard."

He then had taken down the car's license plate number and asked for some identification. He had handed them each a carbon copy of a speeding ticket. Returning to his motorbike, the policeman drove off.

A few days later, they had each received phone calls from the press. Their tickets were on the public books at the police station. One paper had said Russ had received the speeding ticket, while another had said it was Carole. They never spoke of it again, as they had each felt themselves to be at fault.

The dangerous incidents seemed to be ominous portents leading up to the warning Russ had experienced in the church. It was now hovering over their lives.

"Darling, I'm certain you and I feel this way because we've not had any fun lately," she said, trying to reason out why they had both felt so down.

"What do you mean?"

"You know, Russ, we've both been working day and night, nonstop, on one picture or another. We're both tired. What do you say to a party? Something to cheer us up and take our minds off work and my always being so sick and tired."

Her sapphire-blue eyes lit up with an idea. "Oh, boy, I have the perfect remedy for our depression! I'll invite a few couples over, and we'll have one my famous little shindigs. It's been ages since I hosted one."

"A small shindig, you say? One to which you'll invite half of Hollywood to attend, knowing you." He indulgingly agreed, and then frowned. He must have noticed the dark circles under her eyes, the result of time she'd spent filming at night at the studio due to the heatwave.

"Angel, I don't want you tiring yourself out by exhausting yourself from throwing a huge party."

"I promise I'll only invite a couple of our closest friend, maybe twenty or thirty people, instead of the usual hundred. Won't that be fun?"

"If that is what you want, so it shall be."

"Oh, Russ, you're the best. We'll have the party right after the last reshoot for *Wake Up and Dream.*" She threw her arms around him and kissed him enthusiastically. She was going to host a terrific party, something to help them get rid of these blues.

"And I already know what the theme will be, a Roman dinner. I'll have a hand at cooking all the finger food, and everyone will wear togas. Maybe I'll come as Diana the huntress and walk around with a bow and a quiver of arrows, shooting everybody."

"Shall I worship at your feet, Angel?"

"No, Roogie, you won't have to do that," she said, giving him a kiss.

He spent as much time as possible with her on the set. He watched her perform, and between takes they would chat. She felt more at ease when he was near; it was only then that her heart felt light.

He said that everything was fine, but the fear in his eyes told her the truth. He was afraid. He paid a visit to a Catholic priest to discuss his salvation and how he wanted his funeral service to be conducted if the ominous warning should come true.

He started taking trips in his car up into the nearby hills with a land agent and talked of buying property for a house he wanted to build for his mother.

She heard him tell his writer friend William French, as they were driving around in the Hollywood hills looking at properties, "Maybe I'm funny about it, but I want to grab some of the nicest things for my sick mother now. I want to spoil her, while I can. You know how it is, the old fellow with the black hood and scythe is always creeping around the corner."

Several days later, Russ happily informed Carole, "I've found the piece of property where I'm planning to build a place. I'm going to design the house myself. It'll have lots of nooks and gadgets, everything Mother's heart could desire."

"Darling, don't you think it would be best to wait until after you've finished your picture?"

He had started preparing for *Men Without Fear*, the next musical he was to star in. His character was a singing Don Juan, a fearless toreador who mixes romance with bullfighting, parties, and song. He had begun darkening his skin by sitting under sunlamps to make himself look more Spanish for the role.

"I don't want to wait, because you never know what might happen. I'm going to begin negotiations for the piece of land tomorrow." Russ didn't have to say anything more, as Carole knew what he meant by *might happen.* She continued to organize the party, although a dark foreboding hung over their lives.

Chapter Fourteen

Yours to Command

On August 24, the day before the party, Carole's house was abuzz with preparations. Her garden at the back of the house was to be transformed into a Roman villa. The tiled patio area was perfect for parties. She had commissioned a specially constructed low quadrangular table at which her guests would eat. Cushioned lounge chairs were stationed around the table, where her guests would recline. A big pit for roasting a pig was dug in the back corner of the yard next to an unused chicken coop that the previous owners had left behind.

"Fieldsie, you invited Walter Lang, didn't you?" she asked her friend.

"Yes, I did. He'll be here tomorrow."

"Perfect. Would you be a darling and ask him to supervise the carving of the pig for me?"

"Sure thing." Fieldsie wrote it down on her list of things to do.

"I'm afraid I'm going to be keeping Russ busy playing the piano, singing, and schmoozing our guests. Louella wanted me to invite her boss, Ivan St. John. Did we?"

"William Ivan St. John and his wife, Marcia…" Fieldsie checked her guest list. "He's also in charge of publicity for *Photoplay Magazine*, in case you forgot. And yes, we did. They'll both be here. I've got the acceptance card right here." She handed her the small card.

Carole bit down on an edge of it in thought. "Now, why does his last name sound so familiar to me?"

"Because he was the writer, Adela St. John's first husband, that's why. She's married to some sportswriter fella by the name of Richard Hyland, at least for now. I hear that marriage is coming to a rocky end."

"No kidding. Then I can't wait to meet Lolly's boss! But remind me to invite Adela to lunch later this week—we wouldn't want her to think I snubbed her in favor of her ex. Better do it when Russ isn't around. We mustn't forget the last time she was here. She made a huge fuss over the latest bauble he gave me, actually grabbing my hand at one point to get a closer look at it."

Fieldsie chuckled. "And he's given you some real humdingers, too. At the rate he's going, you could open your own jewelry store if you wanted."

"Now, isn't that the truth?" She was happy that Russ enjoyed spoiling her. If you defined being well loved by the number of gifts a person received, which she knew most of Hollywood did, then she was the most loved and adored woman in town.

"You know what Russ said to keep Adela quiet?"

"Did he tell her to mind her own business?"

"He's too polite to do that. No, he told her to make certain she wrote down that he sleeps in the nude and that he gets his best inspiration at night. And then he gave her one of his famous winks."

"He didn't!" laughed Fieldsie.

"She nearly dropped her plate!"

"He's definitely nothing like Bill, that's for certain. Russ is discreet and a bit shy, but once he warms up to you, he's very nice."

"Why, Fieldsie, what a nice thing to say, I'm so glad you two are hitting it off. Don't you think he and I make a swell team?"

"Like Ginger Rogers and Fred Astaire." Fieldsie held up an entertainment magazine. "The wags say you two are 'the most charming couple in Hollywood.' Speaking of which, Cinderella, you came home awfully late last night from Wilshire's Gold Ballroom. I thought maybe you two were going to stay the entire night."

"Nearly did. Russ paid the band extra to keep playing, we could have danced all night long if we wanted to. The only reason I came home was so that I could supervise the workers today." She thought of the lovely suite she and Russ had stayed in at the Ambassador Hotel. "Maybe next time we'll stay overnight. I hear they have some pretty nice bungalows there."

"Hey, I just realized something funny about the day you chose to have the party," said Fieldsie, handing her the newspaper. She put her finger on a picture of a cartoon of a volcano exploding and people running down a cobbled street. "Did you know your party is on the anniversary of the eruption of Mount Vesuvius—you know, the volcano that destroyed Pompeii?"

Carole glanced down at the cartoon and felt a cold heaviness envelope her. "Well, if that isn't the strangest."

She stepped outside to shake the feeling off, observing the workers putting the last-minute touches on the banqueting area. A few men were setting up the tall plaster pillars she had rented from a prop company in the back garden.

"No, Ralph, don't place it there!" Carole waved her hand to get the attention of a bald, mustached man who was carrying one up to the pool area on the hill. "That pillar should go on the other side, behind the table on the hill by the stairs, flanking the one over there between the torches."

He stepped down and placed it opposite the first. "Here, Carole?"

"Yeah, that's right, thanks." She looked down at her list. "We'll come inside later in the evening and take tea and coffee in the drawing room. You'll have to have a couple of the fellas move the piano in there." She had picked the Roman theme because she knew the furnishings of the room fit with it.

For the remainder of the morning, she continued to direct everyone about where she wanted the props for the party to be placed. She planned several Italian side dishes to be served with the pig. In the late afternoon she gave her cook a helping hand in the kitchen, preparing food and supervising the hired helpers.

Russ's family delivered casks of wine in a truck that he had insisted on providing. There was enough to satisfy a Roman legion. She had ordered colored goblets with metal feet, a novelty that made the wine look purple.

Torches were lit around the yard when dusk fell, adding to the atmosphere. The arriving guests were serenaded by musicians seated above them. Everyone wore togas and Roman breastplates with helmets or garlands of laurel leaves woven around their hair. Several beautiful actresses were present, including: Ann Sothern, Arline Judge, and Gloria Foy, a lovely statuesque beauty.

But everyone turned and stared when Carole stood in her toga between two Roman columns, backlit by burning torches. Her blonde hair was piled high up on her head, and she wore a primitive gold tiara and necklace designed by Eugene Joseff, the Hollywood jeweler.

The garment she wore was belted with a long cord, the sheer

cloth hugging her hourglass figure. Her breasts were barely contained by the low cowl-necked bodice. Shapely legs, one of her best assets, showed beneath the almost sheer embroidered material as two long slits revealed lean calves. On her feet were high-heeled, gold-strapped sandals. The added height made her legs look particularly long. She was a heart-stopping beauty.

Louella, who stood next to Russ, asked him, "What do you think of our Venus?"

He let loose a low appreciative whistle. "I think I'm in love with a goddess, and you can quote me on that." He walked over and placed a kiss on her cheek. "You look wonderful, Angel."

"You don't look half bad yourself, Russ. You're quite the hunk." She returned the kiss, admiring how wonderful he looked in a Roman gladiator's costume, which showed off his bulging muscles and thick, manly legs.

Carole took his arm and stepped down to greet their guests. She picked up one of the goblets filled with wine from a nearby tray and addressed her guests, a gold-hammered bracelet on her arm glittering in the torchlight. "I'm extremely happy that all of you could come tonight. I have only one request to make of you, and that is that you eat, drink, and be merry!"

"Here here!" Her guests then raised their goblets and drank.

A gong was rung. Carole and Russ took their places at the low reclining table laden with exotic fruits, some of which were not normally seen in California.

The table had pineapple slices, a real delicacy, and diced papaya and mangoes, as well as grapes, oranges, strawberries, bananas, and figs. The woven baskets held various flatbreads, and bowls contained dipping sauces along with abundant Italian side dishes. As promised, Walter Lang stood by the cooked pig and carved.

Russ and Carole lovingly fed each other. The couple seated next to them was the immensely successful Lowell Sherman and his date, Geneva Mitchell. Lowell had directed *Broadway Thru a Keyhole*. The director was with the comic "straight" actress who'd recently performed in the Three Stooges picture *Hoi Polloi*. The couple were very close friends with Russ and Carole and confided to them that they were now secretly engaged, although the middle-aged Lowell, who'd been married three times before, appeared to be taking his time about walking down the aisle for a fourth time.

"Carole," said Geneva, "I'm terribly glad we're sitting down. My feet are dead tired from all the dancing Lowell and I did with you and Russ last night. We could barely keep up with you two."

"It was a fun evening, wasn't it? We had such a grand time dancing. Guy Lombardo is one of Russ's friends, and his band certainly is one of the best."

It was then that Carole noticed a scar on her friend's exposed arm. "Honey, were you in an accident?"

"Oh, that," shrugged Geneva, glancing at the scar. "It's an old bullet wound from my childhood."

"You were shot? No kidding. What happened?"

"I lived on the south side of Chicago as a kid, and one day I was skipping rope outside our brownstone when some shooting broke out. Two hit men drove by, and I stopped one of the bullets meant for the mobster Joe Colosimo, who was sitting nearby in his café. My parents told me later that he'd died."

"Holy cow! You could have been killed!"

"Fate has dealt you quite a hand, darling," said Lowell, placing an arm around Geneva. "Now she's stuck you with me, and I'm no grand prize."

"You're being far too modest, Lowell," Carole remarked from her recliner. "We all know you've directed nothing but hits this past year. Why, *Morning Glory* won an Oscar for Katie Hepburn, and *She Done Him Wrong* has made Mae enough money that she's bought her apartment building. It's as if you're on one long lucky streak."

Dave Burton, the director, who'd directed *Lady by Choice* and was seated next to Roger Pryors and Ann Sothern at the middle of the table, joined the conversation. "I agree with Carole. If we all had your luck at directing movies we'd be rolling in dough."

"Fate has indeed smiled kindly upon a couple of other people here, as well," put in Louella, who nodded her head at the long-legged ex-showgirl.

"Are you referring to Gloria?" asked Carole, interested. Gloria Foy was chatting with Jack Moss, who was working for Gary Cooper's manager. On her other side, reclining on his chaise, was Gloria's husband, Alan Edwards.

Carole continued, "I guess you could call it a lucky break that Gloria was in *Dancing Lady* for her first picture. I asked her and Alan here tonight because I wanted to learn more about her aviation experience as a pilot. I'm thinking of taking flying lessons and wanted her advice."

"Really?" asked Louella, clearly surprised.

"Not now, of course—I have too much on my plate. But I figure if Will Rogers can pilot a plane, so can I. Maybe I could ask her to teach me?"

Russ didn't say anything at first, but Carole could tell he was none too pleased with the idea. She knew aviation was considered a risky business, since airplanes were unreliable and accidents occurred frequently.

"If you do take lessons, I'm going with you," he said, an edge of determination in his voice.

She kissed him on the cheek, knowing how worried he was about her. She also knew he would never interfere with anything she wanted to do. He was always supportive of her. "You're the best, Russ."

He raised his goblet. "Here's to you, Angel, may you spread your wings and fly."

"Thank you, darling. Let's drink to it." She hooked his arm with hers, and they each took a sip from the other's goblet.

"Now that is a pretty picture," Louella said, beaming at them with approval. "But no, Carole, that's not what I was referring to. Goodness, I would think there would be at least a half dozen movies based on Gloria's life by now. It's a true-life fairytale."

"All right, Lolly, spill the beans."

"You know, of course, that our little Glory here used to be a dancer in Ziegfeld's Follies, but what you didn't know was that she unexpectedly became an heiress worth more than $1.5 million! I hear she had an immensely wealthy uncle named Richard Foy who was a coffee-plantation owner down in Rio de Janeiro. When he died, all his money went to her."

The gossiping woman stabbed a piece of pineapple with her fork and gestured. "That would be amazing enough, but get this: according to the terms of her late uncle's will, she would inherit one-third of the amount immediately if she married within three years of his death and would be entitled to another third of it if she stayed married for ten years. When we ran the story, she received over five thousand proposals of marriage from all over the world."

"She married in a timely manner, of course, some stockbroker fella whose name escapes me at the moment. She later divorced him and, as you can see, she's quite happily married now to Alan. Yes, fate has indeed played a kind hand to that young woman."

"Wow, I'd say so." Carole's sapphire-blue eyes widened with surprise. She had been completely unaware that her friend Gloria was a millionaire.

"She's not the only one," added Louella's husband, who had been imbibing the wine since the moment the party started. "Tell Carole about your boss, and how, uh…how fate played a hand in changing his fortune, Lolly."

"That's right, I nearly forgot. Ike, my boss, was once married to Adela, as you well know. They were both struggling writers and terribly poor. I believe they had two children. Anyway, she's an extremely gifted writer, but don't ever get on her bad side, Carole. She can be as poison-penned as that Mad Hatter Hedda Hopper." Louella glanced sidewise, as if both gossips might appear from behind the bushes, and shuddered theatrically.

And everyone knows how sweet you can be, Lolly—like a viper. Carole knew full well that her friend could be equally poison-pen. She was well aware that Hollywood gossips wielded their columns like Thompson submachine guns, mowing down the careers of those whom they disliked or felt slighted by.

"Where did I leave off?" asked Louella, taking a healthy gulp of wine. "Oh yes. Well, Adela grew tired of having to support the family and must have decided to divorce him in order to marry that handsome quarterback of a sportswriter, because that's exactly what she did as soon as the decree was signed. The marriage seems to have lasted long enough for her to have one child by him. It's a pity she didn't wait a little longer to divorce Ike, because almost right afterward, fate stepped in and made him immensely rich."

"How so?" asked both Carole and Russ, almost in unison. It made them both smile, since doing this was another one of their little idiosyncrasies.

"Do you remember that sportswriter, Lancaster, I think his name was? Well, he up and died. He left the entire bulk of his estate to Ike, including, incredibly enough, a hotel, stocks, and numerous bonds, all totaling up to be worth about a quarter of a million dollars!"

"That's incredible. I bet Adela was upset when she heard about that." Carole looked down to the other end of the table, where Ike, who worked as an editor for the newspaper mogul William Randolph Hearst was animatedly talking to director Wesley Ruggles and his beautiful wife, actress Arline Judge.

"That's true," said Russ. Everyone agreed how funny fate could be. "Reminds me, I need to renew my life insurance. I received the notice today."

"Do it right away," warned Louella, "you never know what Fate has in mind.

Russ didn't say anything to that remark. His expression was hooded. Carole sensed the dark shadow of worry that was hanging around him like a black cloud.

She announced in a loud voice, "Let's dance, everybody!" She pulled Russ up from his lounge chair. "Come on, Roogie, let's cut a rug!"

The small band that Carole had hired played, and everyone danced. The party went Hollywood, as her guests wildly danced and drank. Then, much to everyone's delight, Arline Judge stood on the low table and began to enticingly sing "If It Ain't One Man, It's Another," from the picture *Sensation Hunters*, which she'd starred in.

Carole could hear drunken whistles and applause from all around the table. Several people threw money at Arline in appreciation.

"Back off, fellas," laughed her husband with good humor. Wesley gallantly helped Arline down from the table when she'd finished. "This gal's mine."

As the fun evening turned to drunken early morning, Carole invited everyone indoors for some more entertainment. The few remaining conscious guests sat in the drawing room. There were so many talented performers present, she heard someone say, that it was like being at a Broadway review. One of the highlights of the evening was hearing the songwriting team of Harry Revel and Mack Gordon play songs from their newest musical, *Shoot the Works*.

They asked Russ if he would sing one of the numbers they'd written, which he'd already sung live on the radio: "With My Eyes Wide Open, I'm Dreaming." He also sang "Star Dust" by Hoagy Carmichael from the same program.

Russ agreed, and everyone in the room became still in order to hear him sing. His voice was superb. There was a depth of feeling behind it that Carole had not heard before.

"That was wonderful, Russ," said Lowell. "How about one of your own songs, something you've written, do you have any new ones you'd care to try out on us?"

"Looking for some music for your next picture?" inquired Wesley, who'd recently finished directing the musical *Shoot the Works.*

"Hey, I want in on this, too," said Dave Burton, who was helping himself to a cup of coffee. "Got anything, Russ? A song not yet spoken for?"

"Sure, I have one—well, actually, two." He took his place behind the piano. "One is finished, but the other…" He didn't finish his thought, and she felt a cold shiver run down her spine. "Well, the other, which I've tentatively titled 'Until Eternity,' I'll have to present some other time."

"Why, Carole, you sly minx," said Louella, who was standing next to her. "You knew perfectly well this was going to happen, didn't you? They'll soon have a bidding war over Russ and his music. That's why you invited all these directors tonight, so they could hear your crooner sing, right? The only other man present who could possibly be Russ's equal is the 'poor man's Clark Gable' over there." The professional gossip nodded her head in the direction of the thinly mustached Roger Pryor. "And we both know he's not nearly as musically talented as Russ—not by half."

"Lolly, would you like some coffee? I think you've had enough to drink, dear." Carole pointedly took the goblet out of her friend's hand in order to stop the chatterbox from embarrassing Roger, who'd recently been given the unflattering moniker by film critics who'd watched him in a series of low-budget, B-grade movies.

She walked over to the coffee carafe and poured. Of course she'd planned this to be an opportunity to showcase Russ's talents, but Lolly's mouth really did need a stop switch sometimes.

Russ sat at the piano. "As many of you in this room are aware, Carole and I are planning on getting married. How soon, Angel?"

"Pretty soon," she called from across the room.

Everyone laughed, for that was the answer she always gave.

"I wrote this song for her while thinking about wedding vows and life commitments and what they all mean. 'With this ring I thee marry. With my body, I thee worship. With all my worldly goods, I thee endow.' I worship and adore you, Carole. I'm yours to command." He played the introduction on the piano and began to sing.

Carole walked over to the piano and stood next to him. He had been working on it for the last month. This was the first time she was hearing the song in its completed form.

He played the piano, improvising a couple of verbal riffs, and then sang the last refrain. He ended the song, and picking up her hand, kissed it. She bent down and kissed him full on the lips. Everyone in the room applauded, smiling at the couple who were so obviously in love with each other.

"What did you think of the song, Carole?" Louella asked when he was done.

"What do I think? I think that only Russ could write a love song as wonderful as that." Russ put his arm around her waist, smiling.

Sometimes it was a bit frightening how much he loved her. What would happen if anything should happen to her? She wasn't certain he could handle the loss.

"Well, my dear," said Louella, "I certainly do hope we hear wedding bells ring for you two soon. Speaking of which, has anyone seen my better half? I've misplaced Docky somewhere."

Everyone looked around the room for her husband. Wesley found the doctor lying on the floor behind the sofa sound asleep, an empty wine goblet next to him on the floor.

"Here he is, Lolly."

Arline laughed and exclaimed, "Look, everyone, there's Louella's column!" She pointed to Docky's tunic, where, underneath the loose fabric, the doctor's very erect penis was plainly visible.

"Should we wake him up?"

"No, don't do that, let him sleep. Poor Docky has surgery in the morning," answered Louella, seemingly not the least bit surprised, as if she'd seen far worse.

The next morning, Carole opened the paper to read Louella's gossip column. Poor Lolly must have dictated it over the phone half-drunk. The paper printed the news that she'd attended a Russian dinner, where everyone wore togas and drank purple wine, and Russ was a "crooning cavalier". Several names of those who'd attended were misspelled. When she finished reading, Carole started laughing.

Oh, Lolly, my dear pal, sometimes you're a real scream.

Chapter Fifteen

Red-Letter Day

Carole and Russ were walking down the street toward the Brunswick Records Studio on Friday, August 31, with a couple of the orchestra musicians. Russ suddenly stopped, turned around, and walked back. A young man was standing on the corner with tears in his eyes, holding a piece of paper in his hands.

"Say, don't I know you?" Russ asked. "Didn't you work on *Wake Up and Dream*?"

"Yeah, I did. My name's Buddy. I was in the picture with you, Mr. Columbo. I was one of the extras."

"It's Russ. Yeah, I thought I remembered you, Buddy. You played the part of the bellboy. Nice to see you. Are you all right? You look pretty shook up. Anything I can do to help?"

"It's this." Buddy showed Russ a paper. It was a telegram. "I just received it. My sister, she's in a bad way. I don't know what to do. It's from the doctor. I don't have anyone I can call to ask for help. My sister and I are pretty much alone in the world. The trouble is I don't have enough money to get back home, since most of my salary went to my landlady for rent. I don't know what to do, I gotta get back home somehow."

"Don't worry, I can help." Russ reached into his jacket and pulled out his wallet. He opened it and took out five tens and handed the money to the young man, whose eyes grew huge. Russ had just handed him about half a month's salary.

"I can't. I'd never be able to repay you." Buddy tried to hand the money back.

Russ refused. "Keep it, and don't worry about paying me back."

The young actor nodded his head, tears of relief in his eyes. "Thanks, Russ."

"My pleasure. I hope your sister gets better soon."

"That was very kind of you," said Carole, as they continued their walk.

"It was simply the right thing to do."

"Are you nervous?" she asked. He was about to have his first recording session at Brunswick Studio, for which he had been preparing for the last couple of weeks.

"No, I think this is going to be fine. I trust Jimmie, completely. Also, the acoustics in the studio are excellent. The sound room should provide a good balance between my voice and the orchestra, not overwhelming either one," explained Russ. "The engineers are considered to be some of the very best in the business. I'm fortunate to be recording there."

The bandleader Jimmie Grier, Carole knew, had arranged the music and was conducting his own orchestra, which worked for Brunswick and a few other recording labels.

"Say, Russ, I don't think you'll be needing a coat hanger today," kidded one of the trombonists who had previously worked with Russ, as he took off his jacket at the studio.

Russ laughed. "No, I think Jimmie has everything well in hand today, Ted."

"What's that about a coat hanger?" Carole asked, wanting to know the full story.

"Oh, it's nothing really. It's just that one time on tour, when I was conducting my own orchestra, I was in such a hurry to get to a performance that I forgot my conductor's baton at the hotel. I had to improvise and use a coat hanger instead."

"Is that right? I bet you were embarrassed."

"Boy, was I! There I was in a tux at a swanky club, conducting with a coat hanger—very high class indeed." Russ raised his eyebrows and laughed.

Carole and Ted joined in his laughter.

"Are we ready, Jimmie?" Russ asked, turning to a round faced man with a slicked back forelock.

"Whenever you are," replied the orchestra leader, who had entered from the control room.

"Okay, let's begin."

They began recording three songs from *Wake Up and Dream*: "When You're in Love," "Let's Pretend There's a Moon, and "Too

Beautiful for Words," all of which Russ had co-written. The last song to be recorded during the session was "I See Two Lovers," by Mort Dixon and Allie Wrubel. As was his habit, Russ came so well prepared that only two live takes were necessary for each song. The first takes, which were in Carole's opinion, nothing less than sublime, were chosen for the record label.

The recordings were made in a single studio room with only one microphone for both Russ and the orchestra. One mistake by either, and Carole had ascertained, they would have to start all over from the beginning. After the men heard the final selections played back in the control room, they shook hands.

"I think that's the best I've ever heard you sing, Russ," said Jimmie when he took his earphones off. "Your voice has matured. It's much deeper than it was a few years ago, a true baritone, very full and rich. It must be all those opera lessons I hear you've been taking. I really enjoyed listening to you sing."

"Thanks, Jimmie, that's a real compliment coming from you. Hey, maybe you'll buy a couple of my records?"

Jimmie and the other men laughed. "Russ, some of the fellas from the orchestra and I are planning to escape out of town for few days and do some fishing, would you care to join us? If I recall correctly, you're a pretty good hand with a gun, as well."

"Sometimes I'm good, that is if the wind is in my favor," said Russ modestly. "But you just reminded me... Ted, you were with me the day I shot a buck from my automobile when we were touring in Pennsylvania, back in 32'. At the time Benny Goodman was fronting my orchestra for me and Gene Krupa, the jazz instrumentalist, was playing on drums. Man, that was something else! I'd spotted seventeen deer within an hour from the road."

"And I bet you that you couldn't shoot one from the car," said Ted.

"That's right. I took you up on the dare and shot one: a seven pointer. Boy, that butcher bill was expensive. Cost me one entire week's salary."

"We all ate venison hamburgers at a grill. You used your smooth-as-glass charm and bribed the owner to cook them up for us in exchange for tickets to the show." Ted smiled in remembrance. "Yeah, that was quite a barter. Say you'll join us for the fishing trip, Russ, it'll be fun."

"I'd like to, but I need to check in on my mother. She's not been very well." Everyone in the room knew that Julia was suffering from heart disease and was sick.

"Sure, we all understand," Jimmie said. "You have my number. Call me if you decide to come."

"Thanks," Russ replied. Everyone shook hands, and Carole and Russ took their leave.

"I went to my specialist's yesterday, and he recommended I take some time off and get some rest," she said. "I'm thinking of taking a week off—maybe as much as ten days. I'm driving up to Big Bear tomorrow. A friend of mine is loaning me her cabin up there. I thought I'd stay a day or two with Fieldsie, and then come back down on Sunday. In the evening we could have dinner with Bessie and Fred. What do you think?"

"Sounds fine by me."

The phone rang, and Fieldsie entered.

"Russ, it's your brother John on the telephone."

"Thanks."

He walked into the kitchen to take the call. When he came back a couple of minutes later, Carole knew by his somber expression that he had received bad news.

"Mother's in the hospital. Her heart ailment is giving her serious trouble."

"Oh, Russ, I'm sorry. Is there anything I can do, darling?"

"Not right now. I'm leaving for the hospital. John and Anna asked me to join them there. Mother is in pretty bad shape, she's barely conscious. The doctor put her in an intensive care unit. The hospital won't let many visitors in—only family. It might be best if you stay here."

"Of course," she said.

He kissed her and left.

"Fieldsie, please send some flowers to Julia at the hospital."

"Will do," said her friend, a notebook in her hand. "Russ's secretary, Virginia Brissac, called earlier. They're doing a sneak preview of *Wake Up and Dream* with a test audience in Inglewood tonight. She thought maybe you and Russ might like to attend. She's leaving tickets for you at the door."

"We'll think about it. I would like to go if I can convince Russ.

It'd be great to see the audience's reaction to the picture. I think it would do him a world of good, help build up his confidence. The studio heads were all very pleased by his performance. This is simply a test run to make certain nothing needs to be edited or reshot."

A few hours later, Russ came back from visiting his mother at the hospital.

"Mother is stable now and resting. There's nothing more I can do. I've decided I'm going to tell her tomorrow that you and I are getting married."

"Russ, I don't think now is the right time for us to announce to your family that we're getting married. I think we should wait until..." The look in his worried eyes, silenced her. It went straight to her heart. He was suffering.

He took her hand and held it.

"Please, let me tell her. What you decide we do after that doesn't matter, but I have to tell her that we're getting married. She's always worried that I would be alone in life. I'd like to give her some peace of mind."

"All right, Russ. When I come back from Big Bear, we'll go together to the hospital and tell her the good news."

"Thanks." He smiled and kissed her.

Later that afternoon, Carole approached him about attending the sneak preview in Inglewood. "I'll have Edgar come fetch us from the movie house if anyone calls about your mother."

"Carole, it's a test audience." He shook his head. "I think it would be best if I didn't attend. I don't want everyone looking at me instead of the picture."

"Zasu Pitts is here," announced Fieldsie, "and she's brought over a tray of fudge for you."

A slim, well-dressed brunette carrying a tray entered the room. Carole and Zasu were working together on the same picture, *The Gay Bride*, at MGM. Carole was again being loaned out by Paramount.

The petite Zasu wore a lovely blue day suit, and Carole suddenly had an inspirational idea. Zasu had been cast as a spinster in the picture. What if she were to ask Zasu to lend her one of her drab character dresses and a wig? And with Russ covered up with a hat and scarf, wearing dark glasses, they could then attend the preview in anonymity.

He resisted at first, but Zasu insisted. "Russ, don't be so

modest. You should see it at least once with a regular audience instead of the usual Hollywood crowd. Carole, I have the perfect dress and wig for you to wear. They're in my car and absolutely hideous. You'll love them."

Russ was still frowning. Carole put her arm around him. "Come on, it'll be fun. Let's see how many people we can fool."

"All right, I'll do it."

He drove them over to Inglewood in his car. Inside the theater, Fieldsie sat next to Carole on one side, and Zasu Pitts sat on the aisle end, blocking them from view on the other. Carole was greatly amused that no one from the picture's cast had noticed them.

Carole held her breath for a moment, thinking she and Russ might be recognized when she spotted Lansing Brown walk down the far-right aisle and take a seat several rows in front of them. She could feel Russ tense up beside her. He relaxed when Lansing did not approach them, and the houselights dimmed. It had been three weeks since the two men had last spoken.

A cartoon was played before the feature film began. It was a seven-minute Merrie Melodies cartoon from Warner Brothers, drawn by Max Maxwell and Rollin Hamilton, titled "Crosby, Columbo and Vallee," with music by Frank Marsales and lyrics by Al Dubin:

When it comes to pale-face enemies
I know of only three
Crosby, Columbo and Vallee!

The cartoon featured a cute cast of Native American characters, including one called Mini Ha Ha, and a group of woodland animals doing various imitations of the crooners while they listened to a radio. Suddenly a forest fire breaks out, and they save a trio of baby birds by using a spider's nest. The cartoon ends with the American Indian boy spitting out the fire and Porky the Pig saying, "So long, folks!"

Russ laughed with the rest of the audience. Carole could tell he was at last relaxing and enjoying himself. Following the cartoon, a newsreel came on showing the World's Fair, which was currently taking place in Chicago. Russ had been offered a lucrative weekly singing contract by promoters of the fair of over $7,500 a week to perform there, but he had turned it down. He remained in Hollywood, where he was already under contract to make motion pictures and phonograph recordings.

A couple of more newsreels were shown, including one featuring a strange man with a short lip mustache posed in front of a wall-length, red swastika flag addressing a large crowd. Adolf Hitler had recently been elected as Germany's *führer* and *reichskanzler* (leader and chancellor of the Third Reich).

He's nothing but a crazed dictator, she thought, looking up at the screen.

"That fella looks like a troublemaker to me," whispered Russ. "Someone is going to have to cut him down to size."

She squeezed his hand. It was exactly what she was thinking. Adolf Hitler reminded her of one of those slick-haired mobsters one saw from time to time about town, hateful men who threatened to kill you if you didn't obey them, a frightening and powerful bully.

Carole watched young people wearing Hitler's insignia throwing books into a bonfire and ransacking Jewish businesses, and shuddered.

Destiny, a voice whispered in her head.

Appalled by what she saw, she thought, *I'd like nothing better than to go a couple of rounds with that S. O. B.*

The feature presentation, *Wake Up and Dream*, followed, the title appearing up on the screen, as the upbeat introductory music piped through the sound system and screen credits began to scroll. She gave Russ's hand a quick squeeze upon seeing his name listed. This was his big moment. At last he was a true headlining movie star!

From the amount of laughter and applause she heard from the audience that night, she knew they were enjoying the movie, too. The reviews that came out later were nothing but complimentary. One of them said, "Audiences applaud Russ Columbo. *Wake Up and Dream* takes a legitimate place among the better musical entertainments."

The head executives of the studio had already begun predicting that it should be a moneymaker: "It's one hundred percent entertainment" and "this musical show has all the assets of a class-A production. It has many hilarious comedy situations and general appeal."

She knew Russ was pleased when he left the movie house. He opened the car doors for the ladies and then hopped into the front seat of the Duesenberg, his smile a mile wide. After all the struggles he had endured from: having a crooked manager, suffering sickness, poverty, and the humiliation of being assigned insipid secondary roles, he had at long last made it as a headlining movie star.

He took off his disguise and turned on the engine of his car. When he spotted William French walking by, he waved a cheery hello to him.

Will returned it and walked over to the car.

"Hey, Russ, how do you feel? I just saw your picture. Man, you have quite a pair of pipes on you. The music was terrific. Great score! Brunswick should be patting themselves on the back for signing you to their label."

"Thanks, Will," Russ said with a grin, knowing he had won the cinema audience's approval. "I feel terrific! It looks as if I'm really going places. Just write today down in bright red. Today I started a whole new chapter in the story of my life. And when you write, put it down that Old Man Hard Luck lost my address. So many good things happened to me today."

"Well, congrats—you earned it."

"Thanks. I'll be seeing you around." Russ gave a friendly beep of the horn and drove off.

Carole felt joyful for him, since everything was indeed finally going his way. At long last Russ was a movie star!

Chapter Sixteen

Until Eternity

On late Saturday afternoon, Carole prepared for her trip up to Big Bear. Russ sat on the end of the bed and watched her. "I wish I could go with you. I don't like the idea of being separated from you, Angel. But, as you know, Mother is very ill."

"It's all right, Russ, I understand. You should stay here. If anything should happen to Julia, you'd never forgive yourself."

"By the way, I tried calling Lansa last night to ask him what he thought of the picture. His mother answered and said he was out photographing a wedding somewhere in Santa Barbara."

"I guess Virginia must have given him a ticket to the preview." She took down one of her walking jackets and laid it out next to her overnight case. She was looking forward to the peace and quiet of the mountain retreat.

"I'm ready to leave," she said.

Russ picked up her overnight case and carried it out to the car for her. "If Lansa doesn't get back in time to call me tonight, I'm going over to see him tomorrow," he said. "I want to know what he thinks of the picture."

She nodded, choosing not to say anything. It was Russ's choice if he wanted to continue to be friends with Lansing.

Her small dachshund, Brownie, stood waiting by the car. Brownie loved road trips. He was the only one, of all the pets she owned, which didn't get carsick when traveling on mountain roads.

Russ gave the small dog a treat from his coat pocket and patted Brownie's light-brown head. "Take care of my girl for me, will ya, fella?"

As if he understood, Brownie gave a short bark. He then scrambled up into the back seat of the car. Fieldsie was already seated up front.

"You two gals have a fun time." Russ leaned through the window and kissed Carole. "I love you, Angel."

"I love you, too, Roogie. See you soon, darling."

She suddenly felt uneasy. Maybe she should stay here instead of going up to the cabin? What if Julia's condition should worsen?

She glanced back and saw Russ standing on the sidewalk, waving good-bye. She blew him a kiss.

A heavy feeling entered her heart and by the time the car reached the highway, she almost decided to turn around and return home. It seemed as if something was telling her not to go up there. Resolute, she dismissed her fears as foolish.

They arrived at Big Bear at a quarter to ten in the evening. It was shortly after the telephone exchange had closed until morning. Otherwise, she would have called Russ to assure herself he was all right.

She went to bed feeling uneasy. Brownie lay in his basket next to her, softly snoozing. *Russ.* she tossed and turned the whole night long. *Russ.* She briefly fell asleep, but in the middle of the night she suddenly awoke, cold and frightened.

"Russ!" She sat up, crying out his name, terrified.

Fieldsie appeared sleepily at her door in her nightgown. "Carole, are you all right?"

"It's...it's nothing," she lied. "I guess I'm just exhausted. I wish I'd been able to call Russ. I've got this terrible feeling that something is wrong."

"I'm sure he's fine. Why don't you call him in the morning?"

"I'll do that." She tried to go back to sleep, telling herself, *I can go back home in the morning. I don't have to stay here.*

On Sunday morning Carole tried to contact Russ by phone, but was unable to reach him. She felt foolish. Nothing was wrong. She was letting her frayed nerves get the better of her. The sun was shining outside, and the natural beauty of the mountain surrounding was peaceful.

She and Fieldsie sat outside on the front porch of the cabin and ate lunch. Afterward they went for a walk around the small lake, enjoying the slow pace and tranquility of the outdoors. It was Sunday, a day of rest. She hadn't had one in a long time.

In the middle of the afternoon, the phone rang. *Russ!* She hurriedly went inside to answer the phone.

"Hello."

She heard Russ's brother John's voice on the other end of the telephone. A doom-filled heaviness entered the pit of her stomach.

In a shaky voice John informed her that Russ had been shot, and would she please speak to the surgeon?

"Yes, of course," she managed. Her hand white-knuckled the telephone receiver. Her heart was pounding with fear.

What had happened?

Dr. George Patterson, a renowned brain surgeon, spoke to her from the Good Samaritan Hospital. Russ's unconscious body had been taken there. The surgeon explained to her in a calm voice that Russ had been accidentally shot in the head by Lansing Brown, who had been handling an old French dueling pistol in his parents' home.

Lansing had fired the loaded pistol in the den, after dropping a lit match into the percussion cap of the weapon, thus igniting it. Unknowingly, a bullet was lodged inside and was discharged. The bullet had ricocheted against a table. It then had penetrated Russ's brain, upon entering above the left eye.

Upon hearing the word *brain*, Carole's heart constricted. She knew that Russ was dying. She wanted, however, to hear the brutal truth. If Russ were still conscious, she would go to him as quickly as possible. She knew her presence at his side would help him.

"Is there a chance he'll regain consciousness? Should I fly down?" she asked.

"I'm sorry, Miss Lombard, he's dying. He will never regain consciousness. There is no use in your taking a plane. He'll be gone soon. I advise you to go home and wait for the inevitable end there."

"I understand. Thank you, doctor." Carole hung up. She informed Fieldsie of the terrible news in a choked voice. "I have to return to Los Angeles. Russ was accidentally shot in the head by Lansing Brown. He's dying."

"Oh, no! How terrible, Carole. I'm so sorry to hear this." Her friend gave her a consoling hug, tears welling in her eyes. "Do you want me to drive you home?"

"No, stay here. I know Walter is on his way to pick you up. You can drive back with him. I'll take Brownie with me for company."

On the way down, Carole knew the very instant when Russ died. Brownie suddenly began a whimpering keen. The dog crawled over to her and put his wet nuzzle up against her neck. She lifted one hand off the wheel to comfort him, her heart sinking. She looked at her watch, checking on the time: 7:30 p.m. She would later learn that Russ had died at that very minute.

Russ was not alone at the very end. She was informed afterwards that keeping vigil at the hospital along with John was Sally Blane and Russ's brother-in-law, Joe Di Benedetti. They had briefly glimpsed Russ's unconscious body as he was wheeled into the operating room. Lansing had earlier suffered a partial collapse and was taken home. They did not see Russ alive again. He entered into eternity.

Carole drove into her driveway, tired, her nerves completely frayed.

Bessie came out of the house with Louella and her husband. She could see the bad news in her mother's sad tear-filled eyes, before she said it. "Carole," Bessie greeted her. "The hospital just called. I'm sorry, darling, Russ has passed on."

Carole remembered how Russ didn't want to be separated from her, the look in his gentle brown eyes when he watched her leave and waved his final good-bye. *If only she had come back when she sensed something was wrong. If only Lansing had called on Saturday. If only she had been here, it would never have happened.*

"Russ!" she cried, slowly sinking to the ground.

"Grab her!" yelled Louella.

Semiconscious, they carried her inside. Carole lay down on her bed and, after taking some sedatives, promptly passed out.

Russ. She woke and stared at the painted walls of her bedroom. The effects of the drugs made her eyes sensitive to the light. The room's colored walls looked like they were bleeding red and pink.

"She's up," someone said, as Bessie, Louella, and her husband entered the bedroom.

"How are you feeling, Carole?" the doctor asked, taking her pulse.

"Like Jonah after the whale spat him out, all gooey and messed up." She squeezed her eyes shut. "All that's missing are the dancing elephants."

He tried to give her more pills, but she pushed his hand away, refusing them.

"No. They're making me feel worse. Tell me what I need to know, Bessie. Help me prepare for what's to come. Start with Russ's family. How are they? How's Julia? Does she know yet about Russ?"

"No, she's still in the hospital. The doctor has advised against informing her. He fears the news would bring on a sudden heart attack. She's been told that Russ is far away on a movie location with you, and therefore unavailable. For the moment, the family is keeping her completely ignorant of what's occurred and has asked you do the same."

"I will. What about the funeral arrangements?"

"They haven't decided anything. Everyone is still in shock. No one knows what to do. Julia is still in the hospital, and his father, Nicola, is in a grief-stricken state. He's taken to his bed and is under doctor's care. The only decision they've made so far is to have a Catholic funeral at the church."

"I'll call them." She felt there was something she could still do for Russ. "I'll tell John and Anna that I'll be making the funeral arrangements at the church where Russ and I…where we would have been married." Instead of a wedding, she was now planning a funeral. Unbidden, tears fell down her cheeks.

"Oh, Carole, I'm sorry for your loss," said her mother. "He was a very nice man. Everyone liked him, and we all know how much he adored you."

"Yes, he loved me. That's why I want to plan his funeral, to honor him. Will you help me?"

"Of course, dear. I'll do whatever you want."

"Thanks."

Bessie's face showed momentary concern. "A reporter from the Associated Press plans to drop by tomorrow. Do you think you'll be up to meeting her?"

"Did the studio send her?"

"I'm not certain. Louella can tell you." Bessie turned toward her friend.

"Yes, they did. They're trying to make certain there's no scandal. Everyone's testimonies are being coordinated by Philip Cochrane of the publicity department, so no manslaughter charges will be brought against Lansing. They want the jury to declare Russ's death an accident."

"I understand." Carole nodded her head, she knew the inner workings of the studio. It was bad enough Russ had been killed, but if the word *murder* was added, it would kill any picture he had performed in. "What about *Wake Up and Dream?*"

"Despite Russ's death, they plan to release it into the cinemas on schedule."

"I'm glad. I think Russ would have liked that. Otherwise, it could take years for it to be shown. I'll make a statement to the reporter."

Wake Up and Dream was released to the movie theaters. The critics used the picture to pay final homage to Russ, noting what a wonderful voice he'd had and remembering his handsome profile. In states where he had legions of radio fans, who'd heard his weekly broadcasts, it did very well. The box office receipts, Carole noticed, were good. In a couple of cities, the movie was held over for two weeks. His popularity had not died with him.

The studio sent Mollie Merrick for the brief interview. Carole greeted the reporter in the blue drawing room looking pale and frail, wearing a black crepe dress. She had refused to speak to any other member of the press but Mollie and Louella.

Mollie asked her gently, "Do you have something you want to say to Russ's fans at this time?"

"Yes. His death is a terrible shock to me, as it must be to all of his millions of friends and admirers. It is particularly tragic at this time, for I knew that he was destined for the most successful year of his career."

"Thank you. I'm terribly sorry for your loss, Carole. Russ will be greatly missed by all of us who knew him and his music. He was such a nice man."

"Yes, he was." Carole looked away, trying not to cry.

"When will the funeral be?"

"Tomorrow, at the Blessed Sacrament Church on Sunset Boulevard. The coroner plans to release Russ's body after the inquest. You wouldn't happen to know what the jury decided about the shooting, would you? Is there to be a trial?"

"The jury has exonerated Lansing. No charges will be brought against him. Here, I wrote down what he told the detectives for my column." She handed Carole the notepad. "I tracked it down from the police records."

Carole read the statement:

I was absent-mindedly fooling around with one of the guns. It was of a dueling design and works with a cap and trigger. I was pulling back the trigger and clicking it time after time. I had a match in my hand and when I clicked evidently the match caught in between the hammer and the firing pin. There was an explosion. Russ slid to the side of his chair. It was almighty fast. I thought he was clowning.

The rest of the statement went on to describe how Lansing had called his parents, who put ice on Russ's head, and then contacted an ambulance to take him to the hospital. "I bought these pistols at an antique store. I've had the collection for seven years. I had never made an examination to see whether or not they were loaded, they were so old. I had no idea they were loaded."

She handed the paper back to Mollie.

"There was some question as to whether they were heard quarrelling beforehand, but testimony from Russ's secretary, Virginia, and Lansing's family made it clear that it was an accidental death. The two men were friends, after all."

Carole knew that Russ had planned to tell Lansing that he could no longer photograph him or sell the pictures. Universal had an exclusivity clause about their star that wouldn't permit it. The two men may have quarreled—especially if she added in the fact that Lansing resented her helping Russ run his career—but she said nothing.

She was secretly relieved that she had not been asked to attend the inquest as a witness. She did not think her nerves would have held out.

She spent the rest of the day preparing for Russ's funeral, meeting with the priests who would lead the service and choosing the Bible passages to be read.

The funeral at the Blessed Sacrament Catholic Cathedral was a solemn occasion; as a capacity crowd of three thousand mourners attended the service, another one thousand respectfully stood outside. Unlike other Hollywood funerals, which often bordered on mayhem, the assembly of people was uncommonly solemn and quiet.

A motorcycle escort arrived with the black hearse. She noticed as her car drove up to the cathedral that a police force had set up barricades, and officers directed the crowd where to stand.

When the bronze casket covered by a large blanket of white

gardenias and a simple card bearing Russ's name was taken out of the hearse, the onlookers (who were mostly teenage girls) quietly wept. Carole stepped out of the car and, following behind, saw the bedecked casket. She had personally ordered the flowers, remembering how much Russ had loved the smell of the gardenias from her garden, she would sometimes bathe in gardenia oil to please him.

Near the cathedral steps, a magazine photographer who managed to squeeze off a couple of shots was chastised by the young mourners.

"This is Russ's funeral," a young girl hissed. Her companion, a teary-eyed fan holding a framed picture of Russ, glared at the photographer.

No more photos were taken.

Russ's sister, Anna, who Carole had been told by Russ had been like a second mother to him when he was young, broke the silence outside. She cried aloud in her grief as she stumbled while walking up the steps. "He was just a baby doll," Anna loudly wept. "No one will know how much we loved him!"

Anna had to be led into the sanctuary by relatives who'd come from all over the United States to attend the service.

At ten o'clock the bells of the church rang as the pallbearers: Bing Crosby, Zeppo Marx, Walter Lang, Carole's brother, Stuart Peters, and actors Gilbert Roland and Sheldon Keate Calloway, slowly carried the heavy casket into the sanctuary, placing it between two lit vigil candles. Beside the casket stood several large floral arrangements that had been sent from entertainment colleagues, friends, and admirers. A heart-shaped one with a profusion of gardenias and orchids with a large card attached from her was signed, *Your Angel.*

Among the floral arrangements was one from the studio extra, Buddy, who Russ had loaned money to. He had written in the attached note: *He was a real man.*

The pews and side aisles of the cathedral were overflowing with those who had come to pay a respectful good-bye to Russ; with his golden voice and songs, he had caused them to dream and be comforted by his wonderful music. At the same hour, Carole was informed, at Universal Studio the work would be stilled on the lot. A solemn period of silence was held out of respect for their lost star.

The famous big-band leaders Gus Arnheim, Jimmie Grier, and

Guy Lombardo were present at the funeral, as were many movie personalities, including most of the cast from *Wake Up and Dream.*

Bing Crosby commented on Russ's death. "Few people felt Russ's loss more than I did, because somehow it seemed we should be sailing along together, as we had been the last three months of his life… I was proud when asked to officiate at his funeral as a pallbearer, and to play some small part in his last rites."

Carole wore a plain black coatdress with a twisted white-leather belt, a fox stole, and a beret with a small diamond stickpin. She kept her head down as she walked up the steps of the cathedral, wearing dark sunglasses to conceal her tear-filled eyes. She entered the sanctuary with Russ's family, supported by his brother John, and sat in the widow's pew in front with Dr. Harry Martin on one side and Bing seated on the other.

It was respectfully quiet. There was no organ music, per Russ's request.

"I am the resurrection and the life, saith the Lord. He that believeth in me, though he were dead, yet shall live," intoned Father Cornelius McCoy at the beginning of the service, standing near the casket.

She tried to remain stoic during the service, which was conducted very simply, as Russ had wished. The Fifty-First Psalm was chanted aloud by the congregation. The words echoed up to the large beamed rafters of the cathedral as thousands of people repeated them.

Father McCoy then slowly walked over to the closed casket and, raising the silver aspergillum of holy water, solemnly blessed it, sprinkling the water. It was a reminder of baptism and the belief that Russ's soul had entered into a new life.

"Thou art dust, and unto dust thou shalt return…"

Russ! He was gone. She was never going to touch or hold him in her arms again. Her eyes blurred with tears as a quartet sang "Lead Kindly Light," a John Henry Newman hymn, sung acapella, the only music that was heard during the funeral. The music was as pure as a light from heaven.

No longer able to contain the sorrow within her heart, she began to sob loudly. Dr. Martin and Bing tried to comfort her, putting their arms around her.

"Into thy hands, O merciful Savior, we commend thy servant, Russ. Receive him into the arms of thy mercy, into the blessed rest of everlasting peace, and into the glorious company of the saints in light." The clergyman then blessed the congregation with a closing prayer: "Christ is risen from the dead, trampling down death by death, giving life to those in the tomb."

He addressed the casket, which was being lifted by the pallbearers, as if Russ were still present. "Into paradise may the angels lead thee; and thy coming may the martyrs receive thee, and bring thee into the holy city Jerusalem."

The congregation then rose out of respect. The pallbearers bore the flower-bedecked casket outside to the waiting hearse. Carole followed behind, walking slowly with John and Bessie nearby.

Russ's remains, it was decided, would be placed the following month in the vault opposite his brother Fiore's, at Forest Lawn Cemetery in Glendale, California. When Carole made her last will and testament, the first instruction she wrote down was her desire to be interred in a modest crypt at the same cemetery, dressed wearing her favorite white gown.

In the last pew of the church stood a gaunt Lansing Brown. He looked down, avoiding Carole's gaze when she walked past. She briefly glimpsed through her tears a pale Sally Blane, wearing a white dress and plain white hat, standing against the back wall of the sanctuary with her own mother.

Carole rapidly lost weight, and friends worried she would have another breakdown. She would become easily upset when anyone talked to her about Russ. Her grief was raw and painful.

Russ had been one of the most popular radio stars and song composers of the 1930s. Many writers wanted to talk to her about his death and their life together, but she wasn't ready. She decided to leave for New York City to escape the reporters hounding her for interviews.

Chapter Seventeen

Tender Deception

In early September, Carole stayed in a luxurious penthouse at the Waldorf Astoria Hotel in New York City. It was the same hotel where Russ and his orchestra had performed nightly in the Empire Room for radio broadcasts. At the height of his career, when Russ had sold-out shows at the nearby Paramount Theatre, he had invited hundreds of Broadway reporters to a celebratory party there.

Fieldsie warned journalists who made appointments to meet Carole, "Under no circumstances are you to ask her any questions about Russ."

Carole, however, didn't remain hidden in the penthouse. In an effort to distract herself from her grief, she eventually went out and met people. Surrounded by a protective entourage, she attended theater performances, and visited the city's nightclubs. She attended with photographer Jake Froelich a press preview of the controversial Broadway play *Tobacco Road*, based on the book by Erskine Caldwell.

They arrived early to the theater with a group of friends. Suddenly, Fred Keating, one of the cast members of the show, came in from the rain-soaked street and entered the dimly lit atrium. She turned to look at him as he shook out his umbrella. He was a tall, handsome man with bright brown eyes. He wore his hair slicked back, accentuating his prominent widow's peak hairline.

Jake Froelich, who had taken many pictures of Russ in the past, stared at Fred, as did she.

"Russ," Jake uttered, paling. In the half-light of the foyer, the resemblance between the living man and the dead one was striking.

Carole looked at the actor and felt a sharp constriction of her heart. *Russ.* For a fleeting, illusionary moment, it seemed as if her beloved had come back to the land of the living.

But when the actor spoke, shaking hands with those he knew, the deep timbre of his voice, and speech pattern, was entirely different than Russ's. Her heart returned to its normal beat. The painful loss of her lover was once again buried deep inside her heart.

When she was introduced to Fred, she managed to smile. "I'm pleased to meet you. I've been told that I have something to look forward to tonight."

The tall actor, who had once worked as a magician, produced a rose by sleight of hand.

"The pleasure is all mine, Carole. I hope you enjoy the show." He handed the flower to her with a slight bow and headed for the backstage entrance to prepare for his role.

After weeks away from Hollywood, Carole was ready to meet reporters and to talk about Russ. She was interviewed early one morning by a lady magazine writer at the Waldorf.

"Carole, what did you think of Russ, did you believe he was talented?"

"I knew of his great talents, as a songwriter and a singer, and I wanted to make sure the world knew them, too. I helped him. He had not only a baritone voice that was potentially operatic, he wrote beautiful poetry in his music and had a true genius of mind and heart. He was a very rare, a very unusual person. I knew it, and loved him for it."

"Do you think he loved you, too?"

"Russ and I loved one another. Eventually, I believe we would have married…" She paused to collect her thoughts. "His love for me was the kind that comes very rarely to any woman. How can I explain this to you? It was unique. I never in a million years expected to have such worship, such idolatry, such kind sweetness from any man."

Carole sat in the carpeted Waldorf penthouse wearing nothing but a long white-fur robe that pooled at her feet. She was completely naked underneath, having just risen from bed.

The lady writer who wore a hat and white driving gloves, Carole could see was slightly startled by her appearance, asked, "Has Russ's mother been told yet about his death?"

"No, she's still very ill," Carole replied. "When I came to New York the family arranged to have wires sent to her signed with both our names. Presumably from here in New York, Russ and I sailed for England. She's been told that we are married and on our honeymoon. Cables are being sent from London to her, signed with both our names."

This personal twist on the ruse had been entirely her idea. She was aided in this by Russ's family members, who read the wires to the nearly blind Julia. Carole was told that the invalid woman was over the moon with joy at the news that she and Russ had married. Julia had always liked Carole and couldn't be prouder of her son, whom she thought was still alive and performing in motion pictures in Europe.

Carole felt a sense of accomplishment. It was a tender deception that allowed her to fulfill one of Russ's last wishes. They were married. She willingly played the role of his wife, sending bouquets of flowers almost daily to his sick mother and writing cheerful, newsy letters from all the different places she visited. Julia blissfully never knew of her son's death.

Although he was dead, Russ was still supporting his family through his $24,000 life insurance policy, which paid out a monthly stipend of nearly $400 a month to his mother during the remainder of her life. His music, records, and movie rights all provided additional income.

When Carole returned to Hollywood, she didn't visit the Columbos, since she and Russ were supposed to still be on their honeymoon. She reluctantly went back to work finishing *The Gay Bride* with actor Chester Morris. The story was about a gold-digging showgirl who marries a series of gangsters in order to inherit their money, eventually falling in love with a nice guy. The era of gangster movies was coming to a close. Despite some amusing moments, to her disappointment, the picture was soundly panned by critics.

Carole never retrieved some of the personal belongings she had left behind at the house on Roxbury Drive, including a notebook she had kept as a diary. She was told that reporters and morbid souvenir hunters had invaded the rental property, peeking in the windows, taking flowers from the yard, and wrecking the garden in an effort to see if she or anyone else was still living there. To add insult to injury, she heard from Anna that Russ's family had received a hefty bill from the landlord for the damages that had been done.

It was a repeat of what had happened when Rudolph Valentino had died, back in 1926. What had been worse in the silent-movie idol's passing, in Carole's opinion, was that souvenir hunters had chipped away at the angel monument that had been placed at the star's grave until it was reduced to a pile of rubble. She was relieved that Russ was safely buried in a vault, which insured that no such desecration would ever occur to his final resting place.

"Carole, how are you feeling?" asked Bessie, upon seeing her return home after visiting the cemetery.

"I am desperately lonely for Russ, to tell you the truth. We were so very close, together so constantly. I'm just beginning to feel the loss. Bessie, I feel as though I were suspended in air, somewhere far, far away from here, only now I'm slowly coming alive, returning to earth and reality."

It helped Carole to stay busy, working. Her sole ambition in life now was to become a headlining star. She started to perform in a series of romantic comedies with the married newcomer Fred MacMurray, notably in *Hands Across the Table*. The picture was directed by her good friend Mitchell Leisen and was filmed by her favorite cameraman, Ted Tetzlaff, who made her look strikingly beautiful.

In *Hands Across the Table*, her first picture with Fred, she played the role of a manicurist named Regi Allen, who daydreams of marrying a millionaire. Her character is befriended by a real millionaire, Allen Macklyn (Ralph Bellamy), an ex-pilot who is paralyzed and enjoys her company. She falls in love, however, with playboy Theodore Drew III (played by Fred), who has the pedigree, but not the money. The picture, although a bit of a cliché, much to her pleasure, did extremely well at the cinemas and advanced all three of their careers.

Carole helped Fred by coaching him, especially during the hopscotch scene at the beginning of the picture, since he was ill at ease with playing the children's game in front of a camera. She taught him how to play, and in the end he had fun performing the scene. She liked Fred, and the two became friends, appearing in several more motion pictures together.

Paramount tried to follow up the success of *Bolero* with another dancing picture, *Rumba,* starring Carole again with George Raft.

"I'm not working as long as Ted is the cameraman," George complained to the male director, Marion Gering. "He makes Carole look ten times better than me!"

He then angrily stomped off the set.

No one in the cast or crew was fooled, including Carole. There wasn't a person present who didn't know how much George hated the Cuban dancer he was portraying in *Rumba.*

The fight had been premeditated. Ted Tetzlaff had been the cinematographer for several of her pictures and was part of her unbreakable contract agreement with the studio. Carole figured George must have thought that a fight like this would give him the excuse he needed to not to finish the picture, or so he must have thought.

His sulking didn't work. George was under contract. After the studio had firmly reminded him of this, he went back to work and finished the picture.

She tried to soothe the insecure and temperamental actor's ruffled feathers by putting stars all over his dressing room and in his toilet. She let him know that he was, in her opinion, a great star. She knew he loved the gesture and from that moment onwards had a life-long crush on her that grew in relative proportion with her fame and legendary status as a film star.

George's dissatisfaction must have shown. The picture did not do well at the box office. It was an outright flop. Paramount never asked her to appear in another film with him.

Fieldsie, seeing how hard she worked, asked her, "Carole, you have enough money now, you could retire. How long do you intend to remain in pictures?"

"I want to work for a few more years," she replied. "I'm approaching the peak of my success right now. I want to enjoy this short period I have at the top, and then I want to retire and watch others have their chance."

Carole was in her late twenties now and nowhere near ready to stop performing. Most of her girlfriends, who were her age, had already retired and had started having families. She was hungry for more roles, however, as stardom had at long last tapped her on the shoulder.

Carole spoke to Lansing Brown only once after Russ's death. She called Lansing over to her table one night at a nightclub. She spoke to him as everyone watched. "I hear you're afraid of me. Don't be silly, Lansing. I don't blame you for Russ's death. Let's be friends." The cool look in her eyes and the tight smile she wore dared him to speak. Lansing quickly walked away, giving her no response. The brief encounter was published in a couple of newspapers the next day.

The studio had pressured her into making this very public reconciliation, ensuring that there was to be no scandal connected to Russ's death. This was the final nail in the coffin

She confessed to Fieldsie, "Even though I have lost Russ, I can't feel that life is at an end. I believe that everything that happens is determined by fate. I truly believe Russ's death was predestined. And I am happy that it came when he was happy in our love. That knowledge has been such a great consolation."

Carole began clowning around again, hosting parties and pulling pranks both on and off the set. In December, as she walked by a toy store, she discovered a large mechanized toy tank with a saluting soldier inside. She grinned, thinking of a wonderful prank to play on Myron Selznick, her manager. She bought the toy and contacted a metalworker to alter it.

Bright and early on Christmas morning, Carole knocked on the front door of Myron Selznick's residence. She then went and quickly hid behind a nearby hedge.

Myron answered the door, his eyes visibly widening in surprise as he looked out. The toy tank she had bought was loudly clattering across his neatly manicured front lawn. It stopped in front of him by the steps and slowly turned around.

The soldier inside the tank faced him. He lifted his arm, saluting the manager by putting his thumb up to its nose. This it did repeatedly and rhythmically until it clattered back across the lawn to her.

"What the hell," Myron started to say, before being interrupted by her giggling. Turning his head, he espied her sapphire-blue eyes peeking at him through an opening in the hedge.

"Carole Lombard!"

"Merry Christmas, Myron!" They both laughed.

She threw a party in her dressing room the day before the studio closed for the holidays, passing out glasses of champagne to everyone who walked by. Her gifts to friends and coworkers were the usual mix of small luxury items and personal gag gifts, such as a bullwhip for one of the assistant directors who was always urging her to be at work on time. Shrieks of laughter rang out throughout the dressing room, until Fieldsie handed Carole a small gift wrapped in gold.

"It's small, so it's bound to be good," Carole said. She tore off the wrapping and opened the box. She lifted the lid and drew out a chain with a small, gold, heart-shaped locket attached. "How sweet. Is there a picture inside?"

"Open it and see."

Carole did, and found herself staring down at a very familiar face. "It's Russ."

She remembered how he had laughed and smiled while posing for it and had drawn her down onto his lap and had pictures taken of the both of them. *Russ!* Tears pooled in her eyes and spilled down her cheeks. Without a word she opened the dressing room door and stepped outside. She began walking down the empty studio lot street, clutching the locket.

"Carole!" Fieldsie called after her.

She shook her head. She didn't want to talk to anyone. *Russ. It was unfair*, she thought, angrily wiping the tears away. *He should have been here tonight, laughing at her jokes and kissing her under the mistletoe.* But Fate had decided otherwise.

She walked until she reached the studio's artificial lake. For several minutes she stood there listening to the lapping of the water under a pale white moon, trying to regain control of her emotions.

She took in deep, cleansing breaths, reminding herself that Russ had always been proud of her and that she had made him happy. Now, she had to go on without him in her life.

"I love to hear you laugh, Angel," he had said.

"Russ, I know you can hear me, darling. And I want you to know that I won't stop laughing and doing all those things you loved me for." After kissing his face in the locket, she closed it and walked back to her dressing room, quietly rejoining the party.

Chapter Eighteen

Two Lovers

Carole took several months off in the summer of 1935. She traveled to Europe with Fieldsie, visiting Rome and the Vatican. Everywhere she walked in Italy reminded her of Russ, especially the music. The Italian opera made her cry.

In an old part of the city, as she meandered through the narrow cobbled streets, she felt drawn to walk down a small side alley. It was as if someone were whispering to her, "Turn here."

It was then that she saw a beautiful gold and red garnet cross sitting in an antique shop window. She asked the shopkeeper if she could examine it. She held the small icon in her hand, and, thinking of Julia, she bought it. During her audience with Pope Pius XI, she asked to have it blessed.

Julia was still very fragile and under a nurse's care. The family had planned to tell their mother about Russ's death after Julia had had an eye surgery, which was supposed to help her to regain her sight. Sadly, the operation was unsuccessful. They chose to remain silent and to continue the ruse, not wanting to upset her.

"Carole, she wants to know how Russ is," said Anna, translating for Julia when she came to visit,

"Tell her that Russ is making movies in Europe and unable to visit. I'm here because I'm still under contract with Paramount. He sends his love and bought her this cross. He had the pope bless it for her." She kissed the blind, almost deaf Julia's wrinkled cheek, handing her the gift.

"*Grazie*, Carole." The sick woman smiled while fingering the beautiful icon.

"Yes, thank you," said Anna, her eyes filling with tears.

Carole knew how much Russ had loved his mother. It made her happy. She believed Russ would have wanted her to do this.

The family kept Russ's death from Julia until the very end. Ten years after his death, when the seventy-four-year-old was dying, Julia's last words to her family were reported to be, "Tell Russ I am so proud of him and happy." She died not knowing that she soon would be joining him.

"I told them I wouldn't take the role of Godfrey, unless you played Irene. You're perfect for the part, Carole. I think you have a real talent for this kind of screwball comedy," Bill said over the telephone. He told her he had convinced Universal to give her the role of Irene in the comedy *My Man Godfrey*.

"Thanks, Philo, I can't wait to start!" she replied, knowing he could have insisted that Jean Harlow play the role. She had heard rumors that the two of them were heading for the altar.

Carole had read the script for *My Man Godfrey*. She knew Irene was a character she could sink her teeth into, using her finely honed comedic talents. The screenplay, written by Eric S. Hatch and his assistant, Morrie Ryskind, was a lighthearted tale about a ditzy society belle, Irene Bullock (Carole), and the "forgotten man," Godfrey Parke (Bill), who is found at a dump during a scavenger hunt and becomes the family butler. It was a screwball comedy with a large cast of eccentric characters.

There was friendly cordiality on the set between her and her ex-husband, but not always so between Gregory LaCava, the director, and Bill. They had a few disagreements.

"Where's Bill?" she asked Gregory, when she showed up for an early-morning rehearsal and noticed that he was missing.

"Bill and I had a late-night discussion about how Godfrey should be played," the hard-drinking director said with a wince, gently touching his head. "A bottle of scotch settled the issue."

He handed her a telegram that read: *We may have found Godfrey last night—but we lost Powell. See you tomorrow.*

Gregory directed her and Bill to use their own personalities, much like Howard Hawks had, and encouraged them not to assume someone else's personalities for their roles. This displeased Bill, since he had spent several days observing his own butler in preparation for the role. In the end he reached a compromise with the director and played his customary urbane self.

The entire cast was very relaxed. At the director's request, a real party took place during the performance of the pretend one, complete with alcoholic beverages and food, to help loosen up the cast before filming. Word quickly spread around Hollywood about this unconventional and off-the-cuff picture.

"What do you think of your fellow actors, Carole?" asked a reporter for a promotional interview during filming.

"I think they're wild, crazy, and deliciously insane. To be truthful, it's the maddest picture I've ever worked in, and I love it!"

When the cast's actors, including Bill, flubbed their lines, they let loose with some wholehearted swearing to release tension. Angry with herself whenever she messed up, Carole likewise exploded without hesitation, uttering the Lord's name in vain quite a few times. She would then calm down and restart from the top, determined to get the lines right until she could utter her part in the fast-paced dialogue without stumbling. What appeared as seamlessly delivered speech took a great deal of memorization, enunciation, and comic timing.

She had an interesting moment with Bill prior to the shooting of the much-anticipated scene in which Godfrey places Irene in a cold shower after she fakes passing out. It was one of the last scenes to be filmed, and she experienced some good old-fashioned ribbing from the entire cast, including Bill.

"I think you need a bath, Carole, dear," he murmured into her ear.

"And you're going to give it to me, eh?"

"As your man Godfrey, that seems to be one of my more pleasant duties—a bath in a nice, cold shower, with all those pretty clothes on." His eyes shone with evil delight at the idea.

"Uh huh," she said, nodding her head in agreement. "That will be nice, our taking a bath *together*." She eyed his neatly pressed butler clothing. "And with all your nice clothes on, too."

He visibly blanched. Taking a bath was not in the script for his character.

"Oh, I'll ruffle your dignity, *Baby*." She openly laughed at his discomfort. She admitted to herself that it felt good to make Bill squirm.

When the film debuted, she was pleased. The critics raved and she heard from her agent that many movie theaters held over the screwball comedy for several weeks, raking in thousands of dollars in revenue.

"Several writers have noticed the similarities between you, and your character, Irene," remarked Fieldsie, looking at the reviews. "They think you're a lovable madcap clown who's enthusiastic about everybody and everything. Your behavior on-screen has been called, and I quote, 'versatile and changeable,' much like your real-life self."

"Really, I'm a lovable clown? Well, they can put a red nose on me and call me whatever they want, Fieldsie, just so long as they don't call me a dull bore."

She soon discovered that the picture was a huge hit with movie critics and audiences alike. Her star's zenith seemed limitless. The picture was nominated by the Academy of Motion Pictures for six different categories, including best actress for her performance, best actor for Bill's, and best director for Gregory. Unfortunately, the picture didn't win a single Oscar.

In December of 1935 she started dating her old beau Bob (Robert) Riskin, the screenplay writer who had won an Academy Award for *It Happened One Night*. She threw him a huge barnyard-themed birthday party. They dated for almost a year, and she wondered whether or not she would marry him after he bought her a pair of expensive ruby-and-diamond clip earrings and a silver-fox stole for Christmas.

He gave her a charm bracelet with little symbols that represented special moments in their relationship. The last one was a question mark. When she figured out that he was never going to pop the question, she walked away for the last time from their relationship.

She renewed her acquaintance with Clark Gable in 1936. He had won a best actor Oscar for *It Happened One Night*. They both attended a party at a friend's house at which the guests had been asked to wear something white. Carole made her grand entrance in a white ambulance, wearing a white patient's gown. At first the romance was kept a secret, but it heated up at the Mayfair Ball.

Mollie Merrick asked, "Carole, are you and Clark Gable, you know, *that* way?"

"Of course not—he's married. We're just friends."

To keep the press guessing about her new relationship, Carole used an old subterfuge by pretending to be dating Walter Lang. The ruse ended when Walter and Fieldsie married the following year. Fieldsie stopped working for her, and began helping her husband with his career.

Carole performed in the Technicolor picture *Nothing Sacred*, another comedic success, costarring Frederic March. She put her boxing experience to good use in the film, when her character, Hazel Flagg, lovingly sucker punches Wally Cook (Frederic March) right in the kisser, knocking him out cold. Within a short period of time, she was earning a phenomenal $35,000 a week and was one of the highest-paid movie stars in Hollywood. She had at last reached the top rung.

Clark Gable was about to become the number-one box-office star because of the epic blockbuster *Gone with the Wind*. Carole saw his face appear in all the newspapers and magazines. To support Clark, she decided to help promote the picture by pretending to audition for the role of Scarlett O'Hara, although no screen test of her was ever made. Her studio and Clark's started to pressure her to be silent about her past relationship with Russ.

"We have to build up Clark's image in the public's eyes, especially now with Rhea finally willing to discuss a divorce. It would make Clark look bad by comparison if you should let the ghost of Russ overshadow him. You have to stop talking about him," said Howard Strickling, the head of MGM's publicity department.

"All right," she reluctantly agreed, "I won't say a word about Russ to the press." But she wasn't happy about the promise.

Carole sat in her living room for an afternoon interview with *Life* magazine wearing a sad, pensive expression. She was being photographed by the noted photojournalist Alfred Eisenstaedt.

"This has to be one of the most honest and heartbreaking portraits I've ever done of you, Carole," said Alfred, when he took the picture.

Noel Busch, the senior editor of *Life*, conducted the interview to go with the series of pictures. Her brother Fred was visiting and sat nearby as she answered the questions.

"Carole, would you say Clark Gable was the great love of your life?" the journalist asked, with what sounded to her like an air of smugness. She knew he was already planning to do a big spread on the male megastar. "Everyone knows you were once married to William Powell."

"No. You're wrong."

"Excuse me?"

"Russ Columbo was the great love of my life." She started to become angry once she remembered her promise. *Drat!*

"And that's definitely off the record," she said sternly, walking out of the room.

"Carole, are you all right?" asked her brother, who followed her into the kitchen.

No, she wasn't. She was angry. "They want me to forget him, Fred. Russ was the great love of my life, and they want me to forget him!"

"You don't have to. He's still there in your heart."

She kept her promise and remained silent about her relationship with Russ. As the anniversary of his death neared, however, she couldn't sit still. She listened to all of her favorite recordings by him. He had been so talented. How could the world forget Russ and his wonderful music? It wasn't possible.

She wanted to publicly remember him, but how? She had given her word not to say anything about him to the press. The needle had reached the end of the record. Looking over at it, Carole's eyes lit up with determination.

She would let her actions speak for her when her words couldn't. She called to her little dachshund Contessa, who enjoyed car rides as much as her father, Brownie. "Come on, Contessa, let's go for a ride, girl! You, too, Brownie. Let's go, boy!"

The two small dogs waddled over and stood by the door, waiting to go outside.

"Where are you going in such a hurry, Miss Carole?" asked her maid, Jessie, as Carole brushed past.

"I'm going out to celebrate a life!"

She drove downtown and walked into the first music store she spotted. A wide-eyed teenaged clerk greeted her. "Can I help you, Miss Lombard?"

"Yes, do you have any recordings by Russ Columbo?"

"We do, several, in fact. Which one do you want?"

"All of them."

She drove up and down Hollywood Boulevard and Rodeo Drive buying the records. She visited every music store she saw, wanting them to remember Russ and his great talent. Piles of music sheets and phonograph records soon filled her car.

After she had returned home, Louella telephoned her. "What's up? I've got reports that you've been spotted all over town buying stacks and stacks of Russ's music and records. Why? Everyone knows you already own all of his recordings."

"I can't comment, Lolly. But could you do me a big favor? Remember the anniversary of his death is approaching, would you?"

"Sure, will do."

Carole made no comment about her actions to anyone, but her buying spree appeared in several newspapers the next day, and her name was once again linked to Russ's. A couple of newspapers, she saw, mentioned her as having once been his fiancée. Russ and his wonderful music were not forgotten, and she had made sure of it.

At the end of March in 1939, after a costly divorce from Rhea, Carole and Clark finally eloped, travelling on Route 66 to Kingman, Arizona, in the Mojave Desert. She and Clark had fun hunting and fishing together. They bought a ranch in Encino, California, where they unsuccessfully raised chickens and had a menagerie of pets, including horses. They continued to make movies separately and tried, without success, to start a family.

Amid upsetting rumors of marital infidelity and discord, on January 16, 1942, Carole was anxiously returning home from a successful US War Bond drive in the Midwest when the military plane she was on crashed, killing everyone aboard. The signal beacon that usually pulsated from the top of Potosi Mountain near Las Vegas had been turned off to comply with the wartime blackout. The plane had slammed into the pitch-black mountain after stopping to refuel. Carole, her mother, MGM press agent Otto Winkler, and fifteen military personnel tragically died in the crash, along with the plane's pilot and crew.

Respectful of her final wishes, Clark Gable had his beautiful wife's remains laid to rest beside those of her beloved mother in the Great Mausoleum at Forest Lawn Cemetery in Glendale. Her favorite white gown was laid inside her casket, which was covered in white gardenias and orchids.

Carole's crypt is located in the Sanctuary of Trust near the Sanctuary of the Vespers, the final resting place of the man she considered to be the greatest love of her life: Russ Columbo.

.

Author's Notes

Websites
The Russ Columbo Society web page, by Damon Leigh:
www.russcolumbo.com

The Russ Columbo Society Facebook web page:
www.facebook.com/RussColumbo

 Beverly Adam's Facebook web page:
www.facebook/Beverly-Adam-60810429592761/

Boxing notes: Carole went to the boxing match with George Raft on January 4, 1934. Primo Carnera was banned from boxing in California in 1933. The boxer's career was permanently tainted by his known mob connections.

Popular myth: Russ Columbo never ran the Pyramid Club; it was owned by his older brother Albert Colombo and

William H. Niendorf. Publicity that was created to promote the club cashed in on his name. He first met Con Conrad at the Ambassador Hotel's Cocoanut Club.

Truth: The garnet red cross Carole gave Russ's mother is passed down from eldest daughter to eldest daughter of the Columbo family.

About the Author

Beverly Adam, an award-winning author, enjoys researching history and likes to weave fact with fiction into her novels. She is the author of *She Rode the Rails*, the true story of traveling railroad photographer Mary Jane Wyatt, which won an Editor's Choice Award. She is also the Regency Romance author of the popular series *The Honorable Gentlemen* (Lachesis Publishing).

Printed in Great Britain
by Amazon

48329836R00112